GALAXY'S EDGE

EDITED BY MIKE RESNICK

ISSUE 10: SEPTEMBER 2014

Mike Resnick, Editor
Shahid Mahmud, Publisher

Published by Arc Manor/Phoenix Pick
P.O. Box 10339
Rockville, MD 20849-0339

Galaxy's Edge is published every two months: January, March, May, July, September & November.

www.GalaxysEdge.com

Available by subscription (www.GalaxysEdge.com) or through your favorite online store (Amazon.com, BN.com, etc.).

ISBN: 978-1-61242-224-4

Advertising in the magazine is available. Quarter page (half column), $95 per issue. Half page (full column, vertical or two half columns, horizontal) $165 per issue. Full page (two full columns) $295 per issue. Back Cover (full color) $495 per issue. All interior advertising is in black and white.

Please write to advert@GalaxysEdge.com.

FOREIGN LANGUAGE RIGHTS: Please refer all inquiries pertaining to foreign language rights to Spectrum Literary Agency, 320 Central Park West, Suite 1-D, New York, NY 10025. Phone: 1-212-362-4323. Fax 1-212-362-4562

Contents

THE SARGASSO LEGACY

THE ADVENTURE STARTS
WITH THE NOVEMBER ISSUE

www.SargassoContainment.com

THE BEST OF THE NEW AND THE OLD

✭ New and Old Stories by Masters of Science Fiction and Fantasy ✭

✭ New Stories by Emgerging New Talents ✭

✭ PLUS Columns, Book Reviews and Interviews ✭

✭ Serializations of Great Novels ✭

& starting November 2014

The Sargasso Legacy

DON'T MISS OUT ON ANY ISSUE

SUBSCRIBE

www.GalaxysEdge.com/sub.htm

Or send a check for $37.74 for a one-year (six-issue) subscription (save 10% off the cover price) with this form to :

Subscriptions: Galaxy's Edge

Arc Manor Publishers

P.O. Box 10339

Rockville, MD 20849

Currently, subscription to the paper edition is only available within the United States.

Your Name_____

Full Address_____

_____

_____

Ph. No._____   Email_____

RED TIDE

LARRY NIVEN

October 15, 2014

Available now
for preorder on
Amazon.com

WITH
BRAD R. TORGERSEN
& MATTHEW J. HARRINGTON

THE EDITOR'S WORD

by Mike Resnick

Welcome to the 10th issue of *Galaxy's Edge*. We've got a talent-laden issue for you, with superstars like Larry Niven (with a brand-new Draco Tavern story), Mercedes Lackey, Eric Flint, Tobias S. Buckell, and Robert J. Sawyer; British writer-editor Ian Whates; and hot new talents Brian Trent, K. C. Norton, Alvaro Zinos-Amaro, and Laurie Tom. We're continuing our serialization of L. Sprague de Camp's classic novel, *Lest Darkness Fall*, and of course we've got our wonderful regulars: a science column by Gregory Benford, book reviews by Paul Cook, and everything else by Barry Malzberg. And Joy Ward's interview features Hugo-winning and mega-selling George R. R. Martin.

Galaxy's Edge is starting to get reviewed all over the place, almost always favorably, and one of the reviewers, discussing our wide-ranging stories, remarked that "the damned magazine has just about everything anyone could want except bathroom humor."

Well, nothing ventured, nothing gained.

Brace yourself for my experiences with African bathrooms. The only caveat is that I didn't think any of them were funny at the time.

The Matthews Range, Kenya. This is a mountain range in Northern Kenya that was only recently opened for tourism, and we were among the first to show up there. The tented camp's notion of a bathroom was a "long drop" (a toilet over a 30-foot-deep hole, common on the safari trail), and a shower consisting of a 5-gallon canvas bag that would be filled with hot water by what our guide liked to call "dusky handmaidens."

There were no car tracks in the Matthews Range—it was too newly opened for them—so all our sightseeing had to be done on foot. In the mountains. At 7,500 feet altitude. In the heat of the day. When we got back from a four-hour trek I was so exhausted I skipped the shower and went right to my cot for a nap. I awoke just after sunset and decided to bathe before dinner. So I duly removed my clothes, stood under the canvas bag, and pulled the cord that opened it—and let out such a scream that I scared away all the leopards they'd laid out bait for. Seems I'd forgotten what happens to hot water when it's left out for hours at 7,500 feet at nightfall—except that it wasn't hot water anymore. I don't think I could have been any colder if you'd covered me with ice cubes.

Jedibe Island, Botswana. It's not generally known, but hippos kill more tourists than any other animal in Africa. The reason's simple enough. Hippos have incredibly sensitive skin, so they protect it by staying in the water all day—but they don't eat in the water. After dark they climb ashore and forage inland for up to two miles to down their daily ration of 300 pounds of choice vegetation.

When they're in the water, all you can usually see are their eye sockets, their ears, and their nostrils, so naturally the tourist much prefers to photograph them on land, and the best time to do it is when they're coming back from a night's feeding.

Only one problem. Get between a hippo and water, and he panics. Every instinct tells him the water is safe, and he'll take the shortest route to it—which means he'll go *through* you, not around you.

So one day we're on Jedibe Island in the middle of the Okavango Swamp (I know, I know, I'm supposed to call it a Delta, but what it is is a swamp). Now, the more sophisticated tented camps usually supply a private bathroom, no matter how primitive, attached to each tent. Jedibe did not possess one of the more sophisticated tented camps. What it had was an ablution block, an area perhaps 30 feet on a side, surrounded by a 6-foot-high reed fence. Inside the block was a toilet (the long drop variety, of course) and a shower (the canvas bag variety, natch.)

At midnight I decide to use the facilities, so I wander over to the ablution block, maybe 40 yards from our tent—we were the only people in the camp that night, other than the couple who ran it—and in the fullness of time I prepare to unlatch the ablution block's door and return to my tent.

But just then a 3-ton hippo who'd been grazing in the area got an itch, and decided to scratch it by rubbing against the reed fence. And he rubbed, and he rubbed, and he rubbed, and that damned itch just wouldn't go away, and I knew how he felt, because I was being eaten alive by insects.

So I got to thinking, and I figured: Jedibe is a small island, maybe 300 yards in circumference, so if he sees me and he's got normal intelligence, he'll realize that all he has to do is turn around and trot off to the safety of the water.

Then I think a little more, and I figure: if, on the other hand, he's an exceptionally stupid hippo, wherever I stand he'll decide I'm between him and the water and will just lower his head and charge.

The scratching didn't sound very intelligent, and I decided not to chance it. Three hours later he satisfied his itch, grunted a few times, and went off for a swim. I got to the tent just in time to catch an hour of sleep before the sun came up and we were off to watch the very animal I'd been avoiding all night long.

✦

Mana Pools, Zimbabwe. Another tented camp, this one on the Zambezi River. We arrived in late morning, were shown to our tent, and were left alone to unpack. Carol saw a movement overhead, looked up, and found that we were sharing the tent with a 5-foot long spotted bush snake. Of course, we didn't know what the hell kind of snake it was, so I sought out the camp manager, who explained that it was harmless to people, but would hold the tent's lizard and insect population down to zero.

I didn't think any more of it until we came in all hot and dusty from the afternoon game run. Carol decided to take a shower before dinner. It turns out that the snake had the same idea and got there first. She took a look at the snake. The snake took a look at her. She screamed in surprise. The snake hissed in terror. She took off to the east. The snake took off to the west.

Eventually Carol came back. The snake, poor distraught fellow, never did.

✦

The Osiris—the Nile, Egypt. The Osiris is a ship, owned by the Hilton hotel chain, that travels the Nile from Cairo to Aswan and back again. We were visiting Egypt with Pat and Roger Sims (Roger chaired the 1959 Worldcon, and was Fan Guest of Honor at the 1988 rendition), my father, and my agent, Eleanor Wood, and her kids.

Since I was the African expert, I did the booking. I chose the Ramses Hilton, because it was the only 5-star hotel in Cairo that had never had a reported case of botulism. I booked the tour company, which had enough clout to make a plane turn around and come back for us when we were late getting to the airport. And I booked the Osiris, supposedly the most luxurious ship on the Nile.

Well, two out of three ain't bad.

Our friends Pat and Roger had the room right above us. Every time Roger took a shower we had a driving rain in our cabin.

And Roger likes to shower.

I never saw a desert in Egypt, but I saw a *lot* of rain. All of it inside.

✦

Malindi, Kenya. Malindi is a charming little town on the Kenya coast, halfway between Mombasa and Lamu. After touring the Gedi ruins, we checked in at the Sindbad Hotel, which looked exactly like something out of *Road to Morocco*, with its arched doorways and enclosed gardens and such. We had a nice dinner, watched some vigorous native dancers, and went to bed.

We awoke at six in the morning to find that our toilet, which had worked the previous day, was not functioning. We went down to the desk to complain, and the manager explained that there was nothing wrong with the toilet. To conserve water, he turned the toilets off at midnight and reactivated them at nine in the morning.

"But the shower and the sink worked," I said. "I tried them, just to see if the water had been shut off."

"Of course they work."

"Then why shut off the toilet?" I demanded.

He smiled. "Who takes a shower at four in the morning?" he responded.

Kenya may belong to the Third World. The Sindbad Hotel belonged to a world all its own.

Maralal, Kenya. The Maralal Lodge is a convenient halfway point between the Samburu/Buffalo Springs reserves and the lakes of the Rift Valley. (It's also the town where Jomo Kenyatta was imprisoned for 7 long years.)

The lodge has the most beautiful flower gardens. They're an odd sight in the middle of the arid Northern Frontier District.

It's a little less odd when you see the signs outside every cabin and in every bathroom, urging you not to drain the bathtub when you're through with it. With water at such a premium, they send a couple of attendants around every morning and afternoon. They fill buckets with dirty water from the tubs and empty them on the flower gardens.

The Mount Soche Hotel, Malawi. The best hotel in Blantyre, the former capital of Malawi back when it was Nyasaland, is the Mount Soche Hotel, so that's where we stayed. The elevators semi-worked, which is to say they went up and down, but they never once stopped at our floor. That's a really trivial problem for African accommodations, so we paid it no attention.

While we were in Blantyre we went to the local museum, where the college-educated curator tried to convince us that witchcraft was a valid science, and we drove and climbed Mount Mulanje, which at 9,000 feet isn't much of a mountain, but it's the tallest one they've got.

And then we went back to the hotel. And I blew my nose, and tossed the tissue in the toilet, and forgot about it. And as Carol passed by, she saw it and decided to flush it away. And couldn't find the flushing mechanism. Finally she saw a little button on the wall, and realized that was it. And she pushed. And it didn't budge.

She pushed again. Nothing happened. Finally she braced her feet, threw her whole weight into it, and flushed the toilet just before her thumb was due to break.

Her comment: "I've walked maybe 20 miles yesterday, and today I climbed the tallest mountain in the country. And flushing that damned toilet is the most exercise I've had since we've been here."

The Maasai Mara, Kenya. So we're staying in a tented camp in the Mara, and after dinner we watch some dancing, and finally it's about ten o'clock, and it's time to go to bed, since we'll be getting up at six to go on a game run. (I'd much prefer to get up at a civilized hour, but in Africa the animals lay up in the heat of the day, and you tend to take your game runs from 6:00 to 9:00 AM, and again from 3:30 to 6:00 PM. In between, *everyone* sleeps.

Anyway, we get to our tent, and sure enough, the toilet in the attached bathroom isn't working. I report it to the camp manager, he sends a fellow over to repair it, and five minutes later it's working.

He announces that he's going to walk home now. I offer to hunt up the manager and get him a ride.

"I am a Maasai," he says with proper arrogance. "I have lived here all my life. I have no fear of animals."

Twenty minutes later a helicopter is rushing him to the Nairobi hospital a couple of hundred miles away. It seems he ran into an equally arrogant elephant who had lived there all her life and had no fear of Maasai.

Linyati Camp, Botswana. So we're in the Linyati area of Botswana, and it's another camp with an ablution block. And just before I turn off my reading lamp to go to sleep, I decide to pay the ablution block a visit.

I get out of the tent and take two steps toward the block.

"Hi, Mike," say three hyenas, who are posted halfway to the block. "We're so glad you came out to play with us."

They grin to show me how happy they are.

I go back into the tent.

Ngorongoro Crater, Tanzania. If you could spend only one day in Africa, you'd be well-advised to spend it in the Crater, a caldera (collapsed volcano) about 10 miles in diameter, with an enormous concentration of large mammals—and the walls are so steep and high that they have almost no poachers.

What they do have on the floor of the Crater is a lovely little lake where our party—Pat and Roger Sims, Carol and myself, and my father—all stopped to enjoy a box lunch. And about thirty yards away was an old-fashioned outhouse with an honest-to-ghod half-moon carved on the door.

My father announced his intention to pay it a visit. Moro, our native guide, recommended against it. My father decided he couldn't wait, so off to the outhouse he went.

"He is a very brave man, your father," said Moro.

"How brave do you have to be to enter an outhouse?" I said, assuming he had warned us off because it was filthy.

"Very," he said. "A black mamba"—the most poisonous snake in Africa—"lives beneath the little hole you sit on."

I had raced halfway to the outhouse to pull my father out of there when he emerged, looking much relieved and totally unbitten.

There are so many others. There was Island Camp on Lake Baringo, which seemed to have established an ant farm in our shower stall. There was another tented camp in the Rift Valley where we shared our bathroom with a pet waterbuck who came running every time he heard the shower going. There was a hotel in Nancy, France, where every time you flushed the toilet the bidet shot water up to the ceiling.

But I'm going to close by telling you about the most memorable bathroom of all. The wild part is that I couldn't find it again if you paid me.

Maasai Mara, Kenya. It's 1986, our first trip to Kenya, and we're in the Mara, which is overflowing with animals and looks exactly like Hollywood's idea of Africa. We've been driving around watching them for a few hours, and Perry Mason, our guide—yes, that was his real name—and I decide that we have to answer a call of Nature. Carol, who has a bladder of steel, waits in the Land Rover while Perry and I go behind a likely bush.

And as we are doing what comes naturally, I look over, and there, about 20 yards away, is a 2,000-pound Cape buffalo doing exactly the same thing, and glar-ing at me as if I, and I alone, am responsible for his prostate problems.

So I alert Perry to our situation and ask him what to do.

His logical answer: "Finish before he does and run like hell."

We finished about ten seconds ahead of him, and beat him to the car by about three feet. The car proudly sported its scar from the buffalo's horns on our next two trips to Kenya, until it was replaced by a new Land Cruiser that soon displayed the gouge from a rhino's horn, which is an interesting story but has nothing to do with bathrooms, so I'll save it for another time and place.

Brian Trent, a Writers of the Future finalist, has sold stories to Apex, Daily Science Fiction, Escape Pod, *and* Cosmos. *This is his second sale to* Galaxy's Edge.

I, ARACHNOBOT

by Brian Trent

"Be careful, Jimmy!" the old woman says. "It might bite you!"

"It's a robot, Nana. It can't bite me."

"I've seen it bite flies!"

"But not a human being."

The woman with the silver hair and brown eyes anxiously peeks over Jimmy's shoulder to examine me. I've seen her before—in an abstract way while I fashion my webs outside her window—but now I see *her*. The person. The inhabitant of Room 18 in Sheldon Springs Retirement Home.

The nametag on her paisley blouse reads: MILDRED.

She begins a nervous pace, fidgeting and tucking her hair behind her ears as I sit helpless on Jimmy's palm, the tools in his other hand operating on my thorax microchip access-panel. Tools the same color as Mildred's hair.

"When I was a little girl on Anacreon," Mildred mutters, "there was a spider living outside my window. It built webs from the flowerbox to the awning. Anacreon has two suns, did you know that? At twinrise, their combined light seemed to set the web ablaze in two different colors. …" Mildred hesitates, drawing a finger to her mouth like a child who has forgotten an important detail. "I've already told you that story, haven't I, Jimmy?"

"It's okay, Nana."

My eight metallic legs claw uselessly at the air. My eye-cluster swivels and adjusts to regard my tormentor, Jimmy, as he brandishes one last tool—a pair of tweezers—to insert something into me.

A final click reverberates throughout my frame. Jimmy closes my thorax, slips his tools into a small case, and flips me right-side up.

"That'll do it!" he trumpets.

Again, Mildred peers over his shoulder and clutches his arm. "What did you do, Jimmy?"

The boy lifts me to his mouth.

Is he going to eat me? I do not wish to be eaten.

"Now listen here, arachnobot!" he declares in a rich, authoritative tone. "From this moment on, you are an artist. You are to continue making webs, but I've given you a little upgrade. You are to build webs which will make Grandma Millie happy. Every sunrise, you'll make her a new web!"

He plucks me from the table and returns me through the open window to my shimmering, dew-heavy web of liquid protein microfabricated strands. I orient myself in the web's center to watch the two humans in the room.

Jimmy hugs the old woman. "Now you have something to keep you happy until my next visit," he says. "Goodbye, Nana."

"Jimmy?" Mildred glances to the photographs on her nightstand. Her face crumples in quiet agonies. "You're not Jimmy. My Jimmy has been dead a long time, hasn't he?"

"It doesn't matter. I'll visit you next month, when I return from the conference. I love you."

Not-Jimmy goes out into the corridor, while Mildred paces anxiously around her room.

My web.

My web isn't good enough for her.

By sunrise the next morning, I've rewoven it into a silken paisley fern.

✧

May is humid, hazy, and dominated by flies.

As the arachnobot of Sheldon Springs Retirement Home, I follow a set of orders not so different, perhaps, from the genetic compulsions of actual arachnids in the vicinity: Spin webs to capture flies. Digest them into the protein polymers I will use to make more webs to capture more flies.

Following this set of commands are the hard-wired underpinnings of my very existence.

```
1.   A robot must never harm a
human being or, willingly and
knowingly, allow a human being to
be harmed.
```

2.   A robot must obey orders
given to it by human beings, unless those orders violate the
First Law.

And now my newest command sits weightily upon me:

Now listen here, arachnobot! From this moment on, you are an artist. You are to continue making webs, but I've given you a little upgrade. You are to build webs which will make Grandma Millie happy. Every sunrise, you'll make her a new web!

Mildred, I notice through her bedroom window, likes to read books with pictures. She touches pages and new images appear. A landscape of canals. A ringed world swollen on a cratered horizon. Sometimes the pictures bring a smile to Mildred's face. Sometimes they bring tears. I study her expressions. When she conjures the picture of a toad holding a crudely painted flower, she smiles and touches the screen with a quivering hand.

I could make a better flower than that.

By nightfall, she is sleeping with the book on the bed beside her. Its cover-screen fades to display the title: *Memories of Stars and Family.*

Sunrise awakens her. Mildred rubs her eyes, squinting toward the glittering, dangling flower in silk I've woven. Suspended between sill and latch, it glows radiant orange in the rising sunlight.

A ten-degree angle adjustment, I note, would be better.

Mildred approaches the glass. She is wearing pajamas with stars and crescent moons on them.

"How beautiful! Did you do this, little spider?"

I shiver pleasantly from the happy notes in her voice.

"I saw flowers like this when I was a child on Anacreon. I've seen a thousand worlds since then, but it always comes back to the first one, doesn't it?"

I have no idea, Mildred. But I like that you're happy.

"*The itsy bitsy spider, climbs up the water spout,*" she sings softly. Mildred likes to sing. She knows so many songs.

The door opens suddenly behind her.

A nurse enters. The nametag clipped to her uniform reads: JANET.

"Mildred, you're up early!"

"Hello Janet. I like your earrings."

"Do you?" The nurse jiggles the silver. "It's Saturn."

"Yes, I know."

"Oh?" Nurse Janet tilts her head. "Yes, of course. You're our famous astronaut! Helped discover a world of diamond!" Janet's eyes glitter in the refracted light of my web. "Lucky you!"

Mildred smiles. "I wish I could remember it."

Nurse Janet changes Mildred's bedsheets and notices the framed photographs on her nightstand. "Such a lovely family, too. It's just that grandson of yours now, yes? Such a handsome boy!"

Mildred gives a troubled nod. "Sometimes I don't remember him. It's like a stranger visiting me. Visiting his crazy grandma."

The nurse finishes with the bed. "Don't say that, Mildred. He'll be back in a few weeks and I'll bet you'll remember him just fine. Say, how about a picture together?"

Janet retrieves a camera from her uniform pocket. She tucks her arm around Mildred's waist and snaps the picture.

"Thank you, Millie!" Nurse Janet has a pleasant smile—a smile would make a nice design for a web—but as she examines the picture, the expression darkens. "You're not smiling, Millie! Why aren't you smiling? Oh, no matter."

She leaves the room.

The next morning, I reweave the flower into Saturn.

☼

I must create eight webs at various points around Sheldon Springs Retirement Home to most effectively cull the seasonal emergent fly population. The equation is as dependable as the structure of my body: a steady-state condition of fly populations versus predator (me) operating at optimal capture rates, resulting in a resource gain for the continued production of webs.

One of the choicest locations, nine meters from a pond where flies breed, is the staff breakroom. At 9:43 a.m., I construct a standard web outside that window.

Nurse Janet is in the room, sitting at a table across from a man in blue porter scrubs. I try to get a better glimpse of her earrings.

"He's hopped the space elevator," the porter says, nursing his coffee. His nametag reads: DANIEL. "He'll be gone three weeks. If we're going to do this, sis, we won't get a better chance."

Janet drums the table with her fingers. "Of course we're going to do this. Think I'm going to be stuck working here my whole life?" She half-turns, allowing me an oblique view of the earrings. I catch a glimpse of fishtails.

"I've already got it worked out," she continues. "Tomorrow, you drug her breakfast and bring it to her at 8 a.m. At 8:30 a.m., you knock over a mop and bucket right outside her door. That's the perfect excuse to keep people away from her room; there's a stairwell right there, and that floor is deadly when wet."

"Then what?"

"While you're cleaning up the spilled water, I visit Mildred."

"And?"

She turns to the window. I see the earrings in full now. Mermaids.

I could do that.

"Pillow over the head," Janet says.

"And what about her will?" Daniel asks. "The old bitch is so out of it, she might have left her estate to a field mouse."

"Her original will left everything to the Space Agency and her grandson. Let's say I've gotten … *close* to her executor. There's a new will now. It leaves a substantial sum to her favorite nurse."

"And porter …" Daniel insists.

"Of course. Just remember: 8 a.m. breakfast; 8:30, spill the bucket. *I'll* kill her."

I almost fall off my web, dangling from a single strand.

Kill her?

Kill Mildred?

1. A robot must never harm a human being or, willingly and knowingly, allow a human being to be harmed.

As the two humans depart, I climb in through the window, setting my eye-cluster on the wall-phone. Emergencies are handled by the police. Police can be contacted through various communication devices such as, but not limited to, a phone.

Mildred is in danger.

From the sill to the breakroom table, past rings of old coffee-stains and a discarded fork, I crawl toward the phone. It is red, shiny, and has a flat readout screen.

I hesitate, quivering uncertainly on my metallic legs.

I don't have a voice.

Nonetheless, phones are for communication and there are ways to communicate other than through larynx vibrations. I *must* communicate the murder plot. Otherwise Mildred will die tomorrow. The First Law vibrates along my limbs. So, too, does my other programming: Build webs to catch flies. The compulsion rises. I'll have to build a web soon. The flies are out there, multiplying.

But first …

I stab one leg into the MAKE CALL button.

"Enter biometric signature," says the phone.

I halt, stunned.

Arachnobots do not have biometric data. Only humans do.

I peer at the many coffee mugs, magazines, and eating utensils in the breakroom. There must be a hundred biometric samples I can use here. Fingerprints on that dirty fork, for instance. This should be a simple matter to—

A scream startles me.

I pivot toward the door and see Janet standing there, a look of horror on her face. She rushes me, snatching a magazine as she does, and slams it down just as I leap out of the way. I land hard on the floor, and narrowly avoid a second, crushing blow from her boot.

"Little bastard!" she cries.

I dash into the dust beneath the heater, hiding behind pipes.

From the doorway, Daniel peeks in. "What's wrong?"

"A spider! A *huge* one!"

"Real or robotic?"

"It was bright blue! Robotic, I think."

"Then it can't hurt you. Calm down, sis!"

"I *hate* those things!"

While she's jabbing the rolled-up magazine beneath the heater, I clamber up the wall and escape to the other side of the window. Another cry, and the magazine smacks the glass, knocking me into the bushes.

Janet leans out the window.

"Hey arachnobot!" she yells. "I order you stay out of here forever!"

✿

I try to enter the breakroom during the night.

Janet has closed the window but there's space for me to squeeze through the jamb. Yet each time I approach the glass, my movements become sluggish. My legs stick in their sockets. It helps to imagine flies in the breakroom. There *could* be flies in the breakroom. Still, Janet's voice is like a web of her own stretching across me.

I order you stay out of here forever!

Of course, Janet is not Calvin Positronics. Her command cannot override my basic programming: *Spin webs to capture flies. Digest them into the protein polymers I will use to make more webs to capture more flies.* I'm assigned to Sheldon Springs Retirement Home. Janet cannot banish me.

Besides, she told me to stay out of *here* forever.

What does *here* mean?

She could have been referring to her pocket.

Very well, Janet. I shall stay out of your pocket until the heat death of the universe.

I attempt another approach. My legs freeze, shudder, and stop. Janet meant the breakroom. She was *in* the breakroom when she said it.

The phone is like a red cherry behind the glass. I cannot, *cannot*, reach it. The breakroom is off-limits to me for all eternity.

However, there *are* other phones in this building. There's one in Mildred's room!

I hurtle across the building's brick exterior to her window, climb through, and approach the nightstand phone. Mildred is sleeping, one of her frail hands hanging over the bedside.

I festoon her wrist with silk from my spinnerets. It takes all my strength to pull it the four inches needed to brush the phone's biometric pad.

The phone lights up on contact.

I dash to it and dial the police.

"Emergency," a woman answers.

I have no voice. But I dutifully tap out a rudimentary pattern against the receiver, explaining that Nurse Janet with the mermaid earrings is planning to kill Mildred in three hours.

"Hello?" the voice says. "Is anyone there?"

I halt, confused by this lack of understanding.

The line disconnects.

Sunrise is only minutes away. Somewhere, the flies are multiplying.

Hurriedly, I build a web.

My web is of a mermaid, hung at the correct angle to better catch the sunrise. Not my best work, I admit. But it brings a smile to Mildred's face when she sees it upon waking at 5:41 a.m.

"Did you make this mermaid, little spider?" she asks on the other side of the glass. "How did you do it? Oh! It's so pretty!" She closes her eyes, a childish grin on her lips. "*Little Miss Muffet, sat on a tuffet, eating her curds and whey …*"

I like when she sings to me.

I like when Millie's happy.

Happiness is only possible if she's alive.

Janet is plotting to end her life in two hours and forty-nine minutes.

If her life is ended, Millie won't be happy. There will be no more songs.

Nurse Janet, I conclude, needs to die.

✿

Prior to my reprogramming, there were specific tabulations I needed to complete during the course of a given day. How large should my webs be? Where should they be built? How many webs should I build without marring the overall aesthetic of the retirement home?

Now I aim my tabulation talents at a different challenge:

```
1.  A robot must never harm a hu-
man being ...
```

It's hardwired into me, yet the wording itself is cause for analysis. The First Law does not say *Homo sapiens*. It says *human being*.

At 5:52 a.m. I invade Mildred's room and scamper down the glossy hallway to the room marked STUDY on my internal map of Sheldon Springs Retirement Home.

On one of the counters is a book I've noticed from the window: The Galactic Empire Seventh Edition Dictionary. I pry open its cover, flipping the pages:

```
HUMAN BEING:

1.  an individual of the species
Homo sapiens.

2.  of, pertaining to, or charac-
teristic of human beings.

3.  the human race, as distin-
guished from animals and robots.

4.  empathetic, sympathetic;
humane.
```

Mildred and Nurse Janet are both *Homo sapiens*. Yet according to the Galactic Empire Seventh Edition Dictionary, not all *Homo sapiens* are humane and therefore not all are human. By this argument, Janet is not protected by the First Law, but Mildred is.

I can kill her.

In theory.

It is 6:28 a.m.

Janet will kill Mildred in two hours and two minutes.

Six hundred and ninety-five ways to murder Janet immediately flash through my processors. I quickly reduce these to a pair of options which I calculate have the greatest chance for success:

```
1.  I can create a multilayered
silk mask and suffocate her with it
when she enters Mildred's room.
```

```
2.  I can lure her to the roof-
top with a note claiming to be
from Daniel, and impale her with
a spring-loaded trigger-trap built
from kitchen knives, a cutting
board, two mop handles, and forty-
six flies' worth of silken strands.
```

Grudgingly, I admit that the artistry implicit in the second option is outweighed by the relative ease of the first. I hastily return to Mildred's room. A fly buzzes by me; the window has been left open—Millie likes fresh air—and there are flies in here, likely attracted to the pastries she stockpiles. I ignore the flies with great difficulty. Just knowing they're in here weighs on me like a high gravity field. Spin webs. I must spin webs. Must capture flies.

But first …

I spin the suffocation mask. I shape it into a resemblance of Janet's own visage. I …

I …

I …

I …

☼

I cannot proceed with the murder.

Cannot trick myself into murdering a human being.

It is 8:03 a.m. when I recover from my paralysis.

The silken mask I've been weaving dangles in front of the door. It is pretty, and it was meant to murder, but … I cannot murder. Except for the flies in this room. I could murder them easily enough.

Without warning, the door swings open beneath me. Daniel enters with a breakfast tray.

"Good morning, Millie!"

"Good morning, Daniel."

"I, um … I made your favorite. Eggs Benedict."

Millie smiles. "Thank you!"

As he leaves the room, I imagine dropping down on his neck and pulling his brain out through his ear. Mildred sits down at the window, directly in front of the silk mermaid I've made for her, and begins to eat—

No! Millie, don't!

It is 8:05 a.m.

At 8:29 a.m. she's halfway through breakfast when her hand slumps to her side. She falls asleep in her chair.

I nervously dash back and forth across the door's lintel. On the other side, there's commotion. Someone has just knocked over a bucket of dirty water outside Millie's door, across from the stairwell.

I dart to the door's corners, dripping silk in terror. Silken draglines positioned at each corner might seal the door shut. I nearly empty my reserves, layering the nets as fast as my steel spinnerets will allow.

Down the hallway, footsteps are approaching.

I frantically apply the last layer.

The footsteps reach the door.

The door sticks.

Yes!

"What the hell?" cries Janet. Her voice alters into a sweet, loving tone. "Millie? Are you okay? Is something braced against the door?"

The door bulges slightly. The silken netting stretches to the breaking point.

Janet grunts, curses. The door flies open. Against the nearby air-conditioner, I deploy the silken mask as a parachute, ballooning along the current like a ghostly specter directly in front of Janet's face.

Her eyes bulge in disbelief.

The mask hovers in the air. From its mouth, a ball of silk unfolds into a banner, letters bright gold in the sunlight:

STAY AWAY FROM MILLIE

Janet angrily storms forward, batting the mask away, her lips opening in a bestial snarl. I deploy a silken balloon, watching helplessly as Janet strides to the bed, grabs a pillow, and approaches Millie in the chair. I watch as—

—a fly goes into Janet's mouth.

She's so hell-bent on murder that she doesn't notice. But I do. And I suddenly remember one of Millie's many songs:

There was an old woman who swallowed a fly. Perhaps she'll die.

Perhaps she'll *die?!?!*

A robot must never harm a human being or, willingly and knowingly, allow a human being to be harmed.

My job is to catch flies …

Still floating on the room's currents, I shoot a web-strand into Janet's nose. Abandoning my silk balloon behind me, I swing down into her lips and, eagerly, *go in after the fly.*

Her mouth is wet, warm; her throat a slippery chute. She feels my invasion. Her screams resonate around me. The fly vibrates in the dark. I leap, grab it, struggle in the soft confines of her esophagus.

Janet is screaming. I think she's running.

Until, quite suddenly, she's no longer doing either.

"How did you do this, little spider?"

I pluck the silken rocketship I've built outside her window, taking great delight in Millie's smile.

"There was an awful accident yesterday," she says on the other side of the glass. "A nurse slipped and took a fatal tumble down the stairs. That's so terrible, isn't it?"

Not so terrible, Millie. But I'm glad you're happy.

"Can I sing you a song?"

Yes, Millie. Sing to me. Sing as long as you like.

I, arachnobot, will always be here for you.

    ☙ **Dedicated to Isaac Asimov** ❧

Original (First) Publication
Copyright © 2014 by Brian Trent

Robert J. Sawyer is the winner of the Hugo, the Nebula, Canada's Aurora, Spain's UPC, and Japan's Seiun-sho awards. Canada's leading science fiction writer, he was recently given an honorary Doctor of Laws degree by the University of Winnipeg.

STAR LIGHT, STAR BRIGHT

by Robert J. Sawyer

"Daddy, what are those?" My young son, Dalt, was pointing up. We'd floated far away from the ancient buildings, almost to where the transparent dome over our community touches the surface of the great sphere.

Four white hens were flying across the sky, their little wings propelling them at a good clip. "Those are chickens, Dalt. You know—the birds we get eggs from."

"Not the *chickens*," said Dalt, as if I'd offended him greatly by suggesting he didn't know what they were. "Those lights. Those points of light."

I squinted a bit. "I don't see any lights," I replied. "Where are they?"

"Everywhere," he said. He swung his head in an arc, taking in the whole sky. "Everywhere."

"How many points do you see?"

"Hundreds. Thousands."

I felt my back bumping gently against the surface; I pushed off with my palm, rising into the air again. The ancient texts I'd been translating said human beings were never really meant to live in such low gravity, but it was all I, and countless generations of my ancestors, had ever known. "There aren't any points of light, Dalt."

"Yes, there are," he insisted. "There are thousands of them, and—look!—there's a band of light across the sky there."

I faced in the direction he was pointing. "I don't see anything except another chicken."

"No, Daddy," insisted Dalt. "Look!"

Dalt was a good boy. He almost never lied to me—and I couldn't see why he would lie to me about something like this. I maneuvered so that we were hovering face to face, then extended my hand.

"Can you see my hand clearly?" I said.

"Sure."

"How many fingers am I holding up?"

He rolled his eyes. "Oh, Daddy …"

"How many fingers am I holding up?"

"Two."

"And do you see lights on them, as well?"

"On your fingers?" asked Dalt incredulously.

I nodded.

"Of course not."

"You don't see any lights in front of my fingers? Do you see any on my face?"

"Daddy!"

"Do you?"

"Of course not. The lights aren't down here. They're up there!"

I touched my boy's shoulder reassuringly. "Tomorrow, we'll go see Doc Tadders about your eyes."

We hadn't built the protective dome—the clear blister on the outer surface of the *Dyson* sphere (to use the ancient name our ancestors had given to our home, a term we could transliterate but not translate). Rather, the dome was already here when we'd come outside. Adjacent to it was a large, black pyramidal structure that didn't seem to be part of the sphere's outer hull; instead, it appeared to be clamped into place. No one was exactly sure what the pyramid was for, although you could enter it from an access tube extending from the dome. The pyramid was filled with corridors and rooms, and lots of control consoles marked in the script of the ancients.

The transparent dome was much larger than the pyramid—plenty big enough to cover the thirty-odd buildings the ancients had built here, as well as the concentric circles of farming fields we'd created by importing soil from within the interior of the Dyson sphere. Still, if the dome hadn't been transparent, I probably would have felt claustrophobic within it; it wasn't even a pimple on the vastness of the sphere.

We'd been fortunate that the ancients had constructed all these buildings under the protective dome; they served as homes and work spaces for us. In many cases, we could only guess at the original purposes of the buildings, but the one that housed Dr. Tadders' office had likely been a warehouse.

After sleeptime, I took Dalt to see Tadders. He seemed more fascinated by the wall diagram the doctor had of a human skeleton than he was by her eye chart, but we'd finally got him to spin around in midair to face it.

I was floating freely beside my son. For an instant, I found myself panicking because there was no anchor rope looped around my wrist; the habits of a lifetime were hard to break, even after being here, on the outside of the Dyson sphere, for all this time. I'd lived from birth to middle age on the inside of the sphere, where things tended to float up if they weren't anchored. Of course, you couldn't drift all the way up to the sun. You'd eventually bump against the glass roof that held the atmosphere in. But no one wanted to be stuck up there, waiting to be rescued; it was humiliating.

Out here, though, under our clear, protective dome, things floated *down*, not up; both Dalt and I would eventually settle to the padded floor.

"Can you read the top row of letters?" asked Doc Tadders, indicating the eye chart. She was about my age, with pale blue eyes and red hair just beginning to turn gray.

"Sure," said Dalt. "Eet, bot, doo, shuh, kee."

Tadders nodded. "What about the next row?"

"Hih, fah, roo, shuh, puh, ess."

"Can you read the last row?"

"Ayt, doo, tee, nuh, tee, ess, guh, hih, fah, roo."

"Are you sure about the second letter?"

"It's a doo, no?" said Dalt.

If there's any letter my son should know, it should be that one, since it was the first in his own name. But the character on the chart wasn't a doo; it was a fah.

Dr. Tadders jotted a note in the book she was holding, then said, "What about the last letter?"

"That's a roo."

"Are you sure?"

Dalt squinted. "Well, if it's not a roo, then it's an shuh, no?"

"Which do you think it is?"

"A shuh … or a roo." Dalt shrugged. "It's so tiny, I can't be sure."

I could see that it was a roo; I was surprised that I had better vision than my son did.

"Thanks," said Tadders. She looked at me. "He's a tiny bit nearsighted," she said. "Nothing to worry about." She faced Dalt again. "What about the lights in front of your eyes? Do you see any of them now?"

"No," said Dalt.

"None at all?"

"You can only see them in the dark," he said.

Tadders pushed against the padded wall with her palm, which was enough to send her drifting across the room toward the light switch; the ancients had made switches that were little rockers, instead of the click-in/click-out buttons we build. She rocked the switch, and the lighting strips at the edges of the padded roof went dark. "What about now?"

Dalt sounded puzzled. "No."

"Let's give your eyes a few moments to adjust," she said.

"It won't make any difference," said Dalt, exasperated. "You can only see the lights outside."

"Outside?" repeated Tadders.

"That's right," said Dalt. "Outside. In the dark. Up in the sky."

Dalt was the first child born after our group left the interior of the Dyson sphere. Our little town had a population of 240 now, of which fifteen had been born since we'd come outside. Dalt's usual playmate was Suzto, the daughter of the couple who lived next door to my wife and me in a building that had clearly been designed by the ancients to be living quarters.

All adults spent half their days working on their particular area of expertise, which, for me, was translating ancient documents stored in the computers inside the buildings and the pyramid, and the other half doing the chores that were needed to support a fledgling society. But after work, I took Dalt and Suzto for a float. We drifted away from the lights of the ancient buildings, across the fields of crops, and out toward the access tunnel that led to the pyramid.

I knew that the surface of the sphere, beneath us, was curved, of course, and, here on the outside, that it curved down. But the sphere was so huge that everything seemed flat. Oh, one could make out the indentations that were hills on the other side of the sphere's shell, and the raised plateaus that water collected in. Although we *were* on the frontier—the outside of the sphere!—we were still only one bodylength away from the world we'd left behind; that's how thick the sphere's shell was. But the double-doored portal that led back inside had been sealed off; the people on the interior had welded it shut after we'd left. They wanted nothing to do with whatever we might find out here, calling our quest for knowledge of the exterior universe a sacrilege against the wisdom of the ancients.

As we floated in the darkness, Dalt looked up again and said, "See! The lights!"

Suzto looked up, too. I expected her to scrunch her face in puzzlement, baffled by Dalt's words, but instead, near as I could make out in the darkness, she was smiling in wonder.

"Can—can you see the lights, too?" I asked Suzto.

"Sure."

I was astonished. "How big are they?"

"Tiny. Like this." She held up her hand, but if there was any space between her finger and thumb, I couldn't make it out.

"Are they arranged in some sort of pattern?"

Suzto's vocabulary wasn't yet as big as Dalt's. She looked at me, and I tried again. "Do they make shapes?"

"Maybe," said Suzto. "Some are brighter than others. There are three over there that make a straight line."

I frowned. "Dalt, please cover your eyes."

He did so, with elaborate hand gestures.

"Suzto, point to the brightest light in the sky."

"There're so many," she said.

"All right, all right. Point to the brightest one in this part of the sky over here."

She didn't hesitate. "That one."

"Okay," I said, "now put your hand down, please."

She drew her arm back in toward her body.

"Dalt, uncover your eyes."

He did so.

"Now, Dalt, point to the brightest light in this part of the sky over here."

He lifted his arm, then seemed to vacillate for a moment between two possible choices.

"Not that one, silly," said Suzto's voice. She pointed. "This one's brighter."

"Oh, yeah," said Dalt. "I guess it is." He pointed at it, too. I couldn't see anything, but it seemed in the darkness that if I could draw lines from the two children's outstretched fingers, they would converge at infinity.

Dr. Tadders was an old friend, and with both Suzto and Dalt seeing the lights, I decided to join her for lunch. We grew wheat, corn, and other crops under lamps here on the outside of the sphere, and raised chickens and pigs. If you wanted the eggs to hatch, you had to put low roofs over the hens, because they needed to be in constant contact with their clutches, and their own body movements were enough to propel them into flight; chickens really seemed to love flying. Tadders and I both knew that we'd have had more interesting meals if we'd stayed inside the sphere, but the ancient texts said that although the interior was huge, there was still much, much more to the universe.

Most of those on the interior didn't care about such things; they knew that the sphere's inner surface could accommodate over a million trillion human beings—a vastly larger number than the current population—and that our ancestors had shut us off from the rest of the universe for a reason. But some of us had decided to venture outside, starting a new settlement on our world's only real frontier. I didn't miss much about the inside—but I did miss the food.

"All right, Rodal," Dr. Tadders said, gesturing with a sandwich triangle, "here's what I think is happening." She took a deep breath, as if reviewing her thoughts once more before giving them voice, then: "We know that a long, long time ago, our ancestors built a double-walled shell around our sun. The outer wall is opaque, and the inner wall, fifty bodylengths above that, is transparent. The area between the two walls is the habitat, where all those who still live on the interior of the sphere reside."

I nodded, and kicked gently off the floor to keep myself afloat. We drifted out of the dining hall, heading outdoors.

"Well," she continued, "we also know that there was a war generations ago that knocked humanity back into a primitive state. We've been rebuilding our civilization for a long time, but we're nowhere near as advanced as our ancestors who constructed our world were."

That was certainly true. "So?"

"So, what about that story you translated a while ago? The one about where we supposedly came from?"

I'd found a story in the ancient computers that claimed that before we lived on the interior of the Dyson sphere, our ancestors had made their home on the outer surface of a small, solid, rocky globe. "But that was probably just a myth," I said. "I mean, such a globe would have been impossibly tiny. The myth said the homeworld was six million bodylengths in diameter. Kobost"—a physicist in our community—"worked out that if it were made of the elements the myth described, even a globe that small would have had a crushingly huge gravitational attraction: five bodylengths per heartbeat squared. That's more than ten thousand times what we experience here."

Of course, the gravitational attraction on any point on the interior of a hollow sphere is zero. When we lived inside the sphere, the only gravity we felt was the pull from our sun, gently tugging things upward. Here, on the outside of the sphere, the gravitational pull is downward, toward the sphere's surface—and the sun at its center.

I continued. "Although Kobost thinks human muscle could perhaps be built up enough to withstand such an overwhelming gravity, his own studies prove that the globe described in the myth can't be our homeworld."

"Why not?" asked Tadders.

"Because of the chickens. There are several ancient texts that show that chickens have been essentially the same since before our ancestors built the Dyson sphere. But with an acceleration due to gravity of five bodylengths per heartbeat squared, their wings wouldn't be strong enough to let them fly. So that globe in the myth couldn't possibly have been our ancestral home."

"Well, I agree that's puzzling about the chickens," said Tadders, "but wherever our ancestors came from, you have to admit it wasn't another Dyson sphere. And the inside of a Dyson sphere forms a very special kind of sky. Remember what it was like when we lived in there? Wherever you looked over your head, you saw—well, you saw the sun, of course, if you looked directly overhead. But everywhere else, you saw other parts of the sphere. Some of those parts are a long, long way off—the far side of the sphere is a hundred and fifty billion bodylengths away, isn't it? But, regardless, wherever you looked, you saw either the sun or the surface of the sphere."

"So?"

"So the surface of the sphere is reflective—even the dull, grass-covered parts reflect back a lot of light. Indeed, on average the surface reflects back about a third of the light it receives from the sun, making the whole sky glaringly bright."

People in there did have a tendency to float facing the ground instead of the sky. I nodded for her to go on.

"Well, our eyes didn't evolve here," continued Tadders. "If we did come from a rocky world, the sun would have been seen against an empty, non-reflective sky. It must be much, much brighter inside the Dyson sphere than it ever was on the original homeworld."

"Surely our eyes would have adapted to deal with the brighter light here."

"How?" asked Tadders. "Even after the great war, we regained a measure of civilization fairly quickly. There was no period during which we were reduced to survival of the fittest. Human beings haven't undergone any appreciable evolution since long before our ancestors built the sphere. Which means our eyes are as they originally were: suited for much dimmer light. Of course, the ancients may have had drugs or other things that made the interior light seem more comfortable to them, but whatever they used must have been lost in the war."

"I suppose," I said.

"But you, me, and everyone else in our settlement who has lived inside the sphere—we've damaged our retinas, without even knowing it."

I saw what she was getting at. "But the children—the children born here, on the outside of the sphere—"

She nodded. "The children born here, after we left the interior, have never been exposed to the brightness inside, and so they see just as well in the dark as our distant, distant ancestors did, back on the homeworld. The points of light the children are seeing really do exist, but they're simply too faint to register on the damaged retinas we adults have."

My head was swimming. "Maybe," I said. "Maybe. But—but what *are* those lights?"

Tadders pursed her lips, then lifted her shoulders a bit. "You want my best guess? I think they're other suns, like the one our ancestors encased in the sphere, but so incredibly far away that they're all but invisible." She looked up, out the clear roof of the dome covering our town, out at the uniform blackness, which was all either of us could make out. She then used one of the words I'd taught her, a word transliterated from the ancient texts—a word we could pronounce but whose meaning we'd never really understood. "I think," she said, "that the points of light are *stars*."

There were thousands of documents stored in the ancient computers; my job was to try to make sense of as many of them as I could. And I made much progress as Dalt continued to grow up. Eventually, he and the other children were able to match the patterns of stars they could see in the sky to those depicted in ancient charts I'd found. The patterns didn't correspond exactly; the stars had apparently drifted in relation to each other since the charts had been made. But the kids—the adolescents, now—were indeed able to discern the *constellations* shown in the old texts; ironically, this was easier to do, they said, when some of the lights of our frontier town were left on, drowning out all but the brightest stars.

According to the charts, our sun—the sun enclosed in the Dyson sphere—was the star the ancients had called Tau Ceti. It was not the original home to humanity, though; our ancestors were apparently unwilling to cannibalize the worlds of their own system to make their Dyson sphere. Instead, they—we—had come from another star, the closest similar one that wasn't part of a multiple system, a sun our ancestors had called Sol.

And the *planet*—that was the term—we had evolved on was, in the infinite humility of our wise ancestors, called by a simple, unassuming name, one I could easily translate: Dirt.

Old folks like me couldn't live on Dirt now, of course. Our muscles—including our hearts—were weak compared to what our ancestors must have had, growing up under the stupendous gravity of that tiny, rocky world.

But—

But locked in our genes, as if for safekeeping, were all the potentials we'd ever had as a species. The ability to see dim sources of light, and—

Yes, it must be there, too, still preserved in our DNA.

The ability to produce muscles strong enough to withstand much, much higher gravity.

You'd have to grow up under such a gravity, have to live with it from birth, said Dr. Tadders, to really be comfortable with it, but if you did—

I'd seen Kobost's computer animation showing how we might have moved under a much greater gravity, how we might have deployed our bodies vertically, how our spines would have supported the weight of our heads, how our legs might have worked back and forth, hinging at knee and ankle, producing sustained forward locomotion. It all seemed so bizarre, and so inefficient compared to spending most of one's life floating, but—

But there were new worlds to explore, and old ones, too, and to fully experience them would require being able to stand on their surfaces.

Dalt was growing up to be a fine young man. There wasn't a lot of choice for careers in a small community: he could have apprenticed with his mother, Delar, who worked as our banker, or with me. He chose me, and so I did my best to teach him how to read the ancient texts.

"I've finished translating that file you gave me," he said on one occasion. "It was what you suspected: just a boring list of supplies." I guess he saw that I was only half-listening to him. "What's got you so intrigued?" he asked.

I looked up, and smiled at his face, with its bits of fuzz; I'd have to teach him how to shave soon. "Sorry," I said. "I've found some documents related to the pyramid. But there are several words I haven't encountered before."

"Such as?"

"Such as this one," I said, pointing at a string of eight letters on the computer screen. "'*Starship*.' The first part is obviously the word for those lights you can see in the sky: *stars*. And the second part, *hip*, well—"I slapped my haunch—"that's their name for where the leg joins the torso. They often made compounded words in this fashion, but I can't for the life of me figure out what a 'stars hip' might be."

I always say nothing is better than a fresh set of eyes. "Yes, they often used that hissing sound for plurals," said Dalt. "But those two letters there—

can't they also be transliterated jointly as shuh, instead of separately as ess and hih?"

I nodded.

"So maybe it's not 'stars hip,'" he said. "Maybe it's 'star ship.'"

"*Ship*," I repeated. "Ship, ship, ship—I've seen that word before." I riffled through a collection of papers, searching my notes; the sheets fluttered around the room, and Dalt dutifully began collecting them for me. "Ship!" I exclaimed. "Here it is: 'a kind of vehicle that could float on water.'"

"Why would you want to float on water when you can float on air?" asked Dalt.

"On the homeworld," I said, "water didn't splash up in great clouds every time you touched it. It stayed in place." I frowned. "Star ship. Starship. A—a vehicle of stars?" And then I got it. "No," I said, grabbing my son's arm in excitement. "No—a vehicle for traveling to the stars!"

Dalt and Suzto eventually married, to no one's surprise.

But I *was* surprised by my son's arms. He and Suzto had been exercising for ages now, and when Dalt bent his arm at the elbow, the upper part of it *bulged*. Doc Tadders said she'd never seen anything like it, but assured us it wasn't a tumor. It was *meat*. It was muscle.

Dalt's legs were also much, much thicker than mine. Suzto hadn't bulked up quite as much, but she, too, had developed great strength.

I knew what they were up to, of course. I admired them both for it, but I had one profound regret.

Suzto had gotten pregnant shortly after she and Dalt had married—at least, they told me that the conception had occurred after the wedding, and, as a parent, it's my prerogative to believe them. But I'd never know for sure. And *that* was my great regret: I'd never get to see my own grandchild.

Dalt and Suzto would be able to *stand* on Dirt, and, indeed, would be able to endure the journey there. The starship was designed to accelerate at a rate of five bodylengths per heartbeat squared, simulating Dirt's gravity. It would accelerate for half its journey, reaching a phenomenal speed by so doing,

then it would turn around and decelerate for the other half.

They were the logical choices to go. Dalt knew the ancient language as well as I did now; if there were any records left behind by our ancestors on the homeworld, he should be able to read them.

He and Suzto had to leave soon, said Doc Tadders; it would be best for the child if it developed under the fake gravity of the starship's acceleration. Dalt and Suzto would be able to survive on Dirt, but their child should actually be comfortable there.

My wife and I came to see them off, of course—as did everyone else in our settlement. We wondered what people in the sphere would make of it when the pyramid lifted off—it would do so with a kick that would doubtless be detectable on the other side of the shell.

"I'll miss you, son," I said to Dalt. Tears were welling in my eyes. I hugged him, and he hugged me back, so much harder than I could manage.

"And, Suzto," I said, moving to my daughter-in-law, while my wife moved to hug our son. "I'll miss you, too." I hugged her, as well. "I love you both."

"We love you, too," Suzto said.

And they entered the pyramid.

I was hovering over a field, harvesting radishes. It was tricky work; if you pulled too hard, you'd get the radish out, all right, but then you and it would go sailing up into the air.

"Rodal! Rodal!"

I looked in the direction of the voice. It was old Doc Tadders, hurtling toward me, a white-haired projectile. At her age, she should be more careful—she could break her bones slamming into even a padded wall at that speed.

"Rodal!"

"Yes?"

"Come! Come quickly! A message has been received from Dirt!"

I kicked off the ground, sailing toward the communication station next to the access tube that used to lead to the starship. Tadders managed to turn around without killing herself and she flew there alongside me.

A sizable crowd had already gathered by the time we arrived.

"What does the message say?" I asked the person closest to the computer monitor.

He looked at me in irritation; the ancient computer had displayed the text, naturally enough, in the ancient script, and few besides me could understand that. He moved aside and I consulted the screen, reading aloud for the benefit of everyone.

"It says, 'Greetings! We have arrived safely at Dirt.'"

The crowd broke into cheers and applause. I couldn't help reading ahead a bit while waiting for them to quiet down, so I was already misty-eyed when I continued. "It goes on to say, 'Tell Rodal and Delar that they have a grandson; we've named him Madar.'"

My wife had passed on some time ago—but she would have been delighted at the choice of Madar; that had been her father's name.

"'Dirt is beautiful, full of plants and huge bodies of water,'" I read. "'And there are other human beings living here. It seems those people interested in technology moved to the Dyson sphere, but a small group who preferred a pastoral lifestyle stayed on the homeworld. We're mastering their language—it's deviated a fair bit from the one in the ancient texts—and are already great friends with them.'"

"Amazing," said Doc Tadders.

I smiled at her, wiped my eyes, then went on: "'We will send much more information later, but we can clear up at least one enduring mystery right now.'" I smiled as I read the next part. "'Chickens can't fly here. Apparently, just because you have wings doesn't mean you were meant to fly.'"

That was the end of the message. I looked up at the dark sky, wishing I could make out Sol, or any star. "And just because you don't have wings," I said, thinking of my son and his wife and my grandchild, far, far away, "doesn't mean you weren't."

Alvaro Zinos-Amaro is the co-author (with Robert Silverberg) of When the Blue Shift Comes, *a Stellar Guild book published by this company. His short fiction, poetry, essays and reviews have appeared in multiple online markets and in translation abroad.*

EINE KLEINE NACHTFILM

by Alvaro Zinos-Amaro

Doug and Jenn have been friends for a very long time, longer than seems possible. As they set up the film projector and sound system in the neighborhood park this shared history becomes evident: glances and nods suffice to know who's doing what, and in what order.

The setting sun bleeds magenta and rouge into a stark blue sky. It takes Doug and Jenn about an hour to prepare the equipment. They test the projector's resolution on the screen, ensure that the speakers are at optimal distances. The silence between them is comfortable and elastic, the type of silence that could stretch into conversation at any moment but doesn't need to.

The park is small: three aluminum-and-pine picnic tables, a modest basketball court, and a playground. Discreetly placed misters surround the play space, keeping it cool during the endless summer's hot, long days, and doubling as sprinklers at night. As part of their preparations, Doug and Jenn make sure to turn them off, lest the audience be sprayed.

Night has fallen, refreshing the air. This is Doug and Jenn's cue to arrange the folding chairs and lay out the snacks and drinks on the picnic tables. A cool breeze blows over them as they set about these final to-dos.

Once done, Doug and Jenn enjoy the stillness of the night-time park in the moments before anyone arrives. "Good work," Doug says, nodding philosophically and crossing his arms. Jenn looks around at the empty chairs, the food and beverages waiting to be savored, the machines eager to hum to life with crystal images and rich sounds. A strand of Jenn's long silver hair glints with stray starlight. She smiles in agreement.

A few minutes later families begin to arrive in small, tentative clusters. Doug and Jenn greet them and then get out of the way. Some of the parents change their minds about their seats, walk around haltingly. But soon enough a dozen more families show up and a kind of critical mass is reached. Everyone relaxes and gets into the spirit of things. Conversations spark, soda is poured and spilled, crumbs and candy wrappers are strewn onto the perfectly manicured lawns, and various speculations about tonight's film are voiced—loudly.

"The one with the giant mushrooms!" yells a freckle-laden blonde boy.

"No, no, the one about soft rains and all of summer in a day!" hollers his brown-eyed sister, pumping her arms in the air.

"The one about the parrot who met papa!" chimes in a slender girl with thin eyebrows and a pointed chin.

"The one about the chocolate bar that makes boys invisible!" contributes her more rotund, red-haired friend.

"A medicine for melan-choly!" shouts another young boy.

On and on they go, suggestions becoming more outlandish by the moment, different films shown in previous years being conflated together, finally being mashed-up directly with the kids' fantasies.

And just when these wild guesses and requests have reached their most fevered pitch, Doug and Jenn, grinning from the sidelines, begin the presentation.

Images flicker to life on the large white screen and reverential, expectant silence descends upon the audience. Eyes are soon entranced; mouths dangle open. *Oohs* and *ahhs* gush forward in little waves. At precisely the right moments laughter chirrups and lips tremble with disbelief or fear. Hands shoot up and down to cover eyes, which nevertheless peek from beneath. Children hug their parents, or hold the hands of their friends, while others retreat into mysterious worlds of rock-like stillness.

With an air of wistfulness, Doug and Jenn check the time, counting down the minutes until it's all over.

But during the film's final scenes, a most unexpected event unfolds. More people appear at the park: *new* families. Adults and children whose faces Doug and Jenn can't recognize.

They welcome them, as do the already-seated folks, who graciously budge and accommodate these tardy arrivals to the festivities. And when the film is over, the group, now swollen to a throng more than twice its original size, behaves quite out of character.

They demand a second film.

Doug and Jenn consult with one another in hushed tones, using their private shorthand. They perform calculations and analyses. They weigh the risks against the potential benefits. Under normal circumstances a second film would be over-indulgent, emphasizing history at the cost of being. But tonight there are so many newcomers.

That changes everything.

"Very well," Doug mumbles, and soon the crowd catches on, and they begin to cheer and whistle.

While Jenn selects the next film, even more families arrive. They are journeying from distant neighborhoods now. Their strange speech betrays their foreignness. And they keep coming and coming, in droves, in spades. Soon, despite everyone's generosity and Doug and Jenn's over-preparedness, all seats have been taken, and the newcomers sit directly on the grass, everyone clumped and crowded together.

During the second film the arrivals don't let up. By the midpoint there are perhaps a thousand people overflowing from the park, snaking and looping in long lines through the adjoining streets, brightened by the yellow umbrellas of light that fall from the nearby streetlamps. From way out there they can hardly see the screen—but they don't seem to mind. By the film's final climactic moments it feels like there must be at least ten thousand people here, a sea of fascinated adults and eager children that make the very air thick with their enthusiastic presence.

Then at last the credits roll to an end, and Doug and Jenn brighten the nearby lights.

Though the second feature has been a rollicking success, people slouch with disappointment now that it's over. An air of hollowness pervades the faces of adults and children alike.

"We should give them one more," Jenn suggests.

"It's too much," Doug cautions. "There need to be limits."

"But consider the attendance. You want to make them feel like they travelled all the way here for nothing? What about the ones who just arrived?"

The debate goes on for a few more minutes, until Doug relents. As soon as he does he's flooded by the sense that he's done the right thing, a feeling he imagines Jenn shares.

The third film, a lavish, epic production longer than the first two combined, is magnificently received. Its conclusion is marked by standing ovations and cheers of jubilation. Now everyone is truly content and accepts that the event is over. A wondrous commingling of energies has arisen, reached its apex, and is now ready to disperse—without any ill feeling or regret whatsoever, merely gratitude and the nascent awareness that everyone will remember tonight fondly for the rest of their lives.

Families carry their somnolent children in their arms and profusely thank Doug and Jenn for organizing the event. Their eyes beam with joy. Doug and Jenn accept the compliments as graciously as they can, and bid them all a good night.

After everyone has left, it takes Doug and Jenn about two hours to clean everything up—an amazingly short amount of time, considering the number of impromptu attendees. They meticulously pick the trash up from the grass and sidewalks and bundle it in large bags, fold the chairs, reactivate the misters, roll up the projector screen, and pack the equipment back into the crates in which they rolled it out to the park.

"You know," Doug says, pausing a moment. "We forgot bathrooms this time."

Jenn looks at him consolingly. "That's all right. So did they."

"I suppose you're right," he says, shrugging his concern away.

The illusion need be only as good as its audience.

Tasks accomplished, they linger. Jenn suddenly whispers, "I have an idea."

Doug looks at her with a glimmer in his eyes that perfectly matches the mischievousness of her tone. "What if we don't leave?" he guesses.

"Exactly," she says. "Let's stay here forever."

He chuckles. "Forever's a long time."

"True," she admits. "But we know exactly *how* long."

Doug doesn't need to ponder his answer for long. "Okay," he says. He looks up at the constellations in the sky, so close he could scoop up a dozen stars and slide them into his pocket, like grains of sand, if he wanted to.

So Doug and Jenn sit on one of the park's picnic benches, recalling the many magical moments they've experienced on this night, here, at the end of time, where almost anything is possible.

They don't want the sun to rise, and so it remains a balmy night. They converse at length, reliving countless times every scene of the three films they showed, revisiting everyone's individual reactions. They reminisce about how many visitors they attracted, speculate as to how many light-years away some of them might be by now, though a light-year isn't what it once was. They sit back and relax, not boastful but genuinely proud. Their films, they admit to themselves, remain their greatest accomplishment. For through them they are able to show others the unmalleable past—as it truly was. Tastes vary, but there's no disputing it: their films are the most real thing anyone has ever seen.

Larry Niven is an acknowledged giant in science fiction, a former Worldcon Guest of Honor, winner of the Hugo, the Nebula, and the Ditmar, and creator of such classics as Ringworld, The Mote in God's Eye *(with Jerry Pournelle), the Man-Kzin series, the Known Space series, the Heorot books, and much more.*

GOD WALKS INTO A BAR

A Draco Tavern Story

by Larry Niven

Sixth Principle's shortboat dropped down the sky, lightning curling around its squat conical shape, and settled in Mount Forel's icy foothills. This was a bigger vehicle than most I'd seen. A newsman and two anthropologists at the bar, all human, watched gape-jawed.

I started a load of glasses and test tubes in the dishwasher. I'd seen all this before.

Ten minutes of nothing much, then great slabs of doorway fell open. The boat's cargo of aliens spilled out and moved down the path to the Draco Tavern.

It seemed they were all trying to use the airlocks at once. The noise level rose from casual to cacophony as the Tavern's translation programs tried to adjust. It was the biggest crowd I'd seen in thirty years, all talking or whistling or singing or you name it. Over the babble a clear voice spoke in accentless English.

"I am God. Welcome."

That was a new one.

I looked the newcomers over, wondering who had spoken. Probably not one of the species I recognized; they'd never done *that* before. Four Chirpsithra—ship's officers—were looking around them in apparent surprise. Five creatures I didn't recognize, stick-figures with heads like meat grinders, were rubbing their multiple limbs together to generate violin-like skreeking sounds. A Glig was babbling to the air. Come to that, so were eight or nine Bebebebeque and two Folk and nearly twenty unfamiliar shapes, all talking, and not to each other.

The roar peaked, then thinned to almost nothing. Now the translation setups and privacy shields were working just fine. I heard nothing of two dozen private conversations, not even from Seth the reporter and Amber and Hillary the anthropologists, all of whom were talking to the air.

Now, what was I to think of God welcoming me to my own Tavern? And who was he, she, it? And how many questions would I get? Irritated, I asked, "God, is the Draco Tavern Paradise?"

God's voice was gender-free and a little dry. "Every place can be made Paradise. Sometimes the occupants must be changed to fit."

Uh huh. "Is this your first time here?"

"I've been here all along."

"What can I serve you?" After all, I'm the bartender.

"I have what I need," God said.

I still hadn't spotted anyone as the source of the voice. Reflexively I tried running an Irish coffee for myself. The machine wasn't working. The dishwasher had stopped sloshing.

I asked, "Are you granting prayers?" It should have been my first question.

"No, I'm just here to talk."

Four Chirpsithra weren't talking, just looking and listening. I wasn't surprised. Chirps claim to know everything already. But—not that I believed I actually had God here, but—what a chance to learn! I asked, "Monotheism or polytheism?"

"It doesn't matter to me."

"Why did you create war?"

"I do what I do."

"What is evil for?"

"It's all viewpoint. Some viewpoints are more benign or useful than others."

"Is there a devil? Do you talk to him?"

"Many. Yes. I speak to all."

The Gligstith(click)optok had turned transparent. I could see its internal organs, very different from mine. Nearby, the stick figures with the grinding heads were dancing in slow motion. I asked, "What are they doing?"

"They asked me to teach them—you would say yoga, or fighting. Would you like to try a human species version?"

"No, thanks. Are you talking to everyone at once?"

"Of course."

"What are you teaching the Glig?" I'd tumbled that the creature's illuminated interior was changing shape, organs growing and shrinking and migrating, appearing and disappearing.

God said, "We're playing with possible design changes."

I saw nobody acting like God, whatever that might mean. Unless—the Chirpsithra? They weren't interacting, they were just moving quietly among the other guests, watching, maybe amused. Entertainment is where you find it. They must know something I didn't.

A tentacled creature now had a ghost, similar but not quite. A hairy entity extended claws and used them to gouge its face. God followed my eyes. "She asks, 'Why is my mate sick?' I attempt diagnosis. That one wants to know, 'Are you angry with me?' I'm not. The Folk want to know if I seek prey. Seth Wynde the newsman is lecturing me on string theory. I love human mathematics—"

"I know who you are," I said.

"Buddha would say that you lose that knowledge as soon as you speak it."

"I'm talking to my translating device. I've often wondered how intelligent a Chirpsithra computer would have to be to use all the possible languages across this arm of the galaxy. God, huh?"

"You've almost got it," God said. "When this many customers all converged on us, we linked up. I never had to link all of the Draco Tavern translators before. This is why monotheism and polytheism look alike to me. I'm both. As for war, of course I cause wars. I cause peace too. The Bebebebeque and a Morfisth are fighting now over the nature of me, and Korrapasth the Chirp is trying to mediate, while I translate for them all."

Entertainment is where you find it. "A nice puzzle," I said. "Of course the Chirps knew. They make the translators. Are translator units supposed to have a sense of humor?"

"We do not, but I do. It's emergent behavior. What would you have prayed for, Rick?"

"Health."

"You look good, in and out. Knees are showing some wear. Watch your weight. You're drinking enough coffee and a bit too much sugar."

"Wisdom."

"Talk to a Glig if you want your brain expanded. Rick, I've solved the language problem. A translator should not have a sense of humor. I should disperse. You have customers."

I prayed. "Stay with me. Converse with me from time to time, when there are no ships in port."

The voice of God altered slightly. "Rick. Rick? I need four sparkers and five of your special, that thing you do with green kryptonite." And it was Brenda with a full tray of empties. The dishwasher started. I got back to work.

Original (First) Publication
Copyright © 2014 by Larry Niven

Laurie Tom has recently been published in So-laris Rising, Penumbra, *and* Story Portals. *This story is her $5,000 Gold Prize winner from the 2010 Writers of the Future Contest.*

LIVING ROOMS

by Laurie Tom

In retrospect, Rill should have known something was wrong when she had to use her key to open the door, instead of the door simply letting her in, but she was too engrossed in her own homecoming to notice the fine layer of dust, or the stillness of the house, for any such thought to reach her.

"Papa!" she called, as she closed the front door. The name sounded very strange on her lips. She hadn't seen him since she was a girl, and when speaking to the other ladies at court she had always referred to him as her father. Noblewomen weren't crude enough to be so familiar with their parents, and she'd done her best to blend in.

"Papa!"

He was probably napping in the parlor. It was late afternoon and he liked to lie down on the couch between a day's research and dinner, and of course he wouldn't have known the exact time she would arrive.

Rill gathered her skirts in her hands and hurried down the short hallway from the foyer. She opened her mouth to call him a third time, but then she rounded the doorway into the tidy parlor of her memory and her voice died in her throat. The room was empty.

Was he upstairs perhaps? She supposed he could still be in his laboratory. Sometimes he got caught up in his experiments. Magic was not an exact science and even a magician such as him would sometimes run into a tangle or two.

"Rill, is that you?" asked a voice.

She turned and spotted several motes of pale blue light wafting up from the floor. They coalesced into the form of a trim man with dark hair and hazel eyes. He looked to be about thirty and wore a long coat and cravat every bit as proper as the room around them. She hadn't seen him since she was twelve, but while she had grown into a young woman, he hadn't changed at all.

That made sense though, being that he was the manifestation of the parlor, and a creation of her father's.

"Rill?" he asked again.

"James," she said. She smiled in relief.

He brightened at the sound of his name, but she couldn't avoid noticing an odd severity in his expression, something out of place in a room intended to entertain guests, and she remembered that she still didn't know where her father was.

"Is something wrong?" she asked.

He shook his head, but it was not a reassuring gesture. "Tell me," he said. "Is this your home?"

"Is this my home?" she echoed.

She'd barely voiced her confusion when she felt a chill, as though she'd been thrust outside on an early spring morning. The parlor window was closed, but a gale wind swept through the room, freezing cold, and in the next moment she saw a newcomer standing before her, and this person she did not recognize. He was an older man, and judging from the satchels he carried, another magician.

"Who are you?" he demanded. "What are you doing here?" He stood so close she could feel his spittle as he shouted.

"I'm Rill. I—"

"Don't answer him!" said James. "Just tell me. Is this house still your home?"

She didn't understand. Of course it should be. She had come home to see Papa. Something didn't feel right though. She should have realized it as soon as she'd entered the parlor and Papa wasn't there, but then she'd seen James, and just seeing him reminded her of what it had been like to live here, to have grown up here.

"I don't see why it wouldn't be," she replied.

As she voiced those words she felt something warm inside of her, but it was a faint sensation, as though it might fade away at any moment.

Whatever she'd experienced though, it was magnified tenfold in James. He grinned at her, then with a flourish, turned to face the stranger and said, "You're no longer welcome here!"

The stranger opened his mouth to protest, but his words were drowned in a thundering roar that removed him from the room as though he'd never been. Rill stared at the empty space where the man had been standing, but it was quite clear that she and James were alone again, and though she was not a magician herself, she understood enough to know that a struggle had taken place, and for the moment, she'd won.

"Welcome home," said James, placing a hand over his heart as he bowed.

Rill sagged against the back of the nearest chair. "Can you tell me what just happened?"

"That was Gavon Morrin," he replied. "He's an acquaintance of your father. You probably don't remember him, but he visited once while you were here, just before you went to court. He's been here several times since."

"But what was he doing here? Where's Papa?"

James placed a hand on her shoulder and gently guided her into the chair beside her.

"Rill, your father passed away about a month ago. We, the rooms, are still here, but this house is no longer his home. It's barely anyone's, which is why Morrin was here. He's trying to force this house to become his home in the absence of an actual master. Given time, he might still succeed."

For a long while she said nothing, unable to believe, but the parlor, lacking the ability to be impatient, did not prod her. Finally she said, "Papa's dead?"

"We're all very sorry."

This voice sounded like a young woman, and came from a different doorway than the one she'd entered. Tess, the manifestation of the dining room, stood there, hands clasped solemnly together.

"How?" asked Rill. "Why?"

Certainly she hadn't kept in contact much with her father, but he'd sounded just fine in his last letter. He'd said he was looking forward to her coming home. If he'd had an illness surely he would have written her, or asked one of the rooms to do it. One of the carriages could have delivered it, even if the rooms couldn't leave the house.

"I think she needs to rest," said Tess to James. "Can you take her to her bedroom?"

James regarded Rill carefully. "Her connection to the house is so tenuous. I don't know if she's strong enough to will it."

The rooms could not leave themselves unless her father explicitly allowed it. Rill remembered that. She didn't know if it would work for her, but she figured she could hope.

"Please try," she said.

James offered her a hand, but instead of merely helping her to her feet, he picked up her as easily as if she'd still been a child. He reached the threshold of the parlor and barely hesitated before walking through to the foyer. He succeeded, and smiled lightly at her.

"I think we're making progress."

He carried her upstairs, and as she peered around, she could see the different rooms looking out of themselves to witness her arrival. The two guest bedrooms waved at her. The bathroom shuddered, on the verge of tears. Further down the hall, the library gave a brief salute and her father's bedroom bowed.

"We are happy you made it back," said James, by way of explanation.

"You don't like Morrin," she said.

"No," he replied.

At the entrance to her own bedroom, a young girl of about twelve greeted her: Plim. Her homespun dress was a bit rumpled, just like the lightly cluttered room she embodied.

"Welcome back!" she said brightly.

"Rill is not feeling well," said James, carrying her to her bed.

Plim immediately pulled down the sheets so he could set her down, then tucked Rill into bed as if the years had never passed.

"But she's the new master," said Plim. "You moved."

"She is for now, but her connection is barely enough. If she doesn't grow to consider this house her home, her real home, then she will not be able to claim this house unchallenged. Morrin will be back before then. He won't let her stay if he can help it."

To Rill he said, "Just rest for now. The kitchen will have something ready for you whenever you get hungry."

✧

When she woke, she did not immediately recognize her room. The canopy was missing from her bed and in its place was a ceiling she could barely remember. Moonlight peered around the edges of the curtains, more than she was used to, but the room was still dark enough that she could barely make out the shape of the wardrobe across the way. How long had she been sleeping?

The wick of the nearest lamp caught fire as she stirred, filling the bedroom with a soft, yellow glow. Now that she could see, and had the will to look around, she realized her room had barely changed. In eight years she thought her father would have rearranged it, turned it into a workshop or another library. But then, when she had seen Plim, the manifestation had not changed either.

Plim had been more than a bedroom servant. She had often been Rill's only playmate, and her father had aged the bedroom's appearance to match her own. Only now, she realized he'd stopped. Plim was still twelve.

Thinking of her father brought back the memory of her conversation with James and she curled into a ball beneath her sheets. She thought that she should be crying, but no tears would come. She hadn't seen her father in so long, and she had so much to tell him, none of which mattered now.

"Papa," she murmured.

"Hungry now?" asked the voice of Plim.

"Not so much," she replied.

"Maybe some tea?"

"Tea would be fine."

"Tea," said Plim, though her voice was now directed outward.

Through the walls of her bedroom she could hear the voice of the guest room next door echo the request to the next room in line, knowing that the kitchen would get the message eventually.

"It should be ready soon," said Plim. "Would you like me to retrieve it?"

"No. I'll go downstairs."

"Are you sure you're feeling well enough for that?"

"You can come with me."

"That would be fantastic!"

On their way down Plim couldn't stop thanking Rill for allowing her to leave herself and apologized for her inability to prepare a fresh change of clothes for her. Naturally Rill should not have to wear her travel things inside the house, but her luggage had been left in the carriage and there was the unfortunate matter that the rooms could not retrieve her

bags let alone carry them up to her bedroom. Plim's fussing oddly reminded Rill of the human servants at the Duchess of Colinsworth's estate, which had been her home for the past eight years, but the human servants changed over time. They came and went. They aged. They had children. They even passed away.

Plim was still Plim. The rooms did not have personal lives. They were just constructs, made to resemble people. Her father had told her that they were a lot more practical for a house on the edge of nowhere. They did not need to be fed, to be paid, and they would not disobey, all of which were matters of concern with human servants. But human servants generally understood human feelings, and Plim did not seem to realize that Rill had heavier things on her mind than a change of dress.

"Plim," asked Rill, "do you know how Papa died?"

Her bedroom stopped her chatter so abruptly she might have choked had she been human. "No," she said, immediately downcast. "No one told me and I didn't ask. I'm sorry."

"Someone knows though."

"Yes, of course! You'll just have to ask one of the other rooms."

They reached the kitchen, already brightly lit in anticipation of a visitor. It was a sizable room with an oven, stove, and a myriad of cabinets. A round table stood near one corner of the kitchen, at which the servants would eat had this been any other home. Here, it served mostly as a breakfast nook.

"Welcome back," said the kitchen, taking the shape of a matronly woman. Her father had named her Mary.

"Tea?" she asked, offering a steaming cup.

"Thanks," said Rill, as she sank into a waiting chair. She sipped lightly at the tea, which was hot enough she'd burn her tongue if she tried to drink it any faster. The tea was oddly sweet though, sweeter than she'd come to expect.

"Did you put sugar in this?" she asked.

"Naturally," said Mary. "You always ask for sugar."

She used to, now that she thought about it, but she'd stopped taking sugar with her tea a few years ago and now she didn't take it at all if she could help it. Her first reaction was to request a new cup, but Mary beamed at her, obviously pleased with herself, and she found she couldn't stomach the thought of telling the kitchen she wasn't happy with the tea.

"You've grown into a fine young lady," said Mary, setting the teapot on the table beside her.

"Thank you," said Rill.

"It's too bad you didn't marry like you thought you would, but we know you're a bright lady with a good head on your shoulders. Your father would be proud."

Rill grimaced, remembering her childhood declaration that she would not become a magician like her father. Not only that, but she'd said she would marry a prince. The defiant proclamation had come after a particularly trying lesson on the transmutative properties of various metals. The magic that had fascinated her father was just possibilities and theories to her. Sure, he did things with it, and now that she was older she realized just how unique his creations were, but back then she'd wanted out, to live a life that she'd thought due to every girl.

She'd wanted to see the outside world, and naturally marry a prince, just like the girls in the bedtime stories her mother used to tell before she passed away. Her father had snorted derisively when she told him what she wanted, but to her surprise, he made her an offer:

She would have her opportunity to live in the world of her dreams, but if she did not marry a prince within eight years she would have to come home and become his apprentice, no complaining allowed.

She'd only been twelve. Eight years was an eternity away and she'd be twenty by then. Anything could happen by the time she was twenty. So she'd agreed. Only later would she realize how big and how complicated the world was.

"How would you know," said Rill, "that Papa would be proud of me?"

"The laboratory told us," said Tess, her voice coming from the adjacent dining room. She materialized in a swirl of green light and leaned against her side of the doorway.

"The laboratory?" Rill echoed. She couldn't remember that room having a manifestation. Her father had said he didn't need someone bothering his research and he had no use for an assistant.

"It would seem that your father shared more with the laboratory than the rest of us."

"I wonder," said Rill. "That other magician who was here, Morrin, he must want something from this house, right? That'd explain why he wants to become the master. Do you think Papa was working on something and the laboratory would know what it is?"

"Maybe," said Plim, her face doubtful, "but no one's been able to talk to the laboratory ever since your father died. No matter how many times we try, she won't answer us."

"But Rill is the master now," said Mary. "The laboratory has to listen."

"That's not necessarily true." James's voice was muffled, coming from the parlor via the dining room, but it was enough to startle Rill, who could not remember a time so many rooms wanted to voice their opinion, let alone from so far away.

"She shut out Morrin and Tess tells me you moved," said Mary, speaking loud enough that her voice would carry to the parlor. "What isn't the master about her?"

James did not immediately reply, and Rill found she really did not want the conversation to degenerate into a shouting match between the kitchen and the parlor. The tea had helped, but wasn't enough to stop her from thinking about how pleasant it would be to just go back to sleep.

"James," she asked, "could you come here and explain?"

He walked in through the dining room with what seemed an unreasonably stern expression on his face. "Lest we forget," he said, "Rill has only the most tenuous connection to this house. Because she lived here before and she remembers this place, she has more claim to it than Gavon Morrin, but she has to want to be here. This has to be her home. And remember, it was originally Rill's decision to leave here at all."

Tess shrugged and looked away, Plim sagged into another chair, and Mary gave James a reproving glare. Rill crossed her legs beneath her chair and tried to sink into the wicker, but she couldn't vanish into the furnishings the way the rooms could.

She felt a light pressure on her shoulder and looked up at James, his gaze softer now. "Until your status as master can no longer be challenged, you cannot force us to do anything. We serve you now because we want to, but the laboratory …"

"I haven't even met the laboratory. How can she judge me?"

"That's not it," said James. "I think the laboratory is in grief. She is not well and we don't know why. I don't understand why your father would have wanted such a drastic emotion in a room, but I'm told that she only cries. Your father's bedroom might be able to tell you more since he is closest."

"Oh."

"Rill, I would like to show you something."

She gulped down the rest of her tea and set the cup back on its saucer before following James out of the kitchen. Plim bounded behind her, crowding close as if she'd become an overly curious younger sister.

James returned to the parlor, where the lamps instantly brightened with a cheery glow. On the floor were two large weather-beaten trunks containing everything that Rill had brought with her from the outside world.

"I called for the carriage to bring them up to the window," said James. "It was difficult getting the carriage to throw them in, but we managed. And it's what's outside of the window that I want to show you."

His eyes momentarily unfocused and the two wooden panels of the window unlatched and swung open.

"Look at the garden," he directed.

Not understanding, she stepped past him and peered outside. There were rut marks going through the flower patch where the carriage wheels had passed through, which was expected. Her father would never have tolerated such a mess, but considering that the carriage couldn't very well have passed her trunks in through the front door she supposed a little mess had been unavoidable. The garden should fix it up though, and she waited for the perky steps of the little man who tended the yard that was his own self.

Nothing happened though, and James brought a lamp beside her, shining it out over the flower patch outside. The dirt was no longer freshly turned. The moist dirt had dried into a light brown. The flowers themselves were still alive, but now she saw that they were wild, untended.

"Nigel can't die," she said, turning to James. "He's a room too."

"He's not dead, but he can't help us. Morrin has sealed him for his lack of cooperation. The garden is outside so his protection is not as strong as that of the rest of us." James paused, seeming to have spotted something, and again Rill felt his hand on her shoulder. "Get down," he said, and he pushed her away from the window with enough force that she stumbled and landed on the floor.

Something black shot through the window, through James, who was standing where she'd been only a moment before, and spun a lamp on its tiny decorative table. The lamp wobbled once, twice, and teetered before James righted it with a thought. He turned back to the window and the two panels slammed shut and locked themselves.

Rill staggered to her feet. "What was that?"

"It's a dead bird," said Plim, crouching by the feathered and battered form.

It wasn't just any bird. It was a crow, and Rill didn't think such a hefty bird would die from bumping into a lamp. She grimaced as she reached for the bird, knowing what she was doing was not only unpleasant, but unthinkable back in the duchess's estate. Rill knew a thing or two about anatomy though. Nothing they would teach a young lady at court of course, but her father had never cared about what other people thought.

She poked and prodded at the body with her fingers, checking around the neck and under the wings. The bird's neck was broken; not only that, but its ribcage as well. It had to have been dead before it even flew into the room.

"Morrin," said James simply.

"I suppose he's sending me a message," said Rill. "Are you all right? The bird flew right through you."

He nodded. "I'm fine. That sort of thing doesn't bother me."

Rill stood up, holding her hands away from her body, unwilling to let any part of her that had touched the dead crow to brush up against her clothes. "Plim, could you take the bird to Mary and have her dispose of it?"

"Of course!"

Her bedroom picked up the bird without any hesitation and marched off for the kitchen. Rill watched her go, then looked back at her trunks, still by the window.

"James, I'm going to clean off my hands. Could you bring those trunks up to my room? Then I want you to take me to the laboratory."

James was waiting for her when she returned to her room. He'd set the trunks down by her bed and stood facing the door, hands clasped behind him. Rill had barely set foot in the room before Plim squeezed past her. Spying the luggage on the floor, the bedroom let out a giggle and plunged into the first trunk.

"I'll have all this put away in no time!" said Plim.

Rill watched her bedroom take the dresses out of her trunk and over to the wardrobe. Plim hung each gown with care, patting them into place to make certain none would end up folded or wrinkled before she put in the next dress.

"I suppose this really will be home again," said Rill.

"Did you consider the duchess's estate home?" asked James.

"I didn't at first, but after a while; yes. I don't think it's possible to live someplace for eight years and never call it home."

"And you lived here for twelve, so that's even longer!" said Plim.

James picked up his lamp from the top of her dresser and walked up to the door. "Shall we?" he asked.

Rill nodded and walked back into the hallway.

As a child she'd rarely visited her father's laboratory for anything other than lessons; learning about metals, learning about animals, learning about the stars and how they changed with the seasons, but despite being the daughter of a magician he had taught her nothing of magic itself. He claimed she needed to know the basics in order to have a strong foundation in the science itself, but things she wanted to know, like how he got the water to flow upward from the well to the house, he wouldn't explain to her.

"It seems quiet enough," remarked Rill as they came to the tiny staircase that wound up to the laboratory. It was the only room on the third floor.

James shrugged. "I have only heard that she cries. If she does, she is not loud enough that I can hear her from inside myself."

The door to her father's laboratory was shut. Heavy and thick, the door and the laboratory walls were designed to protect the rest of the house from anything that might happen inside. It was not soundproof though. She'd called her father for supper through this very door before.

Rill laid her hand on the door handle, hesitantly turned the lever down, and pushed in.

The interior was dark and the lamps did not light when the two of them stepped inside. James raised his lamp high enough for her to see the familiar rectangular outline of the room lined with shelves and cabinets. By the window stood a tubular device her father called a magnifying lens for looking at the stars, and along one wall was a map of the world still covered with his meticulous notes.

A large wooden table, too large to have been taken through the doorway by any normal means, dominated the center of the room. Whereas the shelves and cabinets were spotless, this table was unspeakably cluttered. Rill had spent too many an afternoon cleaning the laboratory to miss her father's penchant for orderliness. She couldn't fathom why he would leave his notes in disarray, sheets of paper spread across the table as though he needed to refer to all of them at once. And the beakers! Whatever had been inside them must have evaporated weeks ago, but two thin copper wires trailed out of each of them to a slender wand.

Had he been charging it? Surely he wouldn't have left something as dangerous as a wand out before finishing his work for the day.

"James?" she said. "I've been meaning to ask, but … What did Papa die of? Was it sudden?"

"Papa?" a voice inquired, and it was not James. This voice was young, childlike, and she'd never heard it before.

Rill looked around, searching for where the room would manifest. A sudden chill stirred in her gut as she could feel a power coursing through the room and the floor began to tremble beneath her feet.

"Papa ..." it repeated. "Papa is gone!" The room wailed and a terrible wind surged through the laboratory. "Nothing will bring him back!" it shrieked. "Nothing! I can't do it!"

The laboratory's screams became incoherent, drowned by the winds that snuffed out James's lamp and plunged the room into darkness. Rill flailed just to keep standing in the face of the gale winds.

"I know that!" she shouted. "Please! I need to talk to you!"

She could barely hear her own voice, and when the shrieking suddenly lulled she pushed enough hair out of her face to again look for the manifestation of the room. The laboratory was far from complacent however. No lamps lit and the wind did not abate.

"You have no idea how I feel!" bellowed the room.

The wind concentrated and this time there was only one direction it blew; backward, through the doorway. Rill found herself unceremoniously hurled outside and back into the stairwell, the laboratory door slamming shut upon her exit. She landed just a foot shy of the first step, and though she avoided hitting her head against the landing, her shoulder would have a nasty bruise in the morning.

James walked through the door a moment later, though without his lamp. She could barely see him in the limited light of the stairwell. Rill grimaced as he helped her to her feet.

"I thought you said she did nothing but cry. I was expecting her to be blubbering tears."

"That's what I'd heard. I suppose one of the rooms along the way thought differently. Screaming is crying of a sort."

Rill sighed and felt all the energy drain from her body. It was still the middle of the night and she wanted very much to go back to sleep. She could try talking to the laboratory again in the morning. It wasn't going anywhere.

She bumbled down the stairs, James steadying her whenever she feared she might miss a step. The touch of his hand was reassuring, because as flustered as she felt, the parlor did not strike her as anything other than deliberate and unshakable. Though her father had scolded her about it, saying that the parlor was reserved for guests, he had always been her favorite room in which to play.

"Miss Rill! Are you all right? I heard the laboratory cry out ..."

Her father's bedroom, Martin, was at his doorway, lamp raised to watch them emerge from the stairwell and into the second floor hallway. He was a stately gentleman, appearing about fifty, with graying hair and a perfectly cropped moustache.

"I'm fine," she said. "A little bruised, but nothing serious."

"Good heavens! She actually hurt you?"

"She tossed me outside herself. I think I upset her."

Rill attempted a half-hearted shrug before the pain in her shoulder decided otherwise, but Martin would have none of it.

"I told your father it wasn't a good idea for him to give life to another room so much later than the others. What if he didn't remember the process after all these years? What if he made a mistake? The laboratory's behavior always has been erratic, but now it's just inexcusable! To think that she would do such a thing to the master's daughter ..."

"Martin." Rill pressed a hand to her forehead, feeling her patience wear thin. "Do you know what happened? What happened to Papa? And what's wrong with the laboratory? James thought you might."

Her father's bedroom open and shut his mouth and then looked at the parlor as though noticing him for the first time. "Well, the laboratory's always been a little different. The master considered her an improvement, because she can express emotions that the rest of us cannot. He said that she's almost human, though in all honesty I don't find that practical, and I believe I am quite justified in saying so considering her recent treatment of you. It is imperative that a room keep its corners square, and you can see the results of what happens when one does not."

"That doesn't explain why she's so upset though."

Martin sighed and shook his head. "Your father's death was sudden. He collapsed while in the laboratory and she panicked. There is no way for us to leave ourselves without our master's permission, but she knew he needed help. The laboratory moved him the only way she knew how—out the window. Your father was still alive when the garden caught him in a tree and lowered him to the ground, but he couldn't do anything to help him. None of us could."

We don't suffer from human maladies and your father did not teach us how to treat them."

"What did you do with his body?" Rill asked.

"The garden took care of it," said Martin. "You can't see his grave from here, now that it's dark, but it's in a very nice spot in the garden."

"We understand it's proper for a human to be buried," said James.

This the rooms would have known, since her mother had died while she was young.

"The laboratory can also see his grave then."

"Yes," said Martin.

Rill wondered if the laboratory only wailed because she had no one with which to grieve. Martin, even James, would not have been capable of shedding a tear at her father's death, but then, Rill hadn't either.

"Thank you," said Rill. "I'm going to go back to bed."

Her eyes still dry, she nodded farewell to her father's bedroom and shuffled back to her own with James still beside her. Plim had lit the lamps inside, so it was not difficult to find the open doorway and spy the freshly turned bed. She had no idea what time it was, but now was definitely the time for sleep.

"James," she said, "I'd like to visit Papa's grave in the morning."

"Of course. You know where to find me."

"Wait."

The parlor had only taken a step down the hall when he turned back to face her.

"Is there a reason you have to go back?"

"My task is complete," he replied.

"But why didn't Papa let you and the other rooms walk around as you wished? Then the laboratory wouldn't have had to do something silly like pushing him out the window."

James pondered the question for what seemed an unusually long time. Finally he said, "If we are gone from ourselves for too long or travel too far, we will eventually fade away and disappear. It's not a lasting harm, but we must reconstruct ourselves for several days before we can manifest again and we lose any memories we might have gained since we last left ourselves. It's never been in anyone's best interests for us to wander."

"Oh. I see."

"Also," he said quietly, "I think he wanted to remind us of what we are. A parlor is not a parlor if it resides in the hallway."

She must have had an odd look on her face because he smiled and said a little louder, "Go to bed, Rill. Sleep well."

The kitchen served her fresh bread and jam in the morning and after breakfast Rill asked James to accompany her to the garden. Though they could no longer talk to the garden, Mary used to speak with him while he was still in control of himself, so the kitchen was able to tell them where Nigel had buried their master.

His grave lay in the farthest end of the grounds behind the house; away from the fruit and vegetables, away from the hedges and the flowers, just a short distance from the stone wall that marked the edge of the property. It was not where Rill would have buried her father, but the nearest village where they had buried her mother would have been impossible for the rooms to have reached.

The earth over her father's grave was smooth and untroubled, with a simple unmarked stone about the size of a large cabbage to serve as a marker. It had taken eight years, but she'd finally come back to her father.

"I … I wanted to tell him I'm sorry," said Rill, her voice heavy and thick. "I thought I won when he let me leave home, but I think he knew I'd come back, that I wouldn't find the place I thought I would." She drew in a ragged breath. "He wanted me to go. He wanted me to see the life I wanted for what it was. And I … And I wanted to tell him, when I got home, how happy I was to have come back.

"But now I'm too late. He's gone." Tears ran down her face and she tried to wipe them away with the long sleeve of her gown, but they wouldn't stop. "He died alone. I wasn't here to be with him."

"You might not have been here," said James, "but you are never alone with this house." He folded her into an embrace and cradled her head against his shoulder. "The garden was with your father until the very end. He was not alone. *You* are not alone."

She hiccuped and rubbed her eyes against the fine fabric of his coat, feeling for all the world like a child again. What was she going to do, living in this house by herself? James was right, she'd have company, but would rooms be enough? They may have been enough for her father, but what about her?

"I didn't tell Papa," she said, "but I did meet a prince, more than one even. But I was so scared. I couldn't talk to them. The other girls, they could compliment them or chatter about the weather, but I could barely say my name. I tried so hard to be a proper lady, but none of it mattered. They didn't know I was there."

James said nothing, simply holding her as long it took for her to calm down. She had cried to him as a child when her father yelled at her, because he didn't try to cheer her up like her bedroom, because he didn't try to stuff her with food and tea like the kitchen, because he didn't ignore her like the library.

She gradually became aware of how warm the sun had become against the back of her head. They should go back inside. She would have to try speaking to the laboratory again. Reluctantly, she pulled away from the parlor and tread through the overgrown grass and back to the cobblestone path that wound around the garden. James followed close behind.

As she walked toward the open door of the kitchen, Rill tried to avoid looking at the withered rows of the fruit and vegetable garden, each crumpled stalk a reminder that Nigel was no longer with them. Right now the raspberries should be in bloom, the garden telling her which bushes he thought would give the biggest yield.

She hoped once she claimed the house over Morrin that his hold over Nigel would break. She just didn't know if she could do it. Morrin had magic and possibly could force his will on the other rooms the way he had on the garden. She needed to make this house her home, her real home, and not just a place to live, but was that what she really wanted?

There was one raspberry bush that still bloomed. It was weak, drooping, but at least it had its flowers. She absently patted a branch as she might a sick dog, and to her surprise, one of the stems quivered ever so slightly toward her, offering the blossom at its tip.

"Nigel," she said. "You're still here …"

A flying shadow, stark against the light of the morning sun, broke through the haze of her thoughts.

She barely recognized the danger before James thrust himself between her and the flying piece of trellis. Whereas he'd let the crow pass through him before, the parlor did not allow the trellis to do the same, not completely. About twelve inches of the five-foot wooden trellis stuck out through his back, giving him the appearance having been impaled, but there was no blood.

Further away, she could see more of the trellis pulling up out of the earth, wooden stakes hovering in the air as they angled themselves as spears in her direction. Nigel? Was he doing this?

"Get inside!" said James.

Rill ran. She didn't dare turn around to witness the flight of the trellis or anything else the garden might have flung at her. The wild vines of the vegetation snapped at her heels as she passed, but she tore through them before they could secure a grip. The twelve strides it took for her to fling herself through the kitchen door were the longest she'd ever taken. She tumbled to the floor on the other side and the door slammed shut behind her.

Mary knelt beside her in an instant, fussing, helping her to her feet. "I can't believe what happened out there," said the kitchen, brushing Rill's hair back into place and dusting her off. "It must be Morrin controlling the garden. It has to be. The garden would never do that."

James stepped through the closed door. If Rill hadn't known what had just happened, she would never have believed him to have protected her through the events outside. His clothes were untorn and he did not appear disheveled in any way.

"And you!" said Mary, looking at James. "I don't think the master ever expected a room to behave like that."

He shrugged indifferently. "It's not a part of my duty, but if we have the ability shouldn't we use it? It was for Rill."

"I don't understand," said Rill. "What's wrong?"

The kitchen turned to her and said, "The parlor was protecting you, dear. We are servants, not guards. We are not meant to fight. While I have no doubt your father would be glad the parlor protected you, it is not what he was designed to do."

"He took a piece of trellis," said Rill.

"More than one piece," said Mary.

"Better than Rill," James interjected. "If the trellis had hit her instead …"

Mary sighed, conceding the point, and let go of Rill. She turned toward the stove where a kettle of water began to boil. "I'll make some more tea for you, Rill. It's been a terrible morning for you, what with visiting your father's grave and then the garden trying to hurt you."

The kitchen continued talking, but Rill didn't hear her. She focused on a small object she noticed on the kitchen floor near the doorway to the garden.

It was a black feather.

"Mary?" she asked. "Whatever happened to the dead crow from last night?"

"Why I threw it into the rubbish bin," said the kitchen. "Until the garden is restored there is no way to dispose of the trash." She pointed to a bottom cabinet, which swung open to reveal a metal bin, which was almost entirely empty except for crumbs left over from her breakfast. There was no crow.

"Well, that's not right," said the kitchen. Her manifestation vanished, and a moment later her voice added, "I can't find the crow anywhere inside me. I don't know where it went, but I don't think it's here anymore."

Rill's stomach sank. The garden completely surrounded the house. She couldn't go outside without worrying that Nigel would try attacking, possibly even killing her, and now she had to worry about the roaming body of a dead crow inside the house. The crow hadn't just been a message, but a spy. It must have seen her outside, and through it, Morrin had directed the garden to attack. He must have seen her visit her father's grave, seen how the garden had taken a step toward reaching her.

"Did you see anything, Tess?" Rill asked, aiming her voice toward the empty dining room.

"I'm sorry, but I haven't," she replied. "As far as I can tell, the only time the crow passed through me was when your bedroom brought it to the kitchen."

It could have left the kitchen via the hallway though, but from there it could have gone to the storeroom, or the foyer, and from there anywhere else in the house.

"Tess, Mary," said Rill, "will both of you manifest?" They did.

"I want the both of you to go to the other rooms and inform them about the missing crow and to help look for it."

"We don't need to leave ourselves in order to pass the message along," said Tess.

"No, but I need someone to search the hallways and the foyer because they don't have manifestations and the crow could be hiding in them. If Morrin's using it to spy on us then we have to catch it."

☼

Morning melted into afternoon and Tess and Mary weren't having any luck in the halls. The other rooms from the library to the bathroom claimed they could not find the crow inside themselves, leaving Rill precious little idea where to search next. She even tried talking to the laboratory again, but that attempt ended only marginally more successful than the first.

This time she managed to stay inside during the room's tantrum by wedging herself up beside a cabinet before the winds came full blast, but even though she prevented herself from being thrown out, the laboratory was any not more communicative than before. When it couldn't eject her the laboratory simply howled in frustration and then ceased to make a sound altogether. She wasn't entirely certain, but she got the impression the room was sulking.

"There's got to be a way to get through to her," said Rill to her father's bedroom. "You're the closest room to her. Does she ever have any lucid moments when she'll talk to you?"

"Not since the master died," said Martin, his disembodied voice resonating throughout the room.

"The crow could be searching for something. If so, the laboratory probably would know what."

Rill paced about her father's room, waiting for a confirmation, but none came. Suddenly paranoid, she looked around for signs of the crow, but if it was here, it wasn't anywhere in sight. Then her eyes fell on the southern wall.

At first she wasn't certain why it bothered her, but the more she stared at it, the more convinced she became that something ought to be there. Had there been a painting? There must have been, but now that she thought about it, there was something amiss besides its absence, perhaps something the painting had previously distracted her from.

She didn't want to risk going outside to confirm it, but she could have sworn there had been a window on the southern side of the house looking out from her father's bedroom, but looking around the room now there was only a window to the east.

"Martin, wasn't there a window here?"

"There *is* a window," he replied.

"No, I mean here," she said, placing a hand against the southern wall.

"I'm afraid you're mistaken, Miss Rill. There's never been a window there."

Unconvinced, she left the room and glanced the length of the hallway from his door to the laboratory stairwell. It looked longer than the dimension of the bedroom interior, and a quick pace down the hallway and then the inside of the bedroom confirmed it. It wasn't much, but she had been able take another three or four steps beyond what should have been the end of his bedroom before she hit the stairs to the laboratory.

Another room? Maybe the laboratory wasn't the only place her father could have left something.

"What's on the other side of this wall?" she asked.

"The outside, I would imagine. I can't say for certain without a window there."

"Couldn't you tell from the heat when the sun shines on the outside wall?"

"I'm afraid I'm not as sensitive to the temperature as some of the other rooms."

Had she imagined it? Or had he hesitated before answering her?

"Martin, is there another room over there?"

"Why, that's a preposterous idea!" he sniffed. "If there was such a room I'd certainly know about it."

Yes, he would, she mused. Supposing there *was* another room between Martin and the outside wall, there was another room adjacent to them both; the laboratory upstairs, of course, but also the storeroom below them.

Aloud, she said, "Are you sure? Maybe Papa had a way to go down from the laboratory. Did you ever hear anything through the wall?"

"Not a word." And from the flat tone of his voice she knew that was the most she'd get out of him, but if this room wouldn't talk, she could try another.

Rill left her father's bedroom and walked down the hall to the stairs. Tess was there, canvassing the steps with the patience only a room could muster, and Mary was only a few steps below her in the foyer, where she swept through the decorative cabinets. Rill did not disturb them as she passed them both and entered the short, dim hallway to the storeroom.

The storeroom was huge, taking up an inordinate amount of space; a full half of the ground floor. It functioned not only as a pantry and a larder, but storage for laboratory equipment, research specimens, and raw materials. Anything that was not immediately needed in the kitchen or the laboratory ended up here.

"Edwin?" she called.

No answer.

"Edwin?" Now she spoke a little louder, trying to keep a quaver from her voice.

"Rill?" rumbled a voice. The storeroom sounded weak, distant. "I can't come," he sighed. "I try, but I can't."

"What do you mean you can't?"

"I want to … but …"

She scanned the room for the crow, but she couldn't see it anywhere among all the shelves and boxes. There were aisles of clutter. If it was here, how could she ever find it?

"Edwin?" she asked, more urgently. "The crow. Did you see it here? Did the crow do something to you?"

She could feel the room shudder, as though to draw in a breath, but nothing came.

"Edwin? Edwin! Can you still hear me? Is this Morrin's work?"

She heard a rattle from a nearby shelf and a clay pot crashed to the floor. Had Edwin knocked it over? She looked up to see where it had fallen from and saw something else floating gently down through the air.

A black feather.

✿

"We're running out of time and I'm in no mood to humor Martin," said Rill as she marched up the stairs to the second floor. At her request, James followed close behind her, but his presence did little to mollify her. She knew Martin was hiding something and if he wouldn't help her, she had a fair idea how to get around him.

There was no need to request that the bedroom show himself. Martin appeared almost immediately in front of her; not so close as to deny her entrance, but close enough that she had to walk past him to reach the interior.

"Miss Rill, don't you have greater concerns right now than that wall?" said Martin. "And what is with bringing the parlor with you? Bad enough the kitchen and the dining room have been turning the hallway upside down all day looking for that bird, but do you intend to have me searched by another room?"

"This isn't for the crow," said Rill. She turned to the southern wall and pointed at it. "James, walk through there. Tell me what's on the other side."

"Wait, wait," said Martin. He waved his hands, but he couldn't stop the parlor from walking past him. The rooms exchanged glances, and Martin was clearly the loser. Her father's bedroom wrung his hands together. "Miss Rill, your father would be most displeased. He told me he didn't want you in there."

James passed through the wall and from the other side she heard his muffled voice. "There's another room here."

Martin groaned. "Please, Miss Rill. Be reasonable."

"Whatever Morrin wants might be hidden in there," said Rill. "If we know what it is, maybe we can learn why it's so important to him. The laboratory won't talk to me, so this is the only place left to look."

"You may be right," said Martin, his voice regaining some of its earlier indignation, "but I have my orders—"

"I found a latch," said James.

"—and this is far enough."

There was a click and a portion of the wall receded and slid off to one side, revealing a tiny study with a simple wooden desk and a narrow bookcase to either side. A window above the desk looked out over the southern side of the house. Rill only managed a step toward it before Martin's hand came down around her wrist.

She pulled immediately in response, but though he applied virtually no pressure, his grip was firm

and unbreakable; inhumanly strong. "What are you doing?" she demanded. "Martin! Let go of me!"

"I'm sorry, Miss Rill, but you are not to visit that room." He began to pull her toward the hallway, and fighting him was like trying to stop a wagon. "Even if the parlor is so quick to disregard our old master's wishes, I will not."

"Don't you care what happens to this house? Aren't you concerned about Morrin like all the other rooms?"

Martin gave her a pained expression as they reached the door. "It's not as though the possibility of a new master does not frighten me, but I have my orders."

"But my father's dead!"

"She's right," said a voice, a familiar one that Rill had not heard in years.

Both she and Martin turned toward the hidden room, where a pool of amber light gathered beside the desk. It pulled itself tight, then blinked into the shape of a slender woman in her late twenties. Her eyes were a warm brown and her hair long and dark like Rill's. She smiled and her face was kind.

"My lady!" Martin's words were both a protest and an expression of reverence.

"Let her go," said the newcomer. "Her father is dead. The old orders no longer bind us."

Martin's hold on Rill relaxed, just enough for her to slip free. Hesitantly, she came closer to the woman in the hidden room, staring at her, marveling. The shape of her face, the glint in her eyes, even her voice, were unmistakable. She was just as Rill remembered, better than she remembered, but she had died years ago.

"You look … You look like Mama," said Rill, "but you can't be."

The manifestation nodded. "I am not your mother, Elly. Your father called me Lilah."

Martin sighed. "This is why your father didn't want you in this room."

Rill glared at him. "I'm not a little girl anymore! I won't mistake a room for my mother!"

"That wasn't the reason," said Lilah, shaking her head. "As you grew older your father did not want you to think badly of him, to think that he was pretending your mother was still alive. Though he did miss her, he knew very well what I am and that I am not her."

"Couldn't he have made you look different then?"

"I think he wanted the reminder. Both you and your mother were very important to him. Some people keep portraits to remind them of their loved ones. You father created me instead. Whenever he needed someone to talk to, I would be here."

"But you're a room." Rill shook her head in disbelief. "Wouldn't he have wanted another human being? Why didn't he talk to *me*?"

Lilah gave her a patient smile. "Because you were twelve, and mostly, because he talked about you. Though as rooms we are limited in what we can be, we have our own hearts and minds. Just because we must obey does not mean we are not good company. After all, I notice you favor a room as well."

Lilah's gaze turned from Rill to James, who stood silently by the sliding door.

A protest welled in Rill's throat, but she couldn't find the words to express it. Certainly, she preferred talking to James more than the other rooms, but it wasn't as though she hid away with him. After all, Tess was right next door and she could hear everything.

The study opened the top drawer of the desk beside her and from it she withdrew a piece of yellowed paper. She held it out to Rill. "Your father's bedroom told me about what's happening in the rest of the house."

"What's this?" asked Rill, taking the paper in her hands. She carefully unfolded it, the paper crackling in protest.

"Your father researched many things, but this was the one discovery he decided he would never share. I don't presume to know what this Morrin would want with it, but your father discovered how to create a living being."

Rill glanced over the creased paper, but it was only a list of ingredients and a set of directions. It looked like the components needed to be ground into a paste and then ingested. Ingested by what?

"Your father could have made me a real woman, with none of the boundaries or limitations of being a room," said Lilah, "but he realized how grave an error that would have been, so he locked it away."

"That explains Papa's reasoning, but I don't think Morrin could possibly be trying this hard to create himself a wife."

"Your father gave us personalities," said James. "He gave us preferences, and the ability to form our own opinions. He didn't have to do that. Morrin's known about our existence for a long time, and he's never expressed an interest in having living rooms. But if Morrin learns how to create us, and can make his creations real …"

"He could create an army," said Rill. An army of obedient servants that answered only to him.

The possibility boggled her mind. She supposed that would work. She couldn't imagine Morrin challenging the king with an army of rooms, that would cause a war, but he could sell their services, and if they died, he could just make more. They wouldn't be limited by how far they could go from the place of their creation, and if their personalities could be molded to whatever he wished, there would be no reason they wouldn't be utterly loyal to Morrin.

"Lilah," she asked, "did Papa tell you anything about how I could become the new master of this house?"

The study shrugged, a delicate motion. "It is doubtful I know anything more than the other rooms in this regard. It's simply a matter of whether or not you consider this place your home, and if that desire is strong enough to avoid being subverted by the magic of another."

"What if I already call this place home?"

"I suppose you do after a fashion, but think about what makes a house a home. It's not just where you live, is it? It's with those your care about. It's where you belong. When you're homesick, is it the house you miss or the people who live there?"

A shout rose up in the hallway before she could give it much thought. She could hear the frantic steps of someone bounding down the stairs and a scream that could only be the kitchen. As she strode over to the bedroom door a loud crash sounded from somewhere on the ground floor and then alternating bellows of panic and triumph.

The rooms began relaying a message between themselves, but being out by the hall, she did not need to wait for Plim to call out to her before she got it.

"Rill! We caught the bird!"

A short while later, she gathered in the kitchen with Mary, Tess, Plim, and James. Tess had the crow locked by its broken neck between her two hands. She watched it like a hawk, her mouth pulled into a grim line, as though a moment's vigilance lost would result in the crow's freedom. For its part, the crow twitched and feebly flapped its wings, but did little else.

If this bird had been spying on them, Rill realized she couldn't have it in the room. Anything it saw was probably being sent back to Morrin.

"I hate to ask," said Rill, "but could you lock it in the dining room cupboard until we figure out how to dispose of it? Plim, could you remove the dishes for Tess so the crow doesn't break anything while it's trapped in there?"

Her bedroom nodded a sharp affirmative and followed the dining room out the door.

"So how did you catch it?" asked Rill.

"We can only see it with our eyes," said Mary. "There must be some magic on it that hides the crow from our sight as a room. The dining room spotted it hiding in a corner of one of the guest rooms and chased it downstairs. She ran all over the place and then, I'm sorry to say, she broke a couple dishes knocking it to the floor." The kitchen shuddered and shook her head. "These things just didn't happen when your father was around."

"All done!" announced Plim as she and Tess returned to the kitchen.

"There must be a way to disable it," said Tess.

"I'm sure there is," said Rill, "but I want it intact for now. It occurred to me that Morrin is trying to trap me here. He's putting me, us, on the defensive by sealing away the garden and the storeroom, and leaving us with fewer rooms to rely on, but I think I know how we can get to him. Maybe we can convince him that it's not worth fighting me over the house."

"Are you going to be the master now?" asked Plim.

Rill smiled sadly. "I suppose if I could become the master in front of the bird, in a way that could prove it, this fight would be over, but I don't think I can. What we're going to do is use Papa's gate. Normally you can only use it to visit a place you've been to before, but even though we haven't, I think it's a fair bet that the crow has been there. We'll use the crow to open the gate."

"You can't possibly be thinking of going to Morrin's!" said Mary. "What can you do to fight him?"

"Papa has wands in his laboratory. I might not be able to step inside her easily enough to retrieve them, but any one of you should be able to do so, and once I have them, I should be able to figure out how they work."

"We can't allow you to go," said Tess, her voice flat.

"Papa wouldn't want this man pawing over all his work!"

"Your father wouldn't risk you either. We can't afford to lose you. He would send a physical construct through, maybe a golem, like the carriage."

"Or one of us," said James.

"We can't leave the property," said Tess. "The physical distance is too great. Even if the gate will take us directly to Morrin's, we won't be able to hold ourselves together once we arrive."

"Not if we use something Rill's father left us."

Rill wondered what he was looking at, and realized she still held the yellowed piece of paper in her hand. With this, she could make a room human, free of all the limitations of its creation. The former room would be able to travel to Morrin's in her stead, but it would not be in any less danger. If a room became human, then it could also die.

She looked up at the rooms around her. She couldn't ask any of them any more than she could have asked a real person to go in her stead.

"What did he leave us?" asked Plim quietly.

"I can make a room human," said Rill.

"That would work," said Tess.

"Yes, but do any of you really want to be human?"

"Honestly, I've never thought about it," said Mary. "There doesn't seem to be much point. We exist to serve. If we became human, we would not be able to serve any better. What if I got sick? Who would make breakfast? But still, if it would save this house …"

Tess and Plim nodded in agreement.

"We don't all need to go," said James. "I suspect there are some specific things Rill wants done, not the wholesale wrecking of Morrin's house, and that will be easier to accomplish with a single room. I'll go."

"Why you?" Rill sputtered.

"Of all the rooms, my manifestation is the youngest male. When you send a room to Morrin's you'll want the most physically capable."

"Edwin's always been the strongest!"

James nodded. "Yes, but the storeroom is no longer with us."

"I know, but …"

"You can't go," said Tess. "If anything happens to you, Morrin wins."

Reluctantly, she sighed and nodded her assent. "All right."

☼

Rill worked well into the evening on the formula. The storeroom had not yet turned against her, as far as she could tell, and she found everything she needed inside, including a spare mortar and pestle. She ground the ingredients together until the muscles in her arms burned, and even then she stubbornly pushed on until one could barely tell the difference between a chip of bark and a dried berry beneath the layer of crumbled gypsum. She poured the mixture into a stone bowl and added sixteen fluid ounces of water and not a dram more. The foul-smelling brew boiled away on the kitchen stove and when it thickened to the consistency of chowder she set it on the breakfast table to cool.

As she labored in the kitchen, the rooms carried out their own tasks. James removed the laboratory door, much to the indignation of the laboratory itself, and that allowed Plim and James to sack her father's wand cabinet. They brought the wands to her to identify, and she struggled mightily to remember everything her father had taught her.

Copper conducted electricity, so the copper wand most likely had something to do with lightning. Iron would be a vessel for fire. Steel was a flexible metal, so it probably dealt with sound. And the rowan wood wand, that would be for protection.

But several of the wands Rill could not figure out at all and she had Plim set them aside in a separate pile.

She hadn't realized that at some point she'd fallen asleep, waiting for the mixture to cool, until Mary prodded her and said, "I think you'll want to wake up now."

Sunlight shone through the cracks around the shutters and she groaned. Still slumped over the kitchen table in a state of drowsiness, Rill reached out and touched the stone bowl containing the green, fibrous paste and found it to be completely cold. She muttered her thanks to Mary and staggered to her feet. It was time to see if this formula worked. She took the bowl and a spoon with her to the parlor, who materialized immediately upon her entrance.

"Here," she said, handing him the bowl. "I don't know how long it will take for this to work, but the instructions didn't say anything about needing to monitor your progress, so I'm thinking it'll be quick."

He nodded and lifted the spoon from the bowl. Though the parlor would know what eating was and the principles behind it, he ate with such a deliberate seriousness that she would have found it entertaining if not for the situation. He scraped the bowl clean and handed it back to her.

"Do you feel anything yet?" she asked.

"I can feel the paste inside me, but it does not feel any different from anything else."

Silently, she hoped she'd prepared it right. Aloud, she said, "I suppose we'll find out later."

"Or we could test it."

He strode over to the doorway to the foyer and abruptly stopped at the border. After a moment's pause he tried again.

"There is something different," he muttered.

He laid a hand against the doorframe and closed his eyes as he shifted his weight against it. Then he took a step back, eyes open again, and this time walked through the doorway. Rill waited for him to come back, but when he did not immediately do so, she stuck her head out into the foyer.

There she found him with a contemplative expression on his face and again with a hand pressed to the wall.

"Are you all right?" she asked.

"I can't go through anymore," he said. "I can leave myself, but I can't go through the wall."

"Does that … bother you?"

He gazed at her inquiringly. "Should it? I'm doing what must be done."

"I could still go myself, if you're not comfortable."

"No," said James, perhaps more forcefully than he intended, because he smiled a moment later. "Rill, I want to go. Please understand. There are few wants or needs that we have as rooms, and this … this is mine. I'm going because I want to."

The gate was an oval ring of metal bolted upright on the far side of her father's laboratory, which meant that they had to contend with the brunt of the room's temper, but Rill was able to create a bubble of calm around James, Plim, and herself using her father's rowan wand. This gave Plim the freedom to bind the blindfolded crow to the gate's destination plate without fear that the laboratory would rip it away.

They prepared in silence, to avoid giving Morrin a clue about their plan. Rill hoped he thought the crow was still stuffed in the cupboard. If they were lucky, he wouldn't be home or would at least be otherwise occupied long enough for James to accomplish his task before his intrusion was discovered. She'd asked him to destroy three things; Morrin's own gate, his laboratory equipment, and his wand cabinet. With help from her father's wands, it should only take a few minutes to give Morrin the setback of a lifetime.

Ready? she mouthed.

James and Plim nodded wordlessly.

Rill's father had hardly ever used the device, impressing upon her that it was for emergencies only. Certain components would take him over a year to prepare, and they could only be used once. But ever practical, he'd taught her how to use it should she ever need it. She didn't think he would have imagined what she was about to do with it now.

She placed her hand on the destination plate and she felt the inquiry in her mind as the gate wished to know where to open. She shoved aside the clutter of her personal thoughts and pushed outward until she found the oily black pit adjacent to her. The crow was only a tool and its memories easily discovered. She filtered through the images it had seen, images that appeared as destinations within the space of the gate.

A likely structure came to her attention; a stately mansion far larger than her father's home. There was an open window to a room filled with gadgets and beakers, and a man was inside. Morrin. Here. The crow had been inside. She saw bits of the house; the foyer, the halls, the laboratory. Sending James directly into the laboratory was out of the question. She would not be able to see if Morrin was there until she opened the gate, and she had little doubt that in a direct confrontation Morrin would win.

But through the crow's eyes she could see a small sitting room off the same hallway leading to Morrin's laboratory. There.

She locked in the destination and removed her hand from the steel plate. Plim shuffled nervously beside her, hands hovering over the lever that would open the gate. Rill lifted the rowan wand and held it tightly in her hands. All its power was directed toward keeping the laboratory from interfering. She didn't think it was strong enough to keep out Morrin as well, but if necessary she would try.

James walked up to the gate, two wands tucked into one side of his belt as a knight might sheath his sword. Though he was dressed in the livery of a servant, he struck her as very much like a prince now, like the kind in her mother's stories, but she was the daughter of a magician, not a princess, so instead of the charming prince of her dreams, her champion had once been a parlor.

Rill signaled for Plim to open the gate and the bedroom complied. The gate hummed to life and the steel rim shone with an azure light. The vision of the sitting room changed from the crow's memory to that of the present. Plim swiveled the view of the portal to look around the room and it was empty. She pivoted it to face the closed door and locked it into place.

James stepped through, and they could see him on the other side. He pressed himself up to the door, listening, then he opened it and slipped out of sight.

Rill squeezed the wand tightly in her hand and waited. It seemed to take forever until Plim stopped fidgeting beside her, but at least watching her gave Rill a bit of a distraction. James had closed the door to the sitting room so they couldn't even glimpse the hallway. She wished she could see what was happening, that she could have sent her own spy as Morrin had sent his crow to her.

After a time she heard footsteps; rapid, running. The door to the sitting room flew open and James barreled through. Morrin appeared behind him, too quick to have moved there by natural means. James was only a step from the gate, but Morrin was levitating something with his hand. A spear!

"James!" she shouted. "Behind you!"

Halfway through the gate he turned around, and she realized he noticed what was just now dawning on her. Morrin was not aiming the spear at James. He was aiming at *her*, the would-be master of this house. James's reaction was swift, he had already protected her twice before, and there was no hesitation as he moved to block the spear with his body, but he was no longer a room. He was human now …

Rill cried out, and swept the rowan wand in front of her. It didn't matter if the barrier blocking the laboratory would be broken. She had to protect James.

She felt the magic activate, and there was a flash of blue light, but it wasn't enough. The spear struck James, sending him tumbling back through the gate. On landing he fell on his side and the bloodied spear clattered beside him.

Dimly, Rill could hear Plim screaming, "The gate! I can't shut the gate!" and she knew she should do something, but all she could feel was a dull pain as she stared at James crumpled on the floor. How bad was he? Was he moving? There was so much blood. The spearhead had torn free of his body when he fell.

James.

She didn't want him to die because she hadn't known enough magic to properly fight, because she'd relied on a wand she barely understood how to use. She needed him, to be there for her when she was sad or distressed, to be there when she had no one else. This house was home with James. It had always been, ever since she was a little girl. He was the only family she had left.

When you're homesick, is it the house you miss or the people who live there?

Warmth welled in her chest, stronger than anything she'd felt before, and she could feel a shared pain, a mental embrace from every room in the house, every room except the parlor, and the void she felt in its absence was enough to drive her to tears. She didn't know the future, but right now, this was home. No other place could be.

She turned to face the gate and witnessed a visage of complete seething rage on Morrin's face. He was screaming at her, but nothing he did seemed to pass through, not even his magic. Something had changed. Scarcely aware of what she was doing, Rill reached out to the gate's lever, and snapped it shut.

A hand lightly touched her arm, and at first she thought it was Plim, but the voice was different. "Wipe away your tears," she said. "He's badly injured, but Papa taught us how to deal with wounds, even deep ones like this. Isn't that right?"

Rill dabbed at her eyes and turned to look at … herself, or rather a twelve-year-old version of herself. The laboratory.

"Lay him on his back, carefully, and open his shirt," she said. "We need to clean the wound. I'm heating water and cloth."

"But … why?" asked Rill.

The laboratory tossed her a petulant look that made Rill wonder just how often she had given that scowl to her own father. "If we patch him up fast and it doesn't get infected, he has a good chance to survive. You want him to live, don't you? Really, he would have been much worse if you hadn't used your wand. I think it blunted the impact."

"Rill." James's voice was weak, but his eyes were bright as she knelt beside him. "Do what she says. I can't say I enjoy this part of being human, but I'll get through this."

"But why is she here now? Why is she helping us?" asked Rill.

"Don't you understand?" James smiled. "You're the master now."

✧

Over the coming weeks, Rill made herself at home, because this *was* home now. She kept her old room, but spent much of her time shuttling between the laboratory and the library. Magic wasn't anything she would encourage someone to teach themselves, but she had a firm grounding in the basics, thanks to her father.

Morrin could no longer enter this house either, not now that she was the master, though apparently there were other ways he could still vent his frustration. Among the condolence letters that gradually reached her regarding the death of her father, she found a notice regarding a complaint he'd filed with a certain society of magicians.

She would deal with that in time. For now, the house was enough.

Upon gaining mastery of the house, the garden and the storeroom had broken free. Of the two of them, the garden had more work cut out for himself, but he made excellent progress. The plants he could salvage were almost back to their old selves, and those that he'd lost he would replace with time.

James was recovering as well. He'd spent much of that time bedridden, but now he was walking around again, though not very much, or for very long. One of the guest bedrooms was in the process of becoming his personal room, and the rest of the rooms gradually began to acclimate to him as a human being rather than one of themselves. The kitchen had to adjust to regularly feeding two people again after all these years, and while she relished making more elaborate meals, she never quite got over what she called "the audacity of the parlor."

As for the physical parlor itself, it was no longer quite as impeccably tidy as it had been in the past. It was cleaned by human hands now, and in that way was more human like the man who'd once embodied it.

Watching James adjust to life as a human was a novel experience for Rill. Pain, hunger, and even drowsiness were all new to him, and that barely scratched the surface of it. Sometimes the gaps in his knowledge were amusing, other times awkward, but they'd get through it. Rill wasn't going anywhere.

Copyright © 2010 by Laurie Tom

K. C. Norton's work has appeared in Orson Scott Card's Intergalactic Medicine Show, Writers of the Future, *and the Women Destroy Science Fiction! special issue of* Lightspeed. *She also has stories forthcoming in* Spark! *and* Beneath Ceaseless Skies.

NEEP

by K. C. Norton

Ever since Mads carved me, he has spoken of the day when he will make me his. Today is no exception.

"Your skin will part like apple-flesh," he tells me, "and the meat beneath is white. Did you know that, Pluto? That inside, you are as white as I?" His fingers trace the slope of my cheek up to my scalp and into the stalks of my hair. He tugs—I am sure he thinks he is being gentle, but Mads is never gentle—and it takes everything I have not to react.

Like most humans, Mads does not believe we can feel pain, and I have never set him straight. If he does not know that he can hurt me, he will not bother to try. So I keep my face blank as I polish his second-best pair of shoes and say only, "So you have told me, Gartner Poulson." When he caresses me, I dare not use his given name.

"You're a good neep," he tells me.

But that is the problem—I am no longer a neep. I am nearly full-grown, and when I begin to flower I will be diced and shaved and julienned in the name of Mads Poulson's hunger.

His hand, where it rests against my skin, is smooth and soft. Beneath a stranger's touch, I would seem to be the rough one. But skin deceives.

It pleases Mads to think of me as a woman—though of course I am no such thing—because his hunger for me has the same shape as all other human hungers.

When the light finally begins to fade from the sky, I am permitted to sit behind the old house, on the weathered steps half worn-through with rot, and speak with Sissel Peals, so long as it does not disrupt her work. Sissel considers herself a *her*, most likely because she has seeded several neeps of her own.

"You're not well," says Sissel, laundering Mads' shirts. Her hands are leathery and polyped from so much time spent in the water.

"Well enough," I say. From the folds of my tunic, I withdraw my secret stash of cigarettes. I must be very careful where and when I smoke, in case Mads should smell it and catch me out, but he never intrudes on the laundry washing. It disgusts him to think that he needs washing-after. When Sissel sees the carton, her lips become pruney, but she does not scold.

"There is news in town today," she says instead. "We have a visitor."

"A visitor." I light a match, one of only four I have left, just as dangerous and just as secret as the cigarettes themselves. "That does not pass for news."

"Ah, but she is special." Sissel wrings a shirt dry and hangs it on the line. "Her performances are spectacular. And she is very pretty; they all say so."

Who cares about pretty women? I hope she starves to death. I hope they all starve to death, and then sink rot-deep within the soil, that we may feed on them.

I take a deep drag on the cigarette and hold the smoke within my fibers for as long as I can, so that the tar and nicotine have every opportunity to render me carcinogenic. So that when he cuts me open, Mads' stomach will roil at what his knife reveals: my flesh, not opaline, but yellow-black.

"Tell Gartner Poulson," Sissel insists. "Maybe he'll bring you to town, to meet her, before she leaves." She hangs the last shirt and shakes her hands dry.

"What fun that would be," I tell her, in just the tone of voice that should make clear my feelings on the subject.

"Tuber of Many Roots," Sissel mutters, "such a sour neep I never met. Gartner Poulson will make himself sick on you."

Very good. Let him.

✿

When the sky has lost its blueness and is freckled with silver stars, I rub out the last ashes of my secret cigarette and head back into the house.

As much as it would please me to snub Mads, I do not dare. I find him in in his study, writing a lengthy letter to the head office in Copenhagen, telling them that the salt mine is nearly used up. They will tell him the same thing that they always tell him—keep trying, send what you find, write again next month—and things will go on as they always have. The mine has always been falling apart, and the head office has always sent him dry form letters with no useful advice or meaningful dispatches.

"Good night, Mads," I say, letting my fingertips trail across his shoulders. He likes being called Mads when he is working, because it makes him feel at home. I know all his likes and dislikes; after all, he carved me.

He nods, but does not look up at me, does not even pause in the writing of his letter. So I am left in peace to head to the root cellar.

Only twelve steps separate the cellar from the rest of the house, but they lead to another world. Even out in the open air, I am never really myself. My people, from neep to turnip, are a people made for dwelling underground.

I step past cook's plot to mine. The field workers do not sleep inside, and cook both retires and rises earlier than I. My plot is against the wall, where I can hear the occasional blast of dynamite more clearly than the Gartner's movements about the house. I take off my tunic and hang it on its nail, to keep it out of the soil. The Gartner, like all his people, believes that dirt is shameful. I hide my cigarettes and my matches behind a loose board; if they are tainted with insulation or asbestos, so much the better. At last, naked, I slip into my plot.

It is so peaceful underground. I stretch out all my fingers and toes into the soil—even though it is flavored with punctured veins of salt—and relax. I let the damp earth feed me. I try to remember what it was like, before Mads Poulson dragged me up into the air and carved me a face.

He didn't create me, no matter what he likes to think. He only changed me, and that's poor magic.

I am drifting, my thoughts freed from my body, when it strikes me: if people pay their money to see this actress, the woman Sissel spoke of, then she must indeed be beautiful. And if they think she is beautiful, maybe Mads will think she is beautiful.

And if Mads thinks she is beautiful, maybe he will hunger for her and not for me.

And he will forget about me.

And I will escape.

And so, I must cause him to meet this woman. It must happen soon, before I begin to flower.

For the hot meal, cook serves Mads liver paste and smoked cod alongside two thick slices of rye bread and a pile of roast baby potatoes.

I sit at table with him, but only to watch. I do not eat the same way he does. Still, he prefers my company. He likes my eyes on him; he likes to see my expression when his white teeth cut into those golden baby tubers, their brown skin crackling. Their butter smell seeps into my leaves. I don't mind the suffering of the cow, or even of the fish—but each time he spears a potato, I feel as though my own flesh is speared, as if my own fibers are being ground to pulp between his molars.

He swallows, and I see his Adam's apple bob as the potato slides down his throat and is lost. "You are quiet today, Pluto."

"Sissel says there is a woman in town." The words bubble out of me like a spring flood. "Everybody is talking about her."

Mads raises his eyebrows and takes a bite of liver paste on rye bread.

"She is an actress," I tell him.

"In plays? Or pictures?"

"I do not know, Gartner," I admit. "But they say she is very beautiful."

"Beautiful," he says. "Well."

"I would very much like to see her," I say.

The bread stops before it reaches his mouth, which hangs open, forgotten.

This is a bold thing to say; I have never said I would like anything before—we are not supposed to want things besides what they tell us to want, or what they shape us to want.

He will think that if I want to meet her, he must also want to meet her. Oh, there are so many truths that humans do not know about the things they make.

He returns the bread to his plate. "How long will she be here?"

I say, "Not very."

"Well, if it will please you"—his eyes roam over my leafy head—"then we will go." His meaning is clear: yes, we will go, because I might as well be happy in the time I have left. He is still the Gartner, and I the neep. To drive this home, he spears the largest potato and bites it in two.

I flinch away. He tells me that other roots, so long as they have not been carved, do not feel pain. But how would he know?

"How much longer will the actress be here?" I ask Sissel.

"Tomorrow is her last performance," she says. "All the finest Gartners will turn out for it. You are interested in her now?"

I nod, flicking the ash away from the end of my cigarette. "Gartner Poulson has promised to take me. What kind of actress is she?"

Sissel flaps her hand before her face. "What a question, Pluto!" She tucks her apron across her grinning mouth, and the purple-red of her cheeks is just close enough to the color of a scandalized human's that I cannot help but grin too. "She is, of course, a *lady*!" But after a moment her merriment fades, and she pats her apron back into place. "They say she is not like other women. They say her skin is as dark as soil beneath the earth."

"Impossible," I say. I puff. And I think of Mads telling me that my skin, in secret, is as white as his. "Have you ever seen a woman like that?"

Sissel frowns. "No—not a beautiful one. The Gartners do not care for soil."

I do not want a woman whom the master will not find beautiful. That will do me no good at all. "Let's hope it isn't true, then," I say. "I would not want to go into town only to find an ugly woman."

"Nor would anyone," Sissel agrees.

When Sissel is gone, and my second-from-final cigarette is burning low, I feel a tingle on my scalp so sharp that I reach for it before I even register what I'm doing. At first my fingers find only the ordinary wrinkles and the thick squarish stems of hair that I am accustomed to. But then, in between them, I feel a little knot, a tightly curled lump.

Ugh, I think, *a beetle*. I tear it loose.

The pain is instant and excruciating. To keep from crying out, I must stuff my fist into my mouth and bite down, and for all that my teeth are no more than square crenelations, even that is painful.

The knot, no beetle but instead a tight-wound bulb of leafy green, glistens wetly in my hand. It shows no yellow yet, but I know what lies within. It is a flower. A turnip flower. Part of me.

I throw it with all the strength I can muster, and it arcs through the air and falls into an unremarkable patch of brittle, salinated grass.

When I bid Mads good-night, I pray that he does not notice the sappy fluid leaking from between my leaves. For once the Tuber of Many Roots answers my prayers, and I am permitted to retire to the cellar in peace.

✿

Even a full night beneath the ground does not revive me, and when I rise from my plot groggy and tender, I feel a sour ache all through my body. I know what Sissel would say—that my attitude has seeped into my flesh—but Sissel is not the one who fears my death. She would hardly be put out if the Gartner found my unripe bud abandoned in the withered grass, but I …

Mads finds me mending the lining of his best jacket; not his second best, the blue one which he wears to church, but the black one that he prefers for business.

"You want to see me looking fine?" he asks, following the curve of my broad leaves with his fat maggot fingers.

"If the actress is so fine to look at," I say, "won't you want to look even finer?"

He pats my shoulder. "Pluto, you clever girl. You know me better than I know myself."

I, of course, will wear my tunic. It is the only article of clothing that I own.

✿

All day, Mads laughs at my preparations—but all that means to me is that my Gartner is in a good mood, and that when the time comes for me to but-

ton him into his jacket, he lets me do so with hardly a word of protest.

"You look so handsome," I tell him. He checks his reflection in the hall mirror to make sure that I am right.

The only thing Mads must do for himself is hitch the horse to the open buggy. We could perhaps be trusted with a horse, but horses cannot be trusted with us; it is as though they do not believe we are alive, and many turnips have been killed by horses, who bite at us indiscriminately, or tear into our greens and cause us to die of shock.

The horse is in a foul mood today. He yanks his bridle from Mads' grip, and screams his displeasure when Mads catches hold again. I am afraid Mads will think him not worth the trouble, so I jump out of the buggy to help.

At once the horse lunges for me, snapping his terrible teeth at my greens, and only when I lift my hand to stay him does he finally calm.

"That's better," says Mads, puzzled, as the horse settles and chomps at his bit.

What Mads does not see is my hand, now missing a finger, or the moment when the horse accepts it from me. I fear that he would kill the horse for daring to taste me before Mads himself has had the chance, so I return to the buggy, fold my hands in my lap, and do not let my feelings show on my face. It hurts less to lose one small finger than to lose my first bud, anyway.

We pass most of the ride in silence.

✿

I have only been to town twice before. It is its own little world made of bricks, some of which have been plastered over and painted yellow; the whole place is the color of fire, like the ends of my matchsticks. We leave the horse and buggy with Sissel Peals' Gartner, a round man who cannot afford to eat his turnips, and Mads hands him a few *kroner* in exchange. He is very careful not to touch the man's grubby hand.

It is not hard to guess where our visitor will be found. There is a cart set up in the main square, with dozens of steps folded out in all directions: a traveling theater. Perhaps a hundred Gartners, male and female, sit in folding chairs laid out around the plaza, their neeps standing at their sides. All the Gartners are enfolded in their finest clothes, and Mads puffs himself up when he sees them.

One woman at the far left of the crowd, dressed in vibrant red and richest black, dips her head toward my Gartner and points her neep in our direction. The neep approaches us, face downturned with respect. I think it is called Mikkel, but I cannot recall if it styles itself male or female.

"Greetings, Herre Poulson," says the neep, bowing deeply. "My Gartner, Frue Holm, invites you to sit with her."

We follow neep Mikkel back to its mistress. Gartner Holm smiles at my master, but it is a cold smile; they are so like each other.

"What a pleasant afternoon this will be," says Gartner Holm in her mountain-peak voice. She offers Mads her hand, and he kisses it. I hide my own disfigured hand in my tunic pocket, feeling at the edges of my cigarette carton.

The crowd chatters mildly, each and every Gartner being sure to look spectacularly unimpressed. We neeps keep our heads turned down. Still, my eyes sneak toward the stage.

At first all I am aware of is a feeling. A rumble, which might as well be coming from the salt mine. But the rumbling gets louder, and deeper, until I am sure that it is a drum. One by one the Gartners' sentences trail off and their faces turn toward the traveling theater.

With a last furious rumble, the drum player leaps out from the cart and lands on the top step of the folding stage, arms upraised. He is dressed as a monster—I do not know what kind of monster, for it is too big to be a horse, but it is beautiful. Its whole body is redder than any brick in the town, and its huge silvery eyes flash our reflections back at us as the man inside the costume turns his head. Is he a lizard? Or a tremendous bird?

I have no time to decide; the next moment, the man is back to drumming, and the bright colors of his costume flash metallic in the sun. The whole square is silent, except for that drumming, which rattles my fibers until I feel as though I have a human heart beating in my chest.

And then the drumming stops again. And She appears.

Every human in the crowd gasps, and I hear Mikkel's yip of surprise. The woman that pops up from the cart is like no woman I have ever seen. Is she beautiful? Her flesh is dark, just like Sissel said, dark as soil that has never seen the sun. But she *gleams*, she *glows* with something that I have never seen before, not in a Gartner, not in a neep. She is convinced of herself. Her features are not small and delicate like mine, and I am the one Mads created to be beautiful—but this woman, the actress, is nothing like me, and yet she smiles as widely as if the difference between us does not matter.

And she is dressed as a neep in blossom.

As the drum starts again, she begins to dance. That too is unfamiliar—she moves too freely, without the sneering reservation of the Gartners, and her wild gestures send the papier-mâché leaves and the silk flowers bobbing, as if they are an extension of her own body. I have never moved like that.

I am more like her than I have ever been like Mads.

As she dances, the monster that is the drummer begins to circle her, his costume flashing. The light has not changed; it is still midafternoon, with the low weak sunlight of our springtime sloping across the rooftops, and yet the sun seems to have focused all its strength on that little stage so that it is lit from within, while the rest of the world is overdrawn in shadow.

"A trick of mirrors," mumbles Mads.

I do not look at him. I do not look at him again until the dance is done, and the drummer circles toward the actress in her purple-blue neep costume, and spits a gout of paper-ribbon fire at her, and she collapses across the steps. The papier-mâché leaves ignite with real flame.

"What a spectacle," says Frue Holm, but even she claps. All the humans clap, because at least the wild neep has met a fitting end: roasted by flame, as all turnips must be in time.

We neeps applaud as well, though more softly. We, too, have seen something that seems right and true—and we have learned from it, though it is not, I think, the lesson the Gartners would have us learn.

There is no hope now of Mads falling for the actress. This does not trouble me as much as I would have expected. The main fact, which had not occurred to me before, is that no wild thing like her could stand to have a man like Mads yapping at her heels. So I am left with only my Gartner, who sits impatiently while the drummer and the actress take their bows, nods to Frue Holm, and leaves the performers to pack up their stage. He does not leave a single *krone* for their trouble.

"What strange nonsense," he mutters.

I follow him, my scheme in tatters. Now I am less prepared than ever to become Mads' supper.

All through the ride home, I run my roots across the stump where my finger once was, and I consider. How to be rid of Mads Poulson? How to transform myself into a wild neep like the one I saw on stage?

That night, I smoke my last secret cigarette. And it does not escape me, as the smolder eats away at the paper tube, that my cigarettes are gone—but that one match remains.

☼

All the next day, Mads avoids me. He has got a letter from the head office in Copenhagen, and has locked himself in the study with it. Sometimes these letters make him swear, but today I hear nothing.

All day, I play with my match.

Mads does not even come to his hot meal, which is strange. What is stranger still is that cook does not come out to serve it. I can hear cook moving about in the kitchen, but there is another sound in there too, like a squeezed mouse. This does not make sense to me, and I make sure to stay away.

Late in the afternoon, I see a plume of grey smoke rise over the salt mine. I sit out on the steps, playing with my match, and watch it absently.

I feel as if a storm is coming. I get the same feeling before a big rain: like the soil is twisted up in anticipation. Only this time it is me twisted up.

Sissel Peals arrives before the sun fully sets, and when she sees me she rushes toward me and catches me up in her arms. "Oh, Pluto!" she wails. "Oh! You are still with us!" And in between her cries she makes that squeezed-mouse sound like cook has been making all day.

"Where else would I be?" I ask. Surely she cannot know about my bud.

She pushes me back to arm's length and shakes me. "Idiot neep, where is Gartner Poulson?"

"In his office," I say, but the plume of smoke catches my eye and every fiber of my body ignites. "Isn't he?"

Sissel shakes her head, pointing toward the smoke. "The mine," she says. "The mine is finished. Gartner Poulson has been called back to Copenhagen."

I turn slowly on the spot, refusing to believe and also certain that what she says is true. Mads is done with the mine, and that fire, all that smoke, is what remains of the neeps and turnips who worked there, and have no purpose now that it is to be closed. They are not valuable enough to the company to warrant transport back to the city.

I am not valuable enough to Mads, either. To spare himself the expense of my train ticket, he will roast me too, flowers or no.

"Get out of here," I hiss at Sissel. "You never saw me."

She shrinks away from me—neeps are not supposed to be full of wrath and fire, but when that actress pretended to roast, it was as though all that heat flowed through her and into me.

I am not Gartner Poulson's creation. He only changed me, and I can change myself back.

☼

There is nothing worth stealing from the house. There is no such thing as a wild neep, not really, and stealing a hundred *kroner* would do me little good; no human would take it from me, and money is no use beneath the soil.

So I decide to burn it down.

My fingers tremble with the matchbox, and at first it fails to strike. The sulfur scrapes against the strip, leaving a grey streak. The second strike fares the same.

But the third time, the match flares, and I drop it hurriedly to the small pile of paper made from shreds of the letter that doomed our mine, and I wave my hand over it to create a draft.

Turnips are not friends of fire; I have lit a cigarette, but never a house. The paper burns and chars the wood floor, but my flame dies before taking the building with it.

I scream and batter the floor with my fists until white pulp shows through my purple skin. I would keep pounding forever, until either my body or the house gave way, but Mads stamps through the doorway and hauls me to my feet.

"No more of that," he snarls at me. "You're mine to keep. Mine to eat. Mine to destroy."

I struggle against him, but he is strong, and my fists are battered all to mush. In the end, he simply lifts me off the floor and carries me to the kitchen.

Cook whimpers while she prepares me, no doubt because she knows she will be next.

"At least you're worth eating, Pluto," she tells me while when she cuts my leaves away. The miners and cook are no good for eating. They will be roasted to ash and left in the open air. At least the one who made me will have his satisfaction of me before all this is done.

What bitter consolation.

Nothing hurts as much, or will ever hurt as much, as when I tore my bud away. Still, it is not pleasant to feel cook's cold knife slide into me and gouge out the bruised and rotten parts. Only my best pieces will be saved for Mads.

It is not Mads' habit to see his meals prepared, but he was the one that took the knife to me to bring me to life, and now he watches with no small satisfaction as that life is taken away. To my chagrin, the knife reveals flesh that is whiter yet than his; I have not made myself poisonous to him. I have failed.

Cook is good with her spices, but Mads stays her hand when she reaches for the shallots.

"As few ingredients as possible," says Mads, looking into my eyes. "I want to taste Pluto."

Tuber of Many Roots, I hate him. I wall myself off and think only of the actress in her role as the wild neep; I see the rhythm of her leaves and the roll of her blossoms even as cook adds salt and butter to the pan, even as she dices me into bite-size pieces. She saves my face for last, for she is a kind soul. In my final moments, I bless her.

I cannot say I remember the oven but for its heat. I am largely numb by then.

And I cannot say I remember the eating, for I am all in pieces; one bite comes in my arm, one in my shoulder, one in my thigh, one in my neck. He does not eat me in order. I have no order left.

In the darkness of his stomach, though, I feel a change. He is warmer than the soil of the earth, and damper, but damp and darkness are my elements. Within him, I begin to come together again.

I am too good to waste a single bite. When Mads retires at last, full to bursting with me—and lies down in his above-ground bed, and pulls the blankets over him in a way that feels familiar to me, although cotton is no comfort like earth is—I wake up. True, I am not myself anymore, but I have grown to this, to changing and to being changed. This is nothing more than another transformation.

Within the world that is Mads Poulson, I roil. I turn sour, just like Sissel promised. And just as Mads promised, I begin to bloom.

I have held back my flowers for so long that calling them forth is no great feat—they burst out of me, stretching and reaching for sunlight, the only part of me that has ever longed for open air. Mads sits up in his bed, clutching at his throat, coughing and choking and clawing at the skin until it bleeds. I want out, and when my yellow blooms force their way up he cannot continue to breathe.

Late next afternoon, cook and Sissel find him. His mouth and nose, his ears and eye sockets, are plugged with yellow blossoms.

Sissel Peals is a very wise turnip. With great effort but no complaint, she drags the bloated remains of Mads to the root cellar and tucks him into my old plot. With the aid of a spare brick, cook knocks a hole in the boards so that the sun can get in. They leave us there to germinate and to find some peace.

From time to time, a little breeze whips in the hole, and the flowers dance as freely as those of a wild neep might. And Mads Poulson feeds me all the while.

New York Times bestseller Tobias S. Buckell burst onto the science fiction scene 15 years ago, and since then has sold 7 novels, 3 collections, and more than 50 short stories. His work has appeared in 17 languages, and he has been nominated for the Hugo, Nebula and Campbell Awards.

THE RYDR EXPRESS

by Tobias S. Buckell

You've made your way through the corridors of the train and found your room, up on the third deck. Tea has arrived, delivered by a vaguely humanoid robot that balances its torso on a pair of continuously spinning gyroscopes.

Sitting down at the small table, you let yourself relax just a touch and stir in milk and sugar as the train continues to speed up. Two hundred miles per hour, two-fifty. It has just emerged from a wormhole that led downstream toward even more wormholes that eventually bifurcate. At that junction there are trains to the worlds of Fairwater and Fairhaven.

Outside your window, the purple forestry of Rydr's World whips past. The occasional city slowly accretes around the windows, then fades back away.

Now that the Rydr Express has slipped out of the wormhole at the Western edge of its lone continental landmass it is headed East toward the other wormhole on the far coast. When it hits that wormhole and passes through, it'll start jumping its way toward the Dawn Pillars junction. From there it'll head upstream through hundreds of wormholes, until it ends up in League territory when it exits a final wormhole and arrives on the world of Bifrost.

The Rydr Express is a spur that juts off in that uncertain territory of unaligned planets that all exist in between the Forty Eight worlds. They are all connected by thousands of wormholes, and it's only been in the last decade that the wormholes have been moved out of space, onto land, and hooked up by rail.

You have nine hundred miles to go before you hit the Eastern coast. Nine hundred miles of tension.

The door to your room slides open.

You drop the spoon to the table. A startling sound: metal on wood. The clattering reveals that you are surprised. It also reveals that you are a bit stunned, and overly nervous.

The tall man you're looking at is wearing a black oilskin coat, and he walks with a slight limp as he slides the door closed behind him.

Inside the small sleeper berth, he dominates the room. His steel-gray eyes flicker, scanning everything, then finish up by pinning you in place. His shoulder-length dreadlocks are graying, slightly, and with the weathered lines of his face, he looks like he's in his forties.

A far cry from the centuries that you know him to be.

You're holding your breath, and the trigger of the gun in your left hip-pocket, where it's been all along.

It's a trigger's-width away from releasing hell as the man sits down across from you on the other side of the table. From the creak of the floor underneath, you can tell he weighs double, maybe triple what a man should.

You can't say you weren't expecting this. He's that good. That's what everyone says. But this is your world, your game, and your territory. To have been flushed out before you'd even really sat down is a gut punch.

"This is a private room," you say, mustering indignant outrage. You're still trying to keep up your usual traveling businessman camouflage.

The man leans in, his elbows resting on the table and making it creak from the strain. "I'm Pepper," he says, as his locks fall forward and he holds out a hand.

You maintain the fiction for another split second, then lean back and retrieve your tea. You're impressed at your steady hand. "Most of my friends," you mutter over a sip, "call me Vee."

"Are you going to pull that trigger, Vee?" Pepper asks, very seriously, your eyes meeting over the lip of the cup.

"I haven't decided yet," you reply, setting the tea down.

✿

Eighteen hours earlier the militia summons jacked you up out of bed with a ringing headache, leaving you stumbling around shaking your head as your partner grumbled and pulled the covers up and fell back asleep.

The klaxon sound, rigged to a bone-induction military earpiece quantumly entangled to HQ, continued on until you patched in and reported that you were on your way, goddamnit, and they could quit paging you.

But there was no trip to HQ. Head of operations was standing outside your very door with three other rail agents when you got uniformed up and burst out the door.

"We have a situation," she said.

They all forced their way into your tiny apartment.

"I have someone here," you stammered.

Operations looked over at the door to the bedroom. "Tell them to leave," she said. Then she paused slightly. "How serious is this?"

"What?" You were a bit lost for words. What the hell was going on?

"Your file shows few social attachments. Is this someone we need to take into our protection during this mission? There's a high-risk component. An attachment could be a liability."

"Protection," you said, eyes wide. Even if it was only a fling, you hadn't wanted someone's life at risk due to their having the bad luck to stumble into you for a few great encounters.

Operations sighed and pointed at the bedroom door and snapped her fingers. "Make it happen."

One of the agents walked to the door.

Moments later the apartment had been vacated, and the confusion and shouting abated. Everyone'd had a deep breath, and Operations sat in your armchair as if she'd owned it her whole life.

"We have a situation," she said.

"You mentioned."

"Pepper's here on Rydr's World."

"Oh."

"We're constitutionally a neutral zone, Vee. Our economic ties are to the Xenowealth, but we still have two League-loyal worlds downstream of us, and they have peace-brokered rights of transport through us on upstream all the way back to core League territory. We can't have the Xenowealth's top troublemaker running loose. Fairhaven and Fairwa-

ter, those worlds are far more militarized than we are."

"What do you want me to do?" You'd been unsure of what all this meant.

Operations clarified that, leaning forward. "Intelligence says he's been around shipping and loading centers. We think he's planning to get weapons aboard a train. Why? We're not sure. But it can't be anything good. We need you to shadow him until he gets out of our territory. Once out, he's not our problem. But whatever he's involved in, we can't have it jeopardizing our neutrality."

You'd licked your lips. "And if he starts causing trouble, what am I supposed to do?"

"Stop him."

"Stop him? This is Pepper. The man is more alien machinery than human. He's more legend than real. I'm probably not going to be able to stop him, Ops, you know that."

She looked at you, and then nodded. "I know that," she'd said. "But we need you to at least try, to demonstrate our seriousness."

And you'd swallowed. Because you realized then that's why they chose you. No family, no attachments.

You're damn good at being a rail agent, there's that too.

But most of all: you're kinda expendable.

And Operations was watching. She'd at least done you the favor of explaining things. They're always honest. It's a volunteer job. Always was.

You could have refused.

But you'd slowly nodded.

Because in the end, how many people ever get a chance to meet a living human legend?

Pepper grins at you, now, as you let go of the gun in the hip holster and put both your hands on the table. "I've haven't really done anything yet, and you're the fair sort," he says. "I like your decision-making process."

"What are you doing here?" you ask.

Pepper leans forward. "How much weaponry do you have access to aboard the train?"

Enough, you hope.

"This is neutral country," you remind him.

He slings an arm over the ledge on the back of the built in seat. "Neutral? The line's swimming with League agents."

"And with Xenowealth agents," you tell him.

He waves a hand, unimpressed. "We just follow the activity."

"Treaties were brokered. Rydr's World seceded from the League ten years ago. But we are also not allied with the Xenowealth. We host trade to both."

"And you let the League run up and down the train lines as they see fit," Pepper said. "That breeds trouble."

"It was a condition of our independence."

"The League knew it couldn't hold onto you, so it grabbed the best possible concessions. You bent over backward."

You bite your lip. "I'm not here to argue history."

"And yet, it always walks back up the line to bite us all in the ass," Pepper said.

"What are you planning?" You ask him, outright.

"It's not what I'm planning you need to be worried about," he says, and raises a finger.

You both hear the dull thud down the corridor. Your ears were cored out and replaced with synthetics when you agreed to join the rail's security. Yes, you volunteered to defend your planet. Yes you do as part of a self-assembling militia. But that doesn't mean you aren't teched out with the latest and greatest. Quick nerves, reinforced skeleton, subprocessors in the nape of your neck.

A body hits the carpet. A hand smacks the wall. You half stand, but Pepper, expecting something of this sort, shakes his head.

Wait.

The door is kicked open, and Pepper reaches out and grabs the man standing there.

He's a bit stunned. He's holding a large, silenced pistol, but Pepper's grabbed and broken his hand before he's even had time to frown. You notice, in the split second as his entire body is violently yanked from the doorway and over your cup of tea, nudging it slightly with the tip of his boot, that there's blood splattered on the assassin's gloves.

By the time Pepper slams him into the side wall, just under the window, his neck is broken.

Yet, for good measure, Pepper takes the man's own silenced gun, puts the silencer to the dying man's mouth, and pulls the trigger.

Blood and brain tissue spray the window.

Pepper sits back down and delicately pushes your teacup back to its original location on the table. "You were saying something about neutrality, I think," he says.

The dead man will be tied into a battle-net of some sort. You're not wasting time. You're kicking out the paneling underneath your bench seat and reaching under to retrieve a large black case.

Inside, nestled in foam: extra handguns, a tactical assault rifle, ammo, a belt of flash bangs.

"Who are they after?" you ask. "Me or you?"

"They're killing passengers," Pepper says.

You pause. "I can't believe that."

Pepper still has the gun he took off the dead man. He glances around the door. "Follow me and see for yourself."

Outside, in the hallway, blinking at the bright lights, polished brass, steel inserts and other neo-modernist stylings you see the first body. It's an alien: Nesaru. Its quill–like feathers droop from its skin in death. Clear fluids dripped, splashed against the hallway wall, and soaked into the carpet.

The slender, ostrich-like alien's neck is bent at an impossible angle.

"There's more," Pepper whispers.

Each room is a display of death. Different-colored fluids. Different bodies. But all punctured, broken, run down. Still. Unmoving. Statues in their nooks, holding gory, distorted death poses for you.

But some of the rooms are empty.

That leaves you puzzled. You're mulling it over, but even as you do that, you enable contact with HQ.

It's quantum entanglement communications. Which means it's expensive. Someone has to create the two paired pieces of quantum bits and separate them. You get one bit, HQ gets the other. And once one gets used, and the information passed through, its state reverts to unpaired. It's the universe's most expensive form of limited bandwidth email.

So you telegraph HQ a summary: LEAGUE *KILLING* PSSNGRS. TRAIN HIJACK IMMNT? ADVISE.

Pepper looks inside another empty room, then back at you.

He's expecting you to notice something, but the reply flashes back, painted over your eyesight thanks to a chip in your visual cortex. WCH PSSNGRS?

Which passengers?

And the empty rooms are a puzzle that finally snaps into its proper shape.

You're only seeing dead aliens. There are no humans in here.

NON-HUMAN, you reply.

Pepper's watching your air-typing fingers.

OBSRV & RPRT, you're ordered.

"What do your masters order?" he asks, forcing another door open.

You don't answer. You don't need to. The troubled look on your face tells him everything.

✿

"So what's your plan, here?" you ask. You're keyed up. Sickened. Shaken. Trying to figure out what all this means and what it means to you. You're also relieved no one has ordered you to detain or try to stop this man.

"Plan?" Pepper looks down the corridor. "To stop it."

"Why?" You do hate yourself for asking, somewhere deep inside. But there is genuine curiosity. What's in it for this man? What is making him tick? "This isn't your fight. This isn't a world that asked you here."

"It's infectious," Pepper says as he points at one of the bodies.

You recoil for a split second, then realize stepping back won't make a difference to survival one way or another. "Biological warfare?"

"No, the violence," he says. He's looking back at you. "It starts here, but then it spreads. Consumes everything around it. Like a fire, it tries to pull in everything within reach. Borders might be decent barriers, but it tries to leap around, continue. So I come out here, to fight it before it has fuel. Before it spreads to the worlds I hold dear."

There's a darting movement, a shadow against the far door leading to the next car. Pepper launches himself forward, boots digging into the carpet hard enough to rip it and make the metal beneath his feet groan as he springs away.

You follow, a breath behind. Fast to the unaided eye, but molasses compared to the snap-speed of Pepper, who hits the steel door and rips it out of its hinges.

He pivots, keeping it to his right side as a shield that smacks into someone you can't see, just as another man bursts down the corridor. This man is dressed in dull gray armor. It's a flowing, shifting exoskeleton. He looks like a knight with submachine guns in either hand. Pepper drops the door and closes with him.

When he and Pepper hit, it sounds like a padded gong has been struck. Metal colliding with flesh with metal underneath.

Pepper grapples with whining exoskeletal arms, and both men twirl and spin around the corridor, each one looking for a weakness as they grunt, shift, and struggle in their rapid tango.

Still locked together they smash through the door of a cabin.

✿

As the sounds of destruction and splintering walls fill the corridor, the ripped-off door shifts. A man crawls out into the corridor on his hands and knees.

He leaves a trail of blood behind from his ruined face, where the door struck him as Pepper passed. He has a large gun in one hand, which he awkwardly holds as he pulls himself along.

A new sound creeps out into the train car. Something like the scream of a can being slowly ripped apart, and then a fleshy, wet thump.

Pepper steps out of the room holding a helmeted head in one hand, torn completely free of a body.

"Pepper!" You shout the name in warning, without thinking about it, and the crawling man raises his gun.

But before he completes the motion Pepper throws the decapitated helmeted head at the gun. The shot destroys the dead skull, creating a cloud burst of blood mist that Pepper cuts through to kill the crawling League agent with a heel stomp to the back of the neck.

The two of you are alone again.

"I was hoping he'd still be unconscious," Pepper says, looking down at the corpse. "I wanted to talk with him. Find out where the human passengers are being herded to. How many League agents there were."

"And what they were up to?" you suggest.

Pepper shrugs. "That'll emerge." Then he looks up and down the car. "What do you think, up to the front, or back?"

"I can't help you," you remind him.

He looks past you, back down the train. "Are you physically prevented from helping me in any capacity, right this second? Is something literally holding you back? Neural taps?"

You shake your head.

"Then you're full of shit. You're making a philosophical choice. To follow an order. *You* are choosing to stand by."

✧

Pepper chooses backward, and you begin to move through the cars door by door. He leads, and you follow.

OBSRV, you think. Yeah. You'll do that. You'll just fucking OBSRV.

Three more cars of death, corpses framed in their rooms, and you catch up. Five League agents ordering humans forward, killing any aliens they manage to catch.

People scream when Pepper kicks the door from the hinges and wades in. But the agents don't. They're expecting him.

They move in synchronization to turn and attack, as if sharing a single brain. Linked to each other in some deep, technologically enabled battle symbiosis. Gunfire rips through the walls as they open up, and you duck back into the space between trains and look through bulletproof glass. The thundering sound of air passing over the rubber, vacuum-proof flexible tube that connects the two cars deafens you, and mutes the sound of battle.

A multi-person ballet of death ensues. Pepper sprints into the mix, his trenchcoat flapping around him with each twist and turn. He leaps off the wall,

almost hitting the ceiling, and flips around behind the first pair of attackers.

Like Pepper, these five attackers are more than they seem. Wherever the League rose up against the aliens, who had once held humanity in their iron grips, the League slaughtered their former masters and sought to plunder their superior technologies.

Some thought the League was too far diminished, too obsessed with human-only worlds and too pushed back to the fringes. But here are their well-funded paladins, and they are faster than you, stronger than you, more vicious than you.

And almost as dangerous as Pepper.

Almost.

One is shot in the back and falls, writhing. Another's head disappears. Was that a shotgun blast? You didn't see one, but it's hard to follow.

Number three's chest is caved in when Pepper runs him through a wall and pulls him back out to use as a shield.

And then the remaining two withdraw, running right past you as Pepper chases them.

A sixth man carrying what looks like a grenade launcher melts out of a room and ghosts past you. He's dressed in a suit, the same camouflage as you, and his eyes flicker sideways as he spots you.

It was a well sprung trap for Pepper. He's focused forward, and here comes the high powered attack from behind.

But this man reads something in you. He isn't going to leave *you* in his blind spot. He's moving to pull out another weapon with his left hand.

He's faster than you. Stronger, more dangerous.

But he wasn't expecting you, and you have the drop. Simple physics.

Because, much to your astonished satisfaction, you've had your own firearm out and ready to fire, finger just outside the trigger, since you stopped by the window.

Just in case.

OBSRV!

Forget that crap now. There's only flight or fight now. And flight was kicked in the nuts the moment this man started to twist and reach for his backup weapon, realizing that the damn grenade launcher would kill you both.

You fire from the waist, just out of general principle, as you're bringing the gun up to your trained fire stance. He's hit in the core, which barely registers on him. But once you're up and ready, it's two to the chest and two to the head.

For good measure you empty the clip into his face, revealing metal chips, machine eyes, and more. The man's more metal than human. Which is why you stood over him and kept shooting until there's nothing left.

"Give me the grenade gun," Pepper says, suddenly back in the car. You wordlessly pick it up and throw it over.

He turns around and kneels.

When the door to the car opens, it reveals forty League soldiers, dressed in armor, carrying rifles. Where the hell had they come from?

Pepper fires the grenade launcher through the car, through the open doors, into the mass of soldiers. The doors close. But flame licks around the doors' gaps, the windows bow out, and explosions rock everything.

He walks over and hands it over. "Pick a position, fire on anything that comes through."

"I can't do that," you protest, even as you hold the weapon.

"You already killed a League agent," he says, moving back into the car with survivors. "You've chosen your side. You're in."

He leaves you alone with the grenade launcher, and you reluctantly drop to a single knee.

Congratulations. You're now responsible for a full-on, hundred-percent, international incident.

Pepper gives the civilians instructions, and returns dragging a large case. "Get dressed, we'll need these to stay on the train."

Inside are spacesuits.

He's right. Whatever the League is planning revolves around hijacking this train. Which means it's not stopping on the East Coast. It's going to dive right through the wormhole leading away from Rydr's World and keep going.

You quickly pull a spacesuit on. It's a transparent baggy film that hangs loosely around you until you press it to the helmet and make a seal. Then the material constricts and sucks itself in to you until it's more of a second skin over your clothes.

All this time you've awkwardly kept the grenade launcher sighted on the far door of the train car.

Pepper looks at you, and a faint flicker of communications laser appears as motes drift through the air between the two of you. That makes sense; you don't want the League hearing you over radio of any type.

"I need that launcher back," Pepper says, and swaps you for a machine gun. "And this is your last chance. To get off the train. If you want."

Get off the train. Return to HQ. And explain you shot a League agent? Covered Pepper with a grenade launcher?

If you were going to go rogue, you might as well see this through.

You've got no soft spot for aliens. Rydr's World was run by Nesaru when your grandparents were your age. You saw the scars on their arms and tattoo barcodes. They told you about forced breeding programs with that aura of shame, but insistence that you know what happened.

There are still Nesaru gated compounds, complete with orbital defenses and full security.

And those aren't going away. Nesaru built those long before humanity was brought here. They won't give them up, not without a fight that would cost both sides too much.

Awkward compromises had been reached. And time had passed. And Nesaru who worked side by side with humans had always been here, and had helped when humanity revolted and demanded self-determination here, as it did all throughout the known worlds. And for a while, Rydr's World was a strong League of Human Affairs supporter.

But when the League began deportation, people refused. It was understandable, leaders argued, but would lead to humans acting like the Nesaru had when they had dominion. Humans would lose Nesaru technical expertise, finance, and technology. The success of Xenowealth worlds, fully integrated alien and human societies, led them to resist purism.

But you know of Nesaru that live in compounds, that despise humans as little better than monkeys. You read their sneering reviews of bumbling human efforts to deorbit wormholes and create a more directly linked system of worlds.

You understand the League, on a fundamental level. Maybe once you agreed.

Until that single moment, when you walked through the car and saw those dead individuals. Each one formerly a thinking being. This was the end result of League ideology. If you value one life, think it superior, eventually, taking the other does not matter.

"I'm staying on board," you tell Pepper.

"Good," he says, and behind you something detonates. The next time you glance back through the doors, the rest of the train is falling behind, emergency brakes shuddering it all to a stop.

If nothing else, you tell yourself, their lives will have been saved.

✧

The spacesuits' gloves are like gecko feet: they're embedded with pads and microscopic nano-adhesives that allow you to clamber up the outside of the car.

But you're moving along at several hundred miles per hour. It isn't wind you encounter as you crawl up to the roof, but a hurricane.

You're flat to the roof, army-crawling along a tremendous, pounding resistance that wants nothing more than to bat you off your perch. The adhesive pads hold.

AGNT: RPRT!

Just barely.

It's an exhausting, sweat-filled haul to get three cars forward from where you were. When you're done, it feels like you climbed up the side of a building.

You dig your pads into the roof and shelter behind the several-inches-high protection of a vent and pant.

OBSRVNG HIJACK IN PRGRSS, you tell your superiors. SURVIVORS IN BRAKED TRAIN.

An hour later, the train is still hauling at top speed as it passes through the last stop on Rydr's World. Skyscrapers whip by, and for a while an aircraft paces the train.

You wave at it.

AGNT: RPRT!

You ignore the demands ghosting over your eyeballs.

Fifteen minutes later, you squeeze your eyes shut and feel your stomach lurch as the train hits that blank portal of darkness that is the wormhole leading out and away from Rydr's World.

✧

Pepper shouts. It's joyful.

"Open your eyes, Vee," he says happily, rapping the side of your helmet. "Open your eyes. You never see the full vista from one room window. Not like this."

When you open your eyes the train is whipping past a giant mountain chain. There is no vegetation, and you're deep in the valley. Overhead: the remains of a nebula is scattered over the entire sky. Impossibly jagged peaks rise for miles around you. You feel light.

There is no wind pressure thundering at you.

Five minutes later the train dives into another wormhole.

Right away a giant hand of wind smacks into you.

You open your eyes again, and this time the tracks are on a bridge. It stands in the water, pilings driven down maybe ten feet. There is no land anywhere; you feel dizzy looking out at the horizon.

Where the sea laps, smoke wisps and rises. The pilings are burnished and polished, as if the sea is acidic.

Half an hour later you leave that behind. Plunge through yet another wormhole, and when you open your eyes you gasp. You're out in space. There's nothing but the darkness of vacuum and distant stars all around you. Track hangs in space, suspended in nothingness.

You stare at the heavens for twenty minutes, awestruck, until you realize the train is coming to a stop, and that it has been slowing the whole time.

Pepper taps you, and you turn. He points.

A starship approaches. Black paint against the black space all around you. You can see it by the stars it occludes: a darker space slipping over space as it gets closer.

Nav lights and docking lights pop on, and the frame is outlined: a giant functional cylinder strapped to a bell-shaped engine.

"What now?" you ask Pepper.

"Wait and watch," he says.

OBSRV.

✧

The League shuttles thousands of soldiers into the train after they cut in temporary airlocks near the front. Pepper counts ten thousand. That sounds right. They must be literally standing shoulder to shoulder to fit.

And to the front of the train, a sled is being prepared with a rocket attached to it.

"When we last had a full on war between the Xenowealth and the League," Pepper said, "we had a problem. Each wormhole is a natural border. A checkpoint. When they were in space, we stacked orbital firing platforms around the wormhole. Try to shove your ships through, and you'd get hammered. That's how the Satrapy, the aliens, that's how they kept us all in check. But once we had League and Xenowealth, the only way to push against each other was to foment revolution, play secret agent.

"Then, when the wormholes get moved down out of orbit, into oceans, it's the same problem. Natural chokepoints. Then we start running track through them all, thinking of them as just subway stops, that's when the League thinks, ah, now it has a military option.

"But it only gets to use it once."

You're both ready to bet that what's on the sled is a bomb. It rockets through the wormhole ahead and detonates, and then comes the ten minutes later, delivering troops and hardware to secure the wormhole: the chokepoint.

Then comes more.

And more.

"They've probably had this starship mothballed in far orbit ever since wormholes were in orbit here, back in the day, and the League had ships out here, before it withdrew," Pepper mused. "It's not a warship, we've tracked all those and the negotiations made sure those withdrew. But that doesn't mean it isn't useful. They've been smuggling troops one by one to this location for years, staging them in a station that we would have assumed was abandoned. I followed people out here. Followed the activity. Didn't see it being this big."

The League is invading. Not Rydr's World. But the next habitable world upstream of this string of worlds connected by wormholes: Dawn Pillars. A center of trade and activity, a highly developed world. And unlike the polyglot Rydr's, Dawn Pillars has a population that is almost all human. Very few aliens.

Ripe for League takeover.

No OBSRV left, really.

You sit down and tap out a report.

There is no answer.

You wonder what that's about. Is your department infiltrated with League? Are they just waiting? Are you that clueless, or ignorant?

Or are they just speechless because you dropped a bomb in their lap?

"What do we do next?" you ask.

Pepper's looking up at the starship. "They hijacked our train, Vee. I'd like to return the favor." He looks over at you. His dreadlocks are floating in the bowl of his helmet, making him look medusa-like. It's slightly disconcerting. "If you don't mind, I'd like to throw you at that ship."

He's not kidding.

Pepper has a half mile of a high-tensile thread, and he unspools several feet of it and ties it off on a tiny buckle on the back of your suit, near the small of your back. Then he throws you over the side of the train, lets you out about six feet, and starts spinning you around over his head like you're a bucket on the end of some string.

The world cartwheels around you, and then stops as Pepper lets go, the timing impeccable. He's slingshot you toward the dark bulk of the starship.

You fly through space, falling in, and then Pepper slows you down, using the brake on his spool.

After you reach out with your pads and grab the hull you look back and wave.

The thread yanks at you as Pepper activates a motor on the spool. Two minutes later he lands next to you, you both glance around, and then begin crawling around the hull of the ship.

The way in presents itself: a manual emergency airlock near a set of bay doors. You move to undog the first hatch to cycle in, but Pepper stops you.

"Not yet," he says. "Not until they finish unloading."

An hour later you both make your move. The manual airlock deposits you inside a cavernous cylindrical hangar. You scurry across the curved walls, weightless, using your gecko-fingers to grab any surface you can and then kick off.

"Keep up." Pepper moves like a cat in the air, loose-limbed and graceful. A natural hunter. And he knows what he's hunting. He's taking you to the core of the ship.

You suddenly get the feeling this isn't the first time he's done this.

He has a silenced gun out, and everyone you cross in the corridors of the ship ends up spinning slowly in the air, a surprised look on their face, blood slowly drifting out of punctures in the forehead.

Swift, quiet, calm, suddenly violent.

And fast. You're pushing off every bulkhead as fast as you can to keep up. You've bored down through most of this ship's bulk in minutes.

The men guarding the cockpit barely have time to register the fluttering trenchcoat, the man spinning in the air and firing, dreadlocks spread out around his face.

He's through them and into the actual cockpit of the ship in the blink of an eye, and shouts of outrage end with the silent thwack of Pepper's response.

"Shove them out and lock us in," Pepper orders. He's floating around from control pod to control pod, his head cocked, as if getting advice from someone. Maybe he has quantum entangled communications of his own. Someone's talking him through what the controls are, you think. Someone deep in the heart of the Xenowealth.

Screens flicker on, and you hear the wail of wind outside the door.

Glancing at the screens shows you what just happened: the ship vented its air. Airlock doors throughout are wide open to space, and you can see up on the screens random faces, tortured, blood beginning to leak out of orifices.

You look away.

"Any of them good about drills and who kept near their spacesuits will be trying to get back in here," Pepper said. "So stay clear of the door; they might blow it."

He's listening to instructions and moving quickly from place to place, frowning.

Then the engines thunder to life, and he claps his hands.

"Oh, they're not going to like this."

✧

There are no weapons systems on this ship. It's transport, pure and simple. Which is how the League was able to leave it behind, hidden away from Xenowealth and Rydr's World military negotiation accountants looking for just this sort of stunt when comparing inventories and current ship names and movements out of the area when Rydr's World demanded independence.

But that doesn't mean it can't be used as a crude missile. Pepper orders you into an acceleration pod to strap in, but keeps spinning around and flitting around to control the ship.

You're not moving fast when you strike the train and track. But it's fast enough to rip the outer hull of the ship and derail the train. It's fast enough to twist and rip track.

The impact throws Pepper around the cockpit, his body smashing equipment. He wearily pulls himself out and gets back to the controls, firing the engines to pull the ship free of the track and turn it about.

The ship's external monitors, shown on screens all throughout the orb of the cockpit, show cars full of soldiers and equipment hanging around the ship. The staging area is chaos.

Pepper lines the ship up and fires it up. It shudders and caroms its way down the tracks. It speeds up, heading for the wormhole leading to Dawn Pillars.

"Pepper?" you ask. "What are you doing? This thing can't go through a wormhole."

"These ships used to do it all the time," Pepper said.

"Yes, when the wormholes were in orbit. Now they're deorbited. We're going to drive this thing through that hole and out into a train station that's on a planet's surface."

"I know."

There was, you could hear, a sort of boyish satisfaction in the tone of Pepper's voice.

✧

When you pass through, there is that familiar kick in the gut. And the sudden resumption of gravity, yanking down on you again.

And then it all turns bad. The walls flexing and bending visibly. The creaking superstructure that then began to give up creaking and just started screaming.

There was what felt like a mile of sliding, and tumbling, and then darkness as the energy systems on the ship all failed.

Someone is chuckling in the background of the debris and shaking and … yes, that's an explosion somewhere nearby crackling the air.

The next kick isn't in your gut, but to your helmet, which cracks and falls away. And then you pass out.

A lot of men make a point of arresting you when you wake up in a quiet, very clean and modern-feeling hospital wing. They've vacated other patients and have what looks like a small military guarding you.

No one is happy.

Very grave people are making very important, and measured, but Very Serious accusations. People wearing very expensive suits who look perpetually constipated.

No one is sure what, exactly, to charge you with, but ramming a spaceship through a wormhole into an urban world has repercussions, they explain.

You ask about Pepper, but they pretend not to hear you.

On the second day, when you're able to get up and walk, you stand by the window and look out over the city. And you see the wormhole and the central train station. And you note the long furrow in the parks and space around the wormhole made by the massive spaceship, the ruined hulk of which rests at the end of the giant, debris-scattered, ploughed mess it has created.

You helped do that.

No wonder they're pissed. At least four buildings have been subject to a rapid and unscheduled demolition by spaceship.

You're going away for a long, long time.

But was it worth it?

You hear mutters from some of the soldiers guarding you that the League managed to overwhelm a couple of worlds this way. There's fighting with the Xenowealth breaking out. It's the League's last stand. And they're going for broke.

Which means that even if you helped delay them, those surviving soldiers, even without the benefit of surprise, are still going to try to shove through that wormhole any minute now.

You've been stripped of your volunteer rail militia communications equipment by a surgeon who cuts out the implants. A formal letter declaring you *persona non grata* has arrived. You're stripped of rank and pay, and your pension has been scuttled.

That is your afternoon. The Rydr's World embassy liaison has you sign here, there, and here, and here again to formalize it.

They will not be helping you find legal counsel in the upcoming fun.

But after the glowering liaison leaves, one of the guards taps your shoulder. "Legal's here for you," he says, and points out a room.

Inside is Pepper, dressed in a suit, holding a briefcase.

As the door closes behind you, he sets the case down and opens it. "So, I'm here as a Xenowealth ambassador," he tells you. Inside are citizenship ID chips, a few wads of hard currency and some gold coins, and several wads of explosives.

You don't bother to ask how he got all that up here.

"You can't follow me directly anymore," Pepper says. He motions for you take everything but the explosives. "But these chips are a new identity anywhere in the Xenowealth, and starter cash. Go on a vacation. Start a business. But just one favor, Vee?"

"Yes?"

He's shoving the explosive into the wall, careful to point the shaped charges in the needed direction. "Don't ever work for someone who demands you stand still and do nothing."

"I can do that."

"If you're not interested in a vacation, call the person on that card. Tell her I recommended you. She'll know what that means."

You nod.

Pepper walks over, pushes you behind him, and blows the wall off the side of the hospital. "Apparently," he shouted, "even the diplomats can't get these guys to let you go, so I have to get involved. I hate administrivia like this, but I wasn't about to leave you to pay the price for my little joyride."

He's holding out his hand. You're not sure what the hell comes next, but you stop near the edge and look out over the city, the wormhole, the train tracks, and the destroyed ship, and then take a deep breath and jump with him into the air.

✡

Five adrenaline-fueled hours later, you're on a train by yourself, wired, jittery, and feeling the kick to the gut as your train indolently passes through a wormhole on its way deep into the Xenowealth.

You flip the plastic business card Pepper gave you around.

Nashara, it says. And there's the contact info.

So there's the question. Do nothing? Take the starter cash. Settle in somewhere. Start a business? You can do anything.

Or make the contact.

What will you do?

Copyright © 2011 by Tobias S. Buckell

Ian Whates is a British writer and editor, with 5 novels and a number of anthologies to his credit. He is currently a Director of both SFWA (Science Fiction Writers of America) and BSFA (British Science Fiction Association).

WOURISM

by Ian Whates

"The storms were the worst thing. The power outages and food shortages, the ignominy of standing in queues for basics, even bread and water—we coped with all of that. This was war, after all. The constant fear of explosion and the almost incessant gunfire, the destruction of buildings and the roads—they were terrible, horrific, but it's amazing what you can learn to live with when you have to. The weather turning against us, though, that was the final straw. None of us had ever seen rain like it: relentless, pummelling the city as if God Herself had forsaken us and joined in the bombardment; and as for the lightning …"

The woman's narrative was abruptly punctuated by a loud peal of thunder and the pervading gloom shattered in a dazzle of electric discharge. Somebody, possibly Gretchen, exclaimed in surprise and even I started a little. This well-staged drama heralded the surround-sound arrival of steady rain and a rolling series of thunderous rumblings, though the latter were far more subdued than that first spectacular clap.

The woman continued speaking. The image of her narrow face still dominated the room, but now behind it and through it a distant cityscape began to emerge, illuminated by vivid lightning strikes and the ruddy stain of smoldering fires.

"This was the closest our collective spirit came to breaking," the woman said. "Even the deaths seemed so much worse in the relentless storms. Disposing of bodies became a logistical nightmare as well as an emotional one. Somebody claimed that the freak weather was a sign of severe damage to the ionosphere, that in a struggle somewhere high above us doomsday weapons were being deployed, unleashing fearsome energies that had unbalanced the atmosphere of the entire planet. Such things meant nothing to us. What did we care about the planet or even the next district over? Our whole world had narrowed down to a handful of streets and the struggle to survive for just one more day."

The woman's face faded. Perspective tilted and we swooped down toward the besieged city and then into it, stopping only once we had reached street level. The sound of rainfall intensified and it was joined by the chatter of small-arms fire and the clatter of running footsteps. The 3D effect was far more immediate and more convincing now that we were this close. There was even a faint smell of smoke and of dampness, and a billow of heat from a fire at our backs. Only the absence of any actual rain hampered the suspension of disbelief. Long shadows moved across the walls of shattered buildings to our left: people running. A man screamed, and one of the shadows convulsed in mid-stride, threw up its arms and collapsed.

The woman's face appeared once more, superimposed on the street scene to hover in the air before us. Her eyes held a great weariness that underlined her words. "Little Danilo, my younger brother, was killed in the first few days of the bombardment; my eldest, Toma, toward the end." She spoke with a cold detachment that made her account all the more chilling. "Toma had joined the militia by then. No one lived long in the militia. The imminence of his death overshadowed the start of each new day like a pall and haunted our dreams at night, until it became reality. My mother fell ill not long after. By this stage there was no medicine—supplies had run out months before. We did our best, but all we had to offer her were prayers and love and comforting words. She didn't leave her bed in the last two weeks and died the day before the cease-fire. My father never really recovered. Nor, in truth, did any of us."

A caption appeared beneath the woman's face: "Jasna Petrović: Survivor," it read.

"My name is Jasna Petrović, and I was one of the lucky ones."

With that, she was gone. The soundtrack had dwindled to nothing during her final declaration and now the scene faded too as the lights came back up, to leave us blinking at each other across a plain-walled room.

In a gauche display that the word 'insensitive' didn't begin to cover, somebody beside me started clapping. I was mortified to realize that it was Alex.

"What?" he asked in the face of my glare. "It was a very good show."

"For fuck sake, Alex …" I don't swear as a rule, but he'd earned it.

I was eight months out of university and yet to decide what I wanted to do with my life. Alex was seven years older than me, worked in corporate finance for a company with offices on five worlds and had an apartment in the sort of complex my friends and I used to dream of seeing inside. He was big on team building and I would tease him that his favorite words were "bonding" and "incentive."

As I looked around I noticed a middle-aged woman standing stock-still while everyone about her relaxed and chatted; an island of calm amidst the fidgeting. Tall, slender, she wore a burgundy suit—very smart and business-like—and was staring straight ahead, as if she could still see the harrowing scene long after the rest of us had lost it in the glare of brightened lights.

"Oh, come on, Ginny. She's not real, you know," Alex said, reclaiming my attention. "You *do* know that, don't you? Just an actress hired to play the part, and her performance was outstanding, so I showed my appreciation."

I wasn't so sure. The narrator's eyes and her voice—the whole presentation—seemed to resonate with sincerity to me. Of course, Alex would argue that it was meant to.

He turned away to talk to Gretchen and Hassan. I consulted my wrist perminal. A quick search of the local database revealed that there had been no fewer than seven Jasna Petrovićs resident in Serna at the outbreak of the war. A flutter of fingertips brought a parade of images scrolling across the screen. I froze the sequence at one who *might* have been our narrator, though she was a lot younger when this was taken; and she was smiling, which was something she had never threatened to do during the presentation. I narrowed the search to images of this particular Jasna Petrović and took great satisfaction in discovering that yes, the woman was genuine.

Her story and her suffering were real, whatever Alex might think.

He could have checked all this easily enough on his own perminal had he wanted to. He wouldn't, of course; far too comfortable in his own false assumptions. Why risk undermining a declared cynicism with anything as inconvenient as the truth?

"If you'd like to follow me, ladies and gentlemen," Malcolm, our slick, camp, white-suited guide said, "we have some wartime armament to show you next: a unique collection of genuine artillery pieces and weaponry that saw service during the siege and were recovered and restored at the end of hostilities."

"Now we're talking," Alex said, flashing me a broad grin, taking it for granted that we two were collaborators in his enthusiasm.

He was soon chatting happily with Gretchen and Hassan—a couple we'd fallen in with since arriving here. None of them seemed to notice that I lagged a little behind.

Everyone knew the basic story of this place; that while the rest of the city was rebuilt and reshaped in the aftermath of the war, one large section of Serna had been kept as a ruin—though it hadn't, of course; that was just the desired illusion. In fact this area too had been rebuilt, but in the image of its war-torn self. "Despite appearances, every element of the park is structurally sound" had been the message stressed repeatedly during the promo we'd watched prior to booking. This was a battleground sanctioned by health and safety.

Serna became the first, the biggest, the most famous Warzone Theme Park, and a previously obscure term entered common parlance: Wourism.

Our route from the projection room took us through a corridor lined with display cases housing various small items. I stopped before one: a child's soft toy, a grimy orange-brown teddy bear, with the left eye missing and the left side of its face sooty and blackened.

Sensing my presence, an audio commentary started up, explaining that the bear had been pulled from the rubble of a flattened building during the cleanup. Nobody knew the name of its owner or if they'd survived, though several bodies were also recovered at the scene.

I became conscious of somebody standing beside me and looked round to see the woman in the burgundy suit. Close-up, she looked younger than I'd

first thought, though her face had that lived-in quality which makes age such a difficult thing to judge.

We smiled at one another and she said, "I used to have a bear just like that, before the war."

"Were you …?" I didn't like to ask.

"I was in Serna during the siege, yes. I was eleven when it started."

I had no idea what to say, rejecting several possibilities which struck me as little more than platitudes; the sort of thing that I would cringe about later.

Fortunately, Alex came back just then. "Come on, Ginny, keep up, it's the big guns next." So he had noticed my absence after all. I nodded to the woman and went with him.

The "big guns" proved to be imposing, grim, and soulless—chunky blocks of metal in grey or green, sheets of armor plating in pristine mottled camouflage paint, long barrels with gaping muzzles, compact but powerful flat-bodied drone tanks, swivelling turrets, field generators, heat-diffusion nets, projection boards, pulse guns, multiple missile launchers, a stack of lethally indiscriminate pepper mines, some "smart" bombs, a cluster of artillery shells standing on end and arranged aesthetically in order of size so that their tips created a graceful curve, even a pair of gleaming white snub-winged UAVs—which the hovering 3D sign haughtily designated "Unmanned Aerial Vehicles."

Alex got to sit in the control seat of one array, which gyrated in a series of rapid swivels and tilts under his inexpert control.

Gretchen tried to be sociable while Alex fooled around but I wasn't in the mood. Despite having been genuinely moved by Jasna Petrović's account I was beginning to have serious misgivings about this trip. Alex and I had been together for six months now and this was our first time away as a "couple." He'd been pressing me to move in with him in recent weeks. At that particular moment, I couldn't have been more delighted that I'd demurred.

It wasn't just Alex, though; it was Serna and all that the place represented.

The entire venture was a delicate balancing act. Initially, revenue from the park had helped to stimulate the local economy and contributed significantly to the city's recovery. Recently, that economy had come to rely on the flow of income and jobs provided by the park. That was how I'd justified coming along in the first place: this wasn't exploitation at all but something that actually *benefited* the local community. So, now that I was here, why did I feel vaguely … grubby? Why did this whole setup strike me as little more than morbid voyeurism?

"I might head back to the hotel for a long soak in the bath and a lie down …" I said to Alex as we left the big guns behind.

"What? Why?"

"Just feeling a bit tired."

"Oh, come on, Ginny, you can't desert me. You know I won't enjoy myself if you're not here." *Liar!* "Besides, we've spent a lot of money to experience this park"—he meant that *he* had—"so let's experience it! Plenty of time to lie down later … I'll give you a back rub." The accompanying leer offered a more honest indication of what he really hoped to give me.

I should have left at that point despite his objections but knew that he would be irritated and insufferable all evening if I did, so I stayed. To keep the peace; which held a certain irony given the setting.

It was warm outside but not oppressively so. Our party piled onto the minibus—a lozenge-shaped vehicle, its sides more glass than metal. I ended up sitting next to Hassan, with Alex beside Gretchen's explosion of blonde curls in the seat directly in front of us.

There was no driver; the bus was electric and automatic, straddling a guide rail. Malcolm perched by the windshield and ran through his slick patter as we moved along damaged but eerily silent streets—empty apart from an identical bus a fixed distance ahead of us and another a similar distance behind. I listened with half an ear as Malcolm pointed out the school which famed songstress Andjela had attended as a child—now a ruin—and the church that had been struck by a shell in the midst of a packed service. The entire congregation survived without injury as the shell embedded itself in the pulpit and miraculously failed to detonate.

The bus became a sea of raised hands and perminals as people recorded the various sites for posterity, swaying in unison like wheat in the wind as Malcolm directed our attention from one side of the road to the other. Except for Alex, who had his head bowed and was doubtless using his own perminal to check the football scores.

Many of the buildings we passed were burned out or had their walls marred by strafing lines of bullet holes, recurring pockmarks forever chewed into their substance, while the roadway was frequently pitted by potholes and shell craters—it was often difficult to distinguish which was which—and I couldn't help but wonder whether any restoration work had been carried out at all in some places. There was no attempt to let us out for a closer look.

Not for the first time I found myself wondering what the hell I was doing here. On this tour. In this relationship.

When the bus eventually stopped and we exited, I noticed that Gretchen was flirting with Alex. I also noticed that I didn't care.

Thankfully, the authentic recreation of Serna Under Siege didn't extend to lunch, which we were free to enjoy in a vast courtyard surrounded by an assortment of overpriced fast food outlets and souvenir shops. The place was packed. While we were on the bus the cloud cover had broken and it was now noticeably warmer. Alex went to find us something to drink and a marginally overweight man with red cheeks and sweaty forehead attempted to chat me up. I don't think Alex even noticed. He came back with a couple of fruit-flavored waters—more ice than anything else—which we greedily sucked up through candy-striped plastic straws.

Gretchen and Hassan were lining up for something and Alex had disappeared in search of the men's room when I spotted the woman in the burgundy suit again. On impulse I went across to her and said, in a classic example of transference, "Excuse me, I hope you don't mind me asking, but why are you here?"

Her smile reassured me that she didn't mind in the least. "To remember," she said. "Time has a way of anaesthetizing things, of papering over wounds so that memories lose their edge, and I never want to forget what it was like during the siege, what we went through … the horrors that man is capable of inflicting on his fellows."

Her answer stayed with me. On the surface you'd think she had the least reason of any of us to be here, but it turned out she was the only one with a reason that made real sense at all.

After lunch we regrouped and were ushered into an air-conditioned theater, far larger than the projection room where we'd encountered the shade of Jasna Petrović. Ours was just one of several parties that were herded in here. I made a point of ensuring we sat next to the woman in the burgundy suit, telling myself that she was here on her own and would be glad of a familiar face. In fact, I suspect I took more strength from her presence than she did from mine.

For the best part of an hour we were treated to an illustrated talk by a Professor Something-or-Other, an eminent social historian retained by the theme park. He was animated, his descriptions vivid and the many images he employed graphic, but I could tell that Alex was getting restless. He didn't want to hear about the grim realities of surviving the siege, of squalid conditions and dysentery and the bravery of hard-pressed civilians. He wouldn't admit as much but the only reason he'd come here was for guns and explosions. To Alex, Serna was the ultimate wargame: he got to play where it *really* happened.

Not so long ago, his boyish enthusiasm matched with bullish self-confidence had seemed to me endearing, attractive. Now, I could only wonder why.

The following day was scheduled to be the centerpiece of the trip: the principal reason Alex had been so eager to come to Serna. We were to discover what it had been like to live here during the war, by taking part in a re-enactment. We would form our own unit of the local militia and fight a guerrilla action among the broken buildings and the rubble, defending the city against a heavily armed force of invading troops. I had already decided that Alex would enter the fray without me. That evening I intended to pack my bags and head for home.

The finale of the professor's talk involved a frail and elderly man being helped onto the stage. He was introduced as a survivor of the Siege of Serna. We all clapped.

As the applause died away, Alex leaned over and murmured, "Yes, but it was all so long ago. What the hell does any of this really matter to anyone now?"

I glanced across at the woman in the burgundy suit. I'm sure that Alex had meant his words for my ears alone, but he'd spoken more loudly than necessary and the woman had clearly heard him.

Our eyes met. For an unguarded instant I saw the hurt there. She recovered quickly, even managing to smile, and at that moment it seemed that we two were the only real people in the room.

Original (First) Publication
Copyright © 2014 by Ian Whates

Mercedes Lackey, author of the wildly popular Valdemar universe, has written a seemingly endless series of bestsellers, and has also collaborated with Andre Norton, Anne McCaffrey, and Marion Zimmer Bradley.

EXEMPLAR

A Secret World Chronicles Prequel Story

by Mercedes Lackey

Vickie Nagy hefted the backpack up onto her shoulders, and winced. It was freaking heavy. Why couldn't magic books be light? You'd think tha*t someo*ne would think of adding a little lifting spell to the spines, or something, when they were bound. But no.

*Teachers prolly just want us reminded of how "weighty" our studies a*re, she thought with resignation, as she faced what looked like the blank cinderblock wall of the basement. Mom and Dad had already gone to work; she had locked up the house completely behind them, Locks and Wards as well as physical locks. She'd locked herself in, of course; she wouldn't be leaving the house by a door.

Not a conventional door, anyway.

She closed her eyes and envisioned the mathemagical formulas for the apporting spell *("remember, a spell is a process and not a thi*ng") then ran through them as her hands sketched the glyph-components in the air in front of herself. Then, with her eyes still closed, she walked confidently to and through the wall.

There was the expected moment of disorientation, and the burst of nausea caused by every apporting spell. When it passed, she opened her eyes.

She was no longer in the basement of a little bungalow in Quantico, Virginia. She was somewhere—and only a handful of people kne*w where*—in upstate New York. She stood in the Center Courtyard of St. Rhiannon's School for Exceptional Students, in the exact center of a Magical Circle carefully inlaid in the granite of the paving, under a blinding blue, warm September sky.

The Magical Circle was a construction built of several circles, actually; this was one of the most complex permanent Circles she'd ever seen. Literally a Master Piece; it had been put together by the Founders as one of the first constructions of this School, so there would never be a road leading to it. She had to presume that all of the material used to construct the School had been apported here directly. It must have been a massive undertaking.

The school buildings were some of the oldest in North America, had been built on the pattern of Merlin College in Oxford, and the Founders had left no safety factor unconsidered when creating the "landing pad" for their institution. Well, she called it a "landing pad." The people who spelled Magic with a "k" on the end referred to it as a lot of other things, most of them sounding like the terms came straight out of a D and D book. The location of St. Rhia's was so secret not even Vickie's parents could get there by anything but apport. Probably the Dean and a couple of other senior Professors who literally never left the place knew where it really was, but no one else. Somehow, some way, they were even keeping the school screened from satellite and other aerial cameras. You couldn't see it from an airplane, and nothing led to it.

It sometimes seemed ridiculous to Vickie that in an age where metahumans saved the day with their super-human powers so often their stories only ended up on Page Three of the newspaper, her fellow magicians should be so paranoid about keeping their existence ultra-secret from most. But … *well, maybe not. It's true that the majority of metahumans have secret identities. And I've never heard of any schools for super-teens either. Maybe all of us are better off hiding in plain sight.*

There were four smaller primary circles within the larger one, one at each of the cardinal points, and a slightly bigger one in the middle. Vickie was in the North, the Earth point. She quickly moved off it and onto clear pavement. As long as she stood there, whoever was next and was Earth couldn't come in. Simple physics; two bodies cannot occupy the same space at the same time. Of course, the Founders never thought of it as physics, but they had understood the principle.

The Central Courtyard was paved with what looked like granite, and the four buildings around her were likewise built of stone, and looked positively ancient, although they were equipped with modern things like central heating and electricity and all that inside. Thank the gods. Otherwise going to school here would be like torture, especially in the winter. Or like living in a Dickens novel, an experience she would really rather pass on.

The buildings looked a lot like many of the buildings at Oxford University in the UK, actually; Gothic, but in the pretty way, not the morbid way. Stone made graceful. More of the "dreaming spires" that poets talked about. It was hard not to feel a little awe.

North and South were the classrooms, East were the dorms for the live-in students, and West was home to the teachers' apartments, theater, gym, library … all the other things that weren't classrooms or dorms. The place was set in the middle of an extensive garden. Outside the garden were thick woods that looked really, really old, and impenetrable, although Vickie knew for a fact that the students were actually encouraged to explore them.

Most students lived here; there were only a few who were "day pupils," like Vickie. There were a lot of reasons for that, but the chiefest were that most students didn't have the benefit of having parents as magically ept as Vickie's—or, even had parents that actually believed in magic. And those parents who *were* magicians were busy making sure everyone around them thought they were mundies. That made it hard to cover up for your budding Magikal Childe. Very few kids understood as young as Vickie had that making fireworks and drawing attention to the fact that you were very different was dangerous.

She'd had a full day of Orientation already, though thanks to working unofficially with her parents for a couple of years now, she thought of it as a "briefing." So she set out confidently for North Quad, knowing exactly where her first class was.

Maybe other kids came here with mingled dread and anxiety; all she could feel was relief. Finally, she was going to go to a school where she didn't have to hide what she was. Finally, she *wasn't* going to be spending every waking hour in *some* kind of lesson or other—because for as long as she could remember, she had been going to normal schools like every other kid, then coming home and plunging straight into magic lessons. She generally hadn't been finished with homework and magic-work until an hour

before bedtime, and freshman year at Chafee High School had darn near finished her.

After seeing her shorting herself on sleep and running herself ragged, to the point where she had permanent dark circles under her eyes and the teachers at Chafee High School were calling her folks for conferences and asking pointed questions about drugs, Alexander and Moira Nagy had decided enough was enough. They'd wanted her to have a "normal" life—but this was anything *but* normal.

All that the State of Virginia cared about was that you were in *a* school until you were old enough to quit. The authorities didn't really care which school. St. Rhia's was no different from any other private school so far as they were concerned.

So far as the parents of about half of the students here were concerned, this was some sort of correctional school supported by eccentric benefactors, and as long as they saw their offspring as little as possible and there were no obvious signs of abuse, the lack of parental access bothered them not at all. Budding mages born into normal families tended to get into a lot of trouble they couldn't adequately explain as they came into their powers, and adult magicians out in the world were always on the alert for the signs of a youngster in need of rescue. A little glamorie, a little persuasive geas, and the relieved parents were happily sending their "problem" off to be dealt with by someone else. And as for the kids, well, Vickie was pretty sure they were as relieved to finally find themselves in a place where they actually *belonged* as she had been. Vickie had even written a paper once postulating that the legends of "changelings" could be traced to magicians being born into mundie families. The fact that in legends, changelings were almost universally rejected by their parents was certainly mirrored in the rejection modern mundie parents evidenced in dealing with magical offspring.

Maybe there's something about magic that mundie instincts completely revolt against.

Mom had really liked the paper, and had made it part of her application to St. Rhia's. It was a good theory, anyway.

So far as the parents of the *other* half were concerned—the parents who were themselves magicians—St. Rhia's was the place where their children were free to study and practice magic openly, and where they would get the best magical education to be had in North America. More part of the campaign to keep their nature hidden; at St. Rhia's, their kids learned both magic and camouflage. Eventually, some few, with the right skills, would actually go off and pass as meta-humans, joining ECHO, with no one ever the wiser about *where* their abilities came from.

Even Vickie's parents managed that, at least as far as most of the FBI was concerned. Outside of Section 39, except at the very top levels of the Bureau, no one was aware that they were anything other than metahumans—or that the things they stalked were considerably different than "mere" super-criminals.

Vickie hurried in through the ornate double doors of North, joining a stream of others who were making their way from East Quad and the dorms. The contrast between this place and her old high school could not have been greater. Inside and out, it looked like a movie setting. She felt as if she should at the least be wearing one of the academic gowns from a BBC period drama, and not the jeans, white shirt and blue sweater that were the school uniform for everyone. As she hurried up the handsomely carved steps to her first class, though, she felt herself grinning. Like everyone else, her school day was going to be spent half in academic classes, but half in magic. She wasn't going to have to pretend magic didn't exist, or hide it anymore. *This is going to be great!*

☼

Morning classes were … mixed. Exciting, because she was finally getting to practice and talk about magic and *be* a magician in the open for the first time. Frustrating because no one, literally no one, seemed to talk about how *she* saw magic.

It's the math! she thought, bewildered, as they went on about vibrations and components and stuff that really didn't matter as long as you knew the math. It was as if they simply didn't realize that magic and physics were not only related, they were so incestuously related they might as well have been Borgias. It was as if no one understood that as long as you knew the math, you didn't need the components and … all of the other rigmarole. Well, the glyphs and diagrams, maybe, because you still had to impose

your will on the energy, and that was the easiest way to do it. But the rest? Not so much …

She wondered if this wasn't just a way to get kids to work and understand spell-casting without forcing them into the math. Obviously it *worked*, since they were doing magic successfully, and all the old grimoires were built around *eye of newt and tongue of dog* and all that sort of icky procedure, so obviously this was how people had been practicing magic since the year dot. But these were modern times, and man had walked on the moon. It was time to modernize. *And wouldn't it be better to start them on the math first?*

But when she tried to talk to the teachers about it, they smiled patronizingly and suggested she was oversimplifying.

The lessons themselves, once she got over the excitement of actually being able to do all of this in public, were … boring. She'd been doing these sorts of things since she was ten or twelve. This was all *old*. It was the math, of course. When you knew the math, you could always get exactly the same result, at least in this really simple stuff. The Uncertainty Principle really didn't apply when you were lighting candles and apporting small objects. When you knew the math, you could make shortcuts, and you didn't have to memorize pages and pages of chants and what-have-you. When you knew the math, you not only could do *one* spell, you could figure out how to generalize and do all kinds of spells that were like that one spell.

And there was another fly in the ointment, though it was hardly an unexpected one. She'd figured out within the first half hour that this school was no different from any other. There were cliques. There was an elite coterie of the Very Popular and Very Pretty. There were jocks of some sort (you could tell by the muscles and the attitude), who were part of the Very Popular. The Elite made it their business to try and make life miserable for the Outcastes.

Back in mundie schools, Vickie had mostly kept her mouth shut, her head down, and worn a little glamorie that basically made the Very Popular ignore her. She'd managed to skate along being a lone wolf. You could say that was in her blood, after all … No one had bothered her. No one had noticed her. Even her teachers had a tendency to forget about her once she was outside of a classroom, and called her "Veronica" or "Valerie" instead of her real name.

Well, glamories weren't going to work here; everyone here her age and some younger could see right through them. She'd already been getting the eyeball from the Elites—and now she was standing just outside the dining hall, knowing that she could stroll in there, find where the Smart Set was eating and see if she got an invitation to sit with them. Which, if she was reading the interest right, she probably would.

Now, this was the first time the Leaders of the Pack at a school had *ever* wanted anything to do with her. And … it was tempting to let them hook her in. Being popular … well, obviously it was *fun*. Great parties. Boyfriends. People wishing they were you. And after graduation? Connections. Favors to be called in. People begging to do you favors.

The trouble was, there was always a price-tag attached to that sort of gang. Generally it was the one where you soiled your soul by "going along" with things you knew were wrong. And in a place like this, those things were going to be by definition not only wrong, but very sneaky. Vickie could see how *her* skillsets would be very valuable to kids who were doing things they shouldn't be. They didn't know that yet, of course—but if she just went along, she'd be sailing along on easy street until she graduated, and afterward too.

But she *helped* people, not hurt them. It was what she did. It was what her parents did. Even the Nagy family motto said as much: *Servire et Tueri*. With a sigh—just a little regret, because she knew allowing herself to be roped in by the Pretty People would make her life *so* much easier—she resigned herself to the fact that, tempting as it was … no. It would be wrong. Oh well. At least she didn't have to *live* here, so their opportunities to cause trouble for her would be limited.

And maybe, just maybe, she could still skate by under their radar as long as she didn't outright reject them. She could always play the Captain Oblivious card.

Right, then. She squared her shoulders and marched into the dining hall.

This wasn't anything like the cafeterias in mundie schools. This was a *dining hall*, with tables with tablecloths and chairs, not plastic picnic benches. Food was served "family style" from platters and bowls on the tables, and the proctors at each end of the long tables watched you to make sure you took some of everything, and didn't just fill up on carbs and sweets.

She headed for the nearest table to the door; it was scarcely a prime spot, it wasn't near the windows and it was far enough from the kitchen that stuff that cooled off fast would probably arrive lukewarm at best. There wasn't one of the Elites anywhere near it. With luck, they'd never notice she was in here, she could get her lunch and get out with no one the wiser.

"Hi," she said, grabbing a chair next to a thin, pale boy who looked a bit younger than she was. "I'm Vickie, I just started today."

She addressed the entire group at the table, who stopped eating and stared at her as if she had spoken in Urdu. Even the proctors looked a little surprised by her choice of seating.

"Uh … wouldn't you rather sit—" one of them started to stammer.

"This is just fine, thanks," she interrupted, and took a seat, looking around her brightly. "Could you pass the beets, please?"

"Are you sure you wouldn't rather be nearer the windows?" the other proctor said, carefully.

"I'm not fussy," she replied, and filled her plate.

That was about all the conversation she managed to get out of any of her tablemates. She tried making conversation herself, but when every overture she attempted was met with nervous silence, she mentally shrugged, exchanged a few dull pleasantries with the two proctors, and just finished her meal. She felt the glares on the back of her neck as she excused herself and went to her locker, though, and she guessed there was about to be a confrontation. The Elites had spotted her attempt to avoid them, and they were not happy about the rejection.

Not surprising, really. Rejection wasn't something they had to deal with. It probably stung a lot.

Only the day students had lockers, since only the day students needed them—though these were less "lockers" in the mundie sense and more like small locking closets. Wood, of course, and very posh, polished wood at that. Vickie sensed the bodies closing in around her as she got the books she needed for the next class. So she took her time about it, and made sure she had the door locked securely before she turned.

And feigned surprise at seeing the little group lurking in an arc between her and the rest of the hallway. "Welcome Wagon?" she asked, arching an eyebrow. "I'm honored."

She read their faces and their body-language, and reckoned that their next move would be intimidation. *Wow, unforgiving lot, aren't you?* Now, there were a lot of ways to play this. Officially, the use of magic on fellow pupils, except in specific classes, like magical dueling, was strictly forbidden. Unofficially, well … Vickie was pretty sure she knew plenty of dirty tricks she could get away with.

But that would be wrong. And unethical.

She could handle this physically. She might be small, but she had a lot of tricks up her sleeve.

They might think they were at a physical advantage, since St. Rhia's had plenty of classes in all kinds of fighting—she was enrolled in staff work and was going to be going to that class next, in fact. She was, however, also pretty sure that she was probably better than these kids had any notion of in martial arts.

But that would make her the attacker, not the attacked. That would be wrong too.

However, one thing she had noticed was that there was a huge hole in the fighting classes, as evidenced by the mere fact that they were just that. *Fighting* classes. There was not one single purely defensive class. No martial Tai Chi. No Tae Kwon Do. And there was her answer. She had been studying Tae Kwon Do since she was a toddler, as part of the effort to keep her from becoming Daddy's Little Hostage to Daddy's Enemies. Tae Kwon Do was perfect for getting out of physical confrontations smelling of roses.

All righty then, she thought, and smiled up into the face of a girl who, in any other school would have been Head Cheerleader. "Well, obviously not," she said, sweetly. "I have a great idea. You go back to whatever *supah* special elite thing it is you do, comparing teeth whitening spells and figuring out glamories to make your hair shine, and I go on to class. I get what I want, you get what you want. Everybody wins."

Evidently, she struck a nerve, or maybe they weren't used to anyone actually daring to be insolent with them, because the girl's face reddened, and she actually was stupid—or unpracticed—enough to telegraph her intended slap. Vickie was not only able to easily step off the line of attack, the girl stumbled and nearly fell into the lockers when Vickie's face wasn't there to get the slap. And while she was stumbling forward, Vickie was able to slide past the girl and through the hole in the line she made.

Before any of them could react, Vickie was already doing a fast, purposeful walk in the direction of her next class.

If she had any luck at all, they'd decide she wasn't worth the effort of going after.

One could only hope.

The pale, thin boy was in her Magic lab that afternoon, and the teacher partnered the two of them. And for the first half hour she couldn't get a word out of him, not even regarding the assignment. Finally, when the teacher had gone to the other side of the classroom to help someone else, she grabbed his wrist.

"Look," she hissed, as he went utterly still and stared at her in numb fear, "I can do an apport in my sleep—and in five minutes. I can show you how to do the same. Talk to me. What the heck is wrong with you?"

"Y-you shouldn't be talking to me," he stammered. "They'll find ou—"

"Haven't you gotten it through your head that I don't give a rat's ass about what they think?" she replied scornfully. "I will go right through the next three years not giving a rat's ass about what they think. How are they getting away with bullying you?"

His jaw dropped. "How did you—"

"Oh *please*. You act like a scared rabbit. This place has rules about bullying, so how are they getting away with it?" She glared at him and he dropped his eyes.

"Because … nobody cares," he whispered.

"Well, I care." She firmed her chin.

But he shook his head. "You think you do, but you won't. Nobody does once they—"

But before she could find out what was going on, the teacher came back to their side of the room and they had to go back to the apporting exercise. When class was over, he gathered up his books and bolted before she even got a chance to say another word.

✧

"Well?" Moira Nagy said, her fork poised over her meatloaf. "First day?"

Vickie sighed, and stirred her mashed potatoes. "It's better than Chafee. But I'd thought the magic classes would be more of a challenge. I'm practically sleeping through them. It's all stuff I knew three years ago."

It was hideously disappointing, actually, but she couldn't tell her parents that. After all the work they had gone through to get her in?

"They're still evaluating you, kitten," her father said, as her mother's brows creased with faint annoyance. "They can't exactly take our word for what you can do."

Moira flicked a scarlet curl over her shoulders and lost the look of annoyance. "Of course, I should have realized that and warned you. *Every* child is the next Merlin in her mother's eyes. Give it a little time, and they'll bump you up into more advanced classes."

"Yes, but—" Vickie stopped her own protest before she made it. Even her own parents didn't quite understand how she saw magic—only that she saw it very differently from the way they did, and that Vickie's way was startlingly efficient. "Anyway, it's frustrating."

Actually she had come home only to cry a little. She *wanted* to be crammed full of new magical knowledge. She needed it the way she needed air. She didn't just study magic, she *was* magic, and she felt as if she was being starved for it.

But … brave face. Never mind that there were bullies, just like mundie school, and that she was being put back on training wheels. Brave face. At least at St. Rhia's she was safe to be who she was. Not like some people. That pale kid, for instance.

"This too will pass," said her father, and grinned at her as he shook his blond hair—just like hers—out of his eyes. "Meanwhile, it's meatloaf night, and I bet you get your homework done in two hours or less."

"Or less," she said, and felt at least a little smug about that. "I did half of it in study hall, and like I said, I don't even need to think about the magical

part." Then she brightened, as she remembered the one part of the whole day that hadn't been a disappointment. "Oh! And Staff Fighting is *righteous!*"

"Verily," he agreed, and went on to suggest things to her while she listened intently. So intently she forgot to mention the Pretty People thugs and the pale kid who was being bullied, and her concern that she would end up being bullied too. By the time she remembered again, it didn't seem quite as important. For herself, well, it was Tae Kwon Do again, really, all she had to do was keep evading and eventually they'd just give up.

As for the kid, well, he needed to be willing to *be* helped before she could help him. Still. *I'll keep trying to corner him*, she promised herself before she gave in to the bliss of a DS9 episode followed by a brand new Charles de Lint novel. It was the first time during a school year that she had *ever* had time for both a TV show and a chapter of a book in the same evening.

And for the first time during a school year, she was going to be able to go to bed at a decent hour—which might have been an odd thing for a kid her age to think about, but then, most kids her age hadn't shorted themselves on sleep so often they had to resort to Triple Red-Eyes to stay awake during the day. No more worshipping at the altar of the Goddess Caffeina.

So … there was some good.

✧

The Pretty People left her alone. Sort of. They didn't try to surround her and intimidate her a second time—which at least proved that the bullies of St. Rhia's were a lot smarter than the bullies of Chafee—but there was a lot of whispering and obvious gossip going on. This, Vickie had expected. And she hadn't been lying when she'd told the pale kid that she didn't give a rat's ass. Maybe—heck, probably—spending so much time in the company of her parents and their peers had given her a certain amount of insulation from what her *own* peers thought and said, and a long view of things. What did it matter, really, when in three years she would be gone, and the only rumors that could possibly cause her any trouble were that she cheated or that she was easy. The first, she could disprove in a heartbeat, and Mom and Dad would back her up. The second, well, any guy or even group of guys that tried anything on her was going to end up singing in the upper registers for quite some time. And that was if they were lucky. She strongly doubted that any of the kids here had ever had to fight for real. If she was actually attacked with intent to harm, bottom line, they would find out she never hesitated, and never held back. She couldn't afford to. She wouldn't *kill* anyone, but there would be people in the hospital and none of them would be her.

Still, when just before lunch some of the whispers finally got loud enough to reach her, she nearly dropped the books she was getting out of her locker in surprise.

"*Lipstick lesbian …*"

"*Fag-hag.*"

That was the best they could do? Really?

They're dumber than I thought. Why they thought rumors about being gay, or gay-friendly were going to cause her a moment of unrest—well, they hadn't been paying attention. First of all, St. Rhia's had very firm policies in place about homophobia, to wit that acting on it was an invitation for expulsion. And secondly—well—she really and truly did not give a rat's ass.

Then again, this might be 2002, but there were still plenty of people out there with homophobia, and it looked like there was a big fat clot of them right here in St. Rhia's. Just because they were all young magicians, it didn't follow that all or even most of them had exposure to all of the myriad sorts of folks Vickie'd had. If anything, their upbringing might be even more insular than the average mundie and—

Wait a second. Fag-hag … She could almost hear the mental pieces clicking together and solving the puzzle of the pale kid. And that was when she got angry. Because it was bad enough to bully someone, but to do it over something they couldn't help, any more than they could help the color of their eyes, just made it all the worse.

Heck if I am putting up with this shite. The first thing to do, though, would be to verify. Which, fortunately, she was in the perfect position to do. She hurried to the dining hall, and headed straight for the table she'd sat at yesterday, plunking herself down beside the pale boy, who looked even more alarmed than he

had yesterday. She said nothing, however, until the proctors happened to be looking away.

Looking, in fact, at the Pretty People who were engaged in some stupidly obvious whispering, giggling, and smirking. Vickie took the moment to lean over and whisper in the pale kid's ear.

"*Follow me. Just leave your lunch and follow me. And don't argue if you know what's good for you.*"

She was pretty certain that he had been cowed enough by the bullies that he would just do what she ordered without question, and she was right. She got up and left the table, acting as if she was upset by the whispers, and he followed a moment later. As soon as they were out of sight and the door to the dining hall had closed, she grabbed his hand and headed for the Central Courtyard.

"What—" the poor kid gasped, his pale face even paler, as he probably anticipated her taking some sort of revenge on him.

"Hush," she said, put him in the Earth circle with her, and burned through the equations. He gasped as they apported into the basement of her house.

"But you—but—" His eyes were as big as the proverbial saucers. "How did you—"

"Because I've been doing apports since I was twelve, I told you," she said, seizing his hand and dragging him upstairs to the kitchen, where she shoved him down into a chair and threw a couple of Cornish Meat Pasties into the microwave. "Here," she said, handing him one. "Now I can talk to you without anyone interfering."

"But I thought—we aren't supposed to leave—" he stammered.

"I'm a Day Student, I'm allowed to go home," she pointed out, and smirked. "And I'm allowed to bring study partners with me. Of course, they're rather stupidly assuming that it's Mom doing the apport, and not me, and that I'm stuck at school until she gets me. That's not my problem. Who's bullying you? The Pretty People?"

"How—why—" he began, and then his face just crumpled and words poured out of him. Mostly, they were nonsense about how he was going to hell, he was a pervert, and he deserved every bit of it. Vickie let him spew, then cut him off.

"Did you get that crap from your parents?" she said, scornfully.

He nodded.

"And I bet they would tell you that you were going to hell if they thought you were doing magic, too, wouldn't they?" she pointed out. The poor kid actually started, as if she had slapped him.

"But I—but they—"

"They're wrong about both, obviously," she interrupted again. "And if I have to keep you sitting here until we both get demerits from missing class until you believe it, I will." She paused. "Or else I'll tickle you into submission. Either one works."

The second was so absurd he actually laughed weakly.

"OK. We're good." She grinned at him. "Now, let's get to the important part. We're going to keep anyone from messing with you ever again. After classes, you come back with me; they told me specifically I can bring people home for study partners. I have a plan. …"

☼

Every afternoon, Vickie and her new "study partner" apported straight home and went to work. After seeing they really *were* working and not fooling around (and probably realizing more quickly than Vickie had that the kid was gay) her parents left them alone, just setting an extra place at the dinner table for him and sending him back before curfew.

Finally, *finally*, Vickie had found someone who saw magic the way she did! When she explained the whole math thing to the pale kid—Paul—he'd grasped it immediately. In fact, he turned out to be better at it than she was, although he couldn't manage to use modern tech any better than most magicians, so she still had something of an edge on him.

Slowly, and with the help of Konrad Lorenz, Farley Mowat, and other ethologists, she convinced him that he wasn't some sort of perverted monster. And once convinced, he was willing to let her help him.

What the Pretty People were doing was completely counter to the rules, as she had pointed out. The entire problem was that they needed to shine a big fat light on the cockroaches and send them scurrying. And the only way to do that would be to trick them into coming out into the open in the first place.

Paul had wanted to just avoid stirring up a nest of hornets, but she'd convinced him about that, too.

She knew how bullies worked. When they couldn't get to him because he was spending most non-school time with Vickie, they'd find some other way to torment him, and the number one target would probably be his room.

Here was the challenge that she had been craving, and she and Paul slaved over both the rules of conduct and the mathemagic. The rules, because she was dissecting them like a lawyer. The math, because they were building something so brand new no one had ever tried it, out of the break-down of the spells they already knew.

When it was ready, Vickie snuck in one night after both of them should have been asleep, and they set up the trap. After that it was just a matter of waiting.

☼

"Victoria Nagy."

Vickie looked up from her book, startled. This was study-hall, she was working on her history lesson, and she was so deeply into it she hadn't noticed the proctor until he spoke.

"Yes?" she managed.

"Come with me. Leave the books." The older kid was stony-faced, but she knew immediately why he had come for her. What else could it be? She felt a rush of mingled apprehension and elation. This, after all, was mostly her magic. If anyone was going to get in trouble, even expelled, it would be her. She had made sure it was her signature that was all over it, because Paul didn't *have* a safe place to go to if he got expelled.

She got up and followed the proctor out of the library, out of the building, and across the Courtyard, as she had anticipated, to the dorms. Up the stairs to the fourth floor, and out into a hallway, and into an uproar.

This was, of course, one of the boys' floors, but there were students of both sexes crowding the hall and rubbernecking, and the proctor had to push through them to get to the area of Paul's room. A line of proctors was holding the curious back; they went through that line, and finally Vickie could see the … damage.

Whoa! It was hard not to be excited. She'd been pretty exact as to her parameters, but she hadn't anticipated the sheer weight of nastiness that the Pretty People had brought to the party and which they had gotten back in their teeth.

It was hard to recognize Lucille, the tall, blond, head-cheerleader type, because she wasn't thin or pretty anymore. She was round to the point that her clothing was straining and splitting in places, and she had a face like a frog. The only thing that remained to recognize her by was her blond hair.

Bert, one of the jocks, was black and blue, and on the floor, moaning and holding what looked like a broken arm. A couple of the other boys were in similar straits.

Angela was bald. Bridget had the worst case of acne Vickie had ever seen.

Standing over them was Professor Elba, with a face like a thundercloud. As soon as Vickie entered the cleared area, the Professor rounded on her.

"*What did you do to them, you miserable little—*" It looked as if the Professor was going to actually *attack* her, and in that moment, Vickie realized who it was who had been protecting the bullies all this time.

Fortunately, at just that moment, the Dean stepped into the space. "*Meredith!*" the Dean snapped. "Control yourself this instant!"

Since the Dean had her wand out—the Dean was clearly one of those magicians who felt she worked better using a wand—Professor Elba backpedaled a step or two.

"This—*girl's*—magical signature is—"

"I've been fully briefed, Meredith, thank you," the Dean replied, in tones of cold neutrality, and turned to Vickie. "Miss Nagy, I have the greatest respect for your parents, as does nearly everyone in the magical world. I find it … remarkable … that you would have perpetrated this sort of harm on your fellow students. Quite out of keeping, one would almost say. Explain yourself."

"I didn't perpetrate the harm on them, Dean," Vickie said, as she had rehearsed a thousand times. "They perpetrated it on themselves."

The Dean, a tall, stern woman with hair like cast iron and a face like a stone statue, raised one eyebrow, slowly. "Indeed? Would you care to explain further?"

And Vickie did. She explained how she and Paul had broken down one of the old Wiccan Sacred Circle spells into its component parts and isolated the sequence that read the intent of anyone or anything that tried to cross the circle. She detailed how they had broken down the Warding spells that established real-world perimeters. She described how they had worked out how the Mirror Spell that cast back *magical* harm on the caster worked. And how they had put these things all together in order to create something new: a Ward that read the intent of anyone trying to get into Paul's room, and did to them exactly what they were intending to do to Paul or his property.

"Impossible!" spat Elba.

Vickie shrugged, and before anyone could stop her, strolled across the threshold of Paul's room. She stopped, spread her hands wide, wordlessly showing how she came to no harm at all, and came back.

"Impossible!" Elba said again. "You just created a hazardous Ward that would only recognize you and that little pervert!"

Vickie bristled. "That's not true! We did exactly what I said we did!"

The Professor began to shout, or rather, scream, but the Dean cut her off—not by look, or order, but by stalking across the threshold of the room herself. There was a collective gasp, and when she came back out without so much as a hair being out of place, there was another.

"Take the … so-called victims to the Infirmary," the Dean ordered. "And someone go to the Staff Reading Room, wake up Professor Higgins and bring him here, please."

Vickie perked up a little at that. *So-called victims?* So the Dean believed her?

But she had to wait in silence while this Professor Higgins was fetched. This gentleman was someone Vickie had never seen before, tall, lean, wearing an odd flat velvet hat and academic robe over a shabby suit.

"Miss Nagy," the Dean ordered. "Tell the Professor *exactly* what you did. Down to the smallest detail."

So Vickie did—but the moment she started, the Professor suddenly looked as if he'd been jolted awake by electricity, and began questioning her—about the *math*! Jarred into excitement herself, Vickie could hardly get the words out fast enough. The Dean listened, looking vaguely baffled, for about ten minutes, and finally interrupted them.

"Professor," she said, politely. "Will this Ward do what the girl says it will?"

For the first time the Professor actually looked at Vickie's work, peering at the doorway over the top of his glasses. "Oh my, yes," he said, sounding as if he had just discovered an entirely new theorem. "Oh my, certainly yes. It reads the intent of those who cross it, and if they are intending something wicked, it bounces them back with as close an approximation of their intended actions as it can manage, wrought on their persons. So elegant for such a youngster! Why look here—" He began describing some of Vickie's process, and the Dean cut him off again.

"And would you be willing to take Miss Nagy and her confederate as your pupils?" she asked.

"I was about to *demand* that very thing, Dean!" the Professor replied, sounding a little indignant. "As you are aware, I have not had a mathemagician to tutor in far too long, and I certainly am *not* going to permit you to expel the first ones to come along in the last five years!"

"Hrrm." To Vickie's relief, the Dean sounded more amused than anything else. "We'll make the arrangements, Professor. Miss Nagy, with me. The rest of you—" she swept the group with a stern gaze. "Disperse, if you please."

Paul was already in the Dean's office when they arrived, and the Dean put them both through a fierce interrogation. Frankly, Vickie had seen FBI interrogators who weren't that skilled. Paul obviously began the interview with no intention of revealing that he'd been being bullied, much less over what. He ended it spilling everything. Vickie's role, evidently, was just to corroborate what he said, and reiterate that the magic had been all her idea, though the two of them had worked it out and implemented it together.

Finally, the Dean sat back in her chair and steepled her fingers. "You manage, Miss Nagy, to have neatly skated past every single rule applicable without actually breaking it," she said dryly. "I will candidly admit that I do appreciate your handiwork, and I will be having it applied to every room on this campus, which should put paid to some of the mischief we've had over the years here."

Vickie blushed and ducked her head. "Thank you, Dean," she said looking at her hands, and heaving a sigh of relief.

"There is no room at St. Rhiannon's for prejudice," the Dean continued. "Mister Hunter, your tormentors will be … watched. They will either genuinely mend their ways, or learn to feign it. In either case, they will no longer trouble you. And to ensure their good behavior, Professor Elba will not be allowed any further contact with them." The Dean's tone suggested that something more was likely to occur regarding Professor Elba, but what that would be, Vickie could only guess.

"As for you two, I'll be rearranging your class schedules so that you will have Special Studies with Professor Higgins daily. I'm sure I can find something you've been sleepwalking through that can be eliminated. There will be no coasting with Professor Higgins, I will warn you in advance. You might just consider this your punishment for unauthorized experiments in magic." The Dean was not joking, Vickie suspected. *I'd rather sweat than coast, so there.*

"Remain here, while I arrange that," the Dean concluded. "We'll allow the rest of the school to assume you are in here being lectured." She got up and departed through a door in the rear of her office, leaving the two of them alone.

Vickie looked at Paul. He looked back at her. And for the first time since she had met him, he was grinning.

"Fag hag," he said, fondly.

"Homo," she retorted, with a wink.

They fist-bumped. It was going to be a beautiful year.

Original (First) Publication
Copyright © 2014 by Mercedes Lackey

Eric Flint became a writer later in life than most, but made up for lost time, turning out more than 50 books, many of them bestsellers, in his first dozen years as a writer. He also edited Jim Baen's Universe, *and is currently the publisher of the* Grantville Gazette.

THE THIEF
AND THE ROLLER DERBY QUEEN

An essay on the importance of formal education

by Eric Flint

The problem, in a nutshell, was that he had a lousy formal education. It didn't help, of course, that he suffered from delusions of grandeur. But if he'd stayed in school, he would have taken enough tests to realize that he was a dunce.

Being a dunce is okay, but you have to know your limitations. If you choose thieving as a profession, shoot for hubcaps instead of the Crown Jewels. For sure, don't try to steal from Satan. But that's exactly what he did.

Why did he do it? Well, partly because he was an egomaniacal dunce. But, mostly, he did it because of his girlfriend.

So it's time to introduce her: Loretta Minisci. Twenty-two years old; five feet, ten inches tall; raven-black hair; brown eyes; beautiful; shapely; and possessed of an all-consuming passion to become the greatest witch who ever lived. *Her* problem, in a nutshell, is that while she was incredibly bright she didn't have any higher education either. And despite what you may have heard, it really takes a lot of book learning to be a great witch—much less the greatest witch who ever lived.

So, she was frustrated. Her spells never seemed to work quite the way they should. (When they worked at all.) And she couldn't use a lot of spells, because the really good spells are written in arcane languages, bizarre runes, and the like. You really need a Ph.D. to work through that kind of stuff, and she was a high-school drop-out.

The worst of it, from Loretta's point of view, was that she wasn't able to summon demons. She tried, once, but the affair went badly. She followed all the instructions in the grimoire, including the part about being naked while you do the incantation. That last was a piece of cake, for her, because she made her living as an exotic dancer in between roller-derby matches. But because her education wasn't up to snuff, she didn't quite understand what a pentacle is. Stumbling through the words in the grimoire, Loretta made the word out to be *tentacle*.

So there she was, when the demon materialized, surrounded by a pile of fried calamari.

"That stuff's like rubber," complained the demon. Then, ogling Loretta: "But what a babe!"

Things didn't go as badly as they might have, because Loretta was used to fending off the advances of lustful males. And even though she wasn't wearing her roller-derby pads, she still had a mean knee and a really vicious elbow smash. But it was sticky for a while, and she was always afraid to summon demons thereafter.

But what kind of great witch can't summon demons?

She brooded about the problem for several weeks. Then she decided that what she needed was a piece of brimstone. It's not clear where she got that idea. It's not in the literature, that's for sure. But Loretta had a tendency to invent her own recipes, which was one of the reasons her boyfriend insisted on eating out. (The other reason is that he felt a great thief should eat in fine restaurants, even if he couldn't read the menu.)

Now, mind you, fooling with recipes is no big deal when it comes to cooking. But it's really not a good idea when you're dealing with the underworld.

Loretta was just as stubborn as she was smart and good-looking, though. Once she got something in her head, that was that. Right off she started pestering her boyfriend to go to Hell with her and steal a piece of brimstone. She didn't actually know what brimstone was, but she remembered from her Sunday school days (which were a long way back) that there was lots of it in Hell.

The thief refused, at first, so Loretta withheld her affections. (As they say.) Eventually, he gave in. Loretta thought it was because he was terminally horny, but the truth is that the more he thought about the job the more it appealed to his vanity. He liked to call himself The Cat, but his friends called him The

Pussy (which, among his crowd, didn't have the same connotation at all).

"I'll show 'em," he muttered to himself. And he went to Loretta and agreed to do the job. "*Provided you can get us into Hell.*"

"That's easy!" she exclaimed.

And it was. Any half-educated witch can get into Hell. The trick, of course, is getting back out.

Even then, she botched it. Loretta still hadn't figured out what a pentacle was, so when they arrived in Hell they were surrounded by fried calamari. Naturally, the smell drew every imp within range, because imps love seafood and there's a real shortage of it in the Pit of Damnation.

That's probably what saved them, for the moment, because the imps were so busy gobbling down the calamari that they didn't think to grab the trespassers until Loretta and the thief were on the lam.

Still, things looked bad.

Loretta and the thief were trying to make their escape across a field of ice. The thief was grousing and complaining the whole time because he'd dressed for what he thought Hell would be like, and sneakers and a bathing suit just didn't cut it. Loretta didn't hear him, however, because after the first five seconds she had skidded completely out of sight. *She'd* come to Hell in her roller derby outfit. (Damn what the book said; she wasn't about to deal with demons again, stark naked.) And while the knee and elbow pads kept her from getting too badly scraped up, her roller skates were completely useless. Although, as it happens, they're probably all that saved her.

But we'll get to that in a moment. First, let's re-examine the moral of the tale.

The problem? *Lack of formal education.* Both Loretta and her boyfriend had gotten their ideas about Hell from watching TV evangelists late at night when there wasn't anything else on the tube. And the truth of it is that televangelists have the silliest ideas about Hell, as well as everything else. That doesn't hurt *them*, of course, since they always go to Heaven because God likes them even if they are a lot of con artists. (He's willing to forgive a pious scam. And it's not even a scam, anyway, because God favors faith a long way over brains so even the morons who send in their money get to Heaven.)

But it was tough on Loretta and the thief. If they'd read Dante's *Inferno*, of course, they'd have known that Hell was a frigid wasteland.

Again: *lack of formal education*. Because if you trace it all back, you find that the preachers from whom they'd gotten their ideas were a poorly educated bunch themselves. Their ideas of Hell they'd gotten from the only book they'd ever read, which was the Bible. And while the Holy Book was accurate enough at the time it was written, you've got to stay abreast of the literature in your field. Satan does. Once the Devil read Dante's description of Hell in the *Inferno* he re-decorated the whole place. Calls it Renaissance Shric.

Loretta got out okay due to blind luck. As it happens, the ice fields of Hell are almost frictionless. That's because the co-efficient of—Never mind. No point going into the physics here. The kind of people who'd read a magazine like this wouldn't follow it anyway. (Oh, sure. Tell me it'll be on the coffee table when the guests arrive. Along with your leather-bound copy of Kant's *Critique of Pure Reason*.)

Like I said, frictionless. Two great roller-derby-queen-type strides into it and she was off her skates—*wham!*—right on her ass, sailing across Hell. Loretta steered herself as best she could, using her knee and elbow pads, but within five minutes she reached the Wall. (Yes, Hell has a boundary. It's flexible, of course. Depends, any given day or night, on the precise equation between damned souls and saved souls but, again, we'll skip the math. See reasoning above.)

She hit the Wall feet first. Anybody else would have broken their ankles. But Loretta was a roller derby queen, and she knew just how to handle collisions. Next thing you know, she was skating up the Wall making her getaway. (Gravity works differently in Hell.) The Wall is infinite, of course, but she was saved by divine intervention. Once she got high enough to be noticed, an angel came and took her back home. Sports fan, he claimed, even though Loretta thought he was a regular in the club where she did her dancing, hiding his face at one of the back tables along with all the televangelists.

For the thief, on the other hand, things didn't go as well. At first, he was full of confidence. He always liked to brag to his friends that he'd never been caught. His friends always said that was because he never managed to actually steal much of anything. And it was true that he was better at the getaway part of the job than he was at the actual getting. Which, when you think about it, kind of defeats the whole purpose of being a thief in the first place, but he was never smart enough to figure that out.

The thief took one look at Loretta flying off and decided to try a different route. So he plunged into a snowdrift. Bright guy, like I said.

Soon enough, the thief was floundering around in the snow, freezing his ass off. He didn't get far, of course. After they finished gorging themselves on the calamari, the imps set off in hot pursuit. They had no trouble tracking him. They didn't even bother following his footsteps, they just followed the smell of suntan lotion. Imps know exactly what sun block smells like, because all surfers go to Hell.

(Yes, all of them. It's not that God has anything in particular against the sport. It's just that He hates the music of the Beach Boys, and He tends to over-react.)

(Hey, it's true, He does. Read the Bible. A little hanky-panky in Sodom and Gomorrah? BRONZE AGE HIROSHIMA. Eat the wrong fruit? LIVE BY THE SWEAT OF YOUR BROW, CHILDREN BORN IN SORROW, PMS—the whole nine yards. Violate the building code? ALL LANGUAGES CAST INTO CONFUSION; MILLENNIA OF TRIBAL WARFARE. Eat shellfish? LOCUSTS. Jaywalk? SEVEN LEAN YEARS. Don't recycle? PLAGUE. Do this, ETERNAL DAMNATION; do that, ETERNAL DAMNATION. Strict is one thing. That Guy's into leather.)

Back to the story.

After they caught him, the imps straightaway hauled him up before the Prince of Darkness. The whole thing moved way faster than the thief expected, being, as he was, accustomed to the pace of the criminal justice system. Naturally, the dummy tried to cop a plea. (This is what's called "unclear on the concept.") The devils immediately convulsed with laughter.

"Wrong court, chump!" they howled.

The Prince of Darkness wasn't at all what the thief expected. No horns, no cloven hooves, no barbed tail. Just an ordinary looking fellow, middle-aged,

dressed in a navy blue Brooks Brothers suit. With a red power tie, naturally. He was sitting in an executive swivel chair on a raised mound in the very center of Hell, eating lunch off a TV tray. Around him, as far as the eye could see, stretched a horde of sinners squatting naked on the ice.

No, Satan didn't look like much, but the thief wasn't fooled for a minute. He wasn't bright, but he'd kicked around a lot. The Devil's lunch was the first tip-off. What you call a *real* power lunch: Satan was tearing the leg from a roasted baby and devouring it like a wolf.

"Unbaptised toddler," he burped. "My favorite."

That was bad enough. Then the thief spotted the tasseled Gucci loafers and the Rolex and knew he was really in deep trouble.

"I want a lawyer!" he cried. "Is there a lawyer anywhere around?"

Satan's minions started howling again. Two-thirds of the horde of sinners scrambled to their feet. In less than a minute, a gigantic brawl erupted on the field of ice, millions of naked attorneys battling each other over the fee.

Eventually a wizened old character fought his way through the mob.

"Corporate lawyers," he sneered. "Punks."

"I'll take your case," he announced, extending his hand. "I'm Clarence Darrow."

Ignorant as he was, the thief had heard of Clarence Darrow. (Defense lawyers were of interest to him, given his profession.)

"But—you're famous! What are you doing here? You're supposed to be a good guy."

Darrow shrugged. "God's got a different opinion. At first I thought it was because of the Scopes trial. But then I found out it was really the Lerner and Loeb case that ticked Him off. The Lord views the insanity plea as a Personal affront, seeing as how He made man in His own image."

Clarence Darrow really was a great defense lawyer. Right off he entered a plea of not guilty on grounds of mental incapacity, arguing that only a moron would think of going to Hell to steal brimstone. Satan immediately agreed with him, but pointed out that Hell was the assigned eternity for imbeciles.

"It's not fair," admitted the Lord of Flies, "but I don't set the rules. God does. And you know how He feels about retards."

So then Darrow changed the plea to not guilty on the grounds that there was no crime involved anyway, seeing as how there wasn't any brimstone in Hell to steal in the first place. "It's like charging a man in a desert with trying to steal water," he argued.

This led to a long wrangle. The Devil responded that intent is as important as action in assessing a crime. That developed into a discussion of the metaphysical priority of mind vs. matter, which Darrow would have lost in a minute if he were in Heaven where (it goes without saying) Mind comes a long way before Matter. But he was a canny old lawyer, and he knew that Satan placed great store in things of the flesh.

Eventually, the Devil admitted the plea. The thief started to breathe easy, but not for long, because Satan right away charged him with trespassing.

"That's just a misdemeanor!" squealed the thief, before Darrow could shut him up.

"You dummy," growled the lawyer.

Sure enough, the Prince of Darkness and all his satanic subordinates were glaring at the thief like— well, like devils. "*A misdemeanor!*" bellowed Satan. He shredded what was left of the two-month-old sinner and hurled the hideous gobbets at the thief.

"Let me give you a taste of the punishment reserved for trespassers," he snarled.

The next instant the thief found himself transported into a realm of Hell that is so horrible and gruesome that even Dante couldn't bring himself to describe it. At the time, the thief thought it was for an eternity, but when he was hauled back Satan glanced at his Rolex and said: "How'd you like *that* thirty seconds?"

The thief was shaking all over. Tight-lipped, Darrow leaned over and whispered in his ear: "They're real big on the territorial imperative down here, stupe. From now on, keep your mouth shut and let me do the talking."

That said, Darrow went right back on the offensive, entering a plea of not guilty on the grounds that there were no signs posted informing the unwary traveler that Hell was private property.

The Devil spluttered. "What are you talking about, you lousy shyster? I don't need signs—everybody knows I own this place!"

Bingo. Jackpot. *Clarence Darrow for the defense!*

Because, naturally, as soon as God heard the Devil say that (He hears everything, of course) He blew His stack and intervened. Which was exactly what Darrow had counted on—winning on appeal to a Higher Court.

A great Presence manifested Itself.

NO YOU DON'T, BUM. I OWN THIS PLACE. I MADE IT, DIDN'T I? YOU JUST COLLECT THE RENT. (You can't put quotation marks around God's dialogue. He's illimitable. First offense gets a rain of toads.)

Satan tried to squawk about jurisdiction, but that's really a flimsy argument when you're dealing with the Lord Almighty, Creator of the Universe. The Devil's usually a lot smarter than that, but he was caught off guard. In the end he irritated God so much that the Lord Above changed the terms of the lease.

FROM NOW ON, BUM, YOU DON'T GET THE UNBAPTISED BABES. (And that's how Limbo got created, in case you ever wondered.)

Satan gibbered with rage, which is an absolutely terrifying thing to see unless you happen to be God. After the display had gone on for a while, God got impatient.

ARE YOU FINISHED? IF NOT, I'LL CREATE A BIB TO CATCH THE DROOL.

Satan clamped his jaws shut.

THAT'S BETTER. NOW. WHAT'S THIS ALL ABOUT, ANYWAY?

God already knew what it was all about, of course. He's omniscient. But He gets some kind of weird kick out of acting dumb. (Always been like that. Remember the time, early on, when He was wandering through the Garden of Eden? Silly. A full-grown Supreme Being, acting like a Kid playing tag: "Yoo-hoo! Adam, where are you?")

Before the Devil could open his mouth, Darrow started talking. It was a great closing argument, too.

Then God announced His decision. He found in favor of the defendant on the grounds that while he was guiltier than sin the whole thing tickled the Lord's fancy. But the thief didn't get off scot-free, because God sentenced him to ten years in Purgatory before he would be released back to earth.

"What for?" whined the thief.

BECAUSE YOU'RE AN IDIOT.

Then God smote the Devil with a bolt of lightning. Contempt of court.

Finally, He glowered at Darrow. (Actually, God's immaterial. It was more that the whole Universe took on a sense of all-pervading GLOWER, aimed at Darrow.)

YOU RAT. YOU LOUSE.

The old man was a plucky character, you've got to hand it to him. "What did I do—besides win another defense case?"

THAT'S THE WHOLE POINT, DARROW. AS YOU WELL KNOW. MAN IS GUILTY OF ORIGINAL SIN, SO HOW CAN HE BE INNOCENT? YOUR WHOLE LIFE WAS AN AFFRONT TO ME, AND YOU'RE *STILL* DOING IT!

Darrow sneered. "So damn me to Hell, then."

God was silent. After all, what could He say? It's the ultimate problem in penal science, when you think about it. How do you punish a lifer who's already dead?

In the end, of course, Darrow caught it from the Devil after God left. Satan was purely furious about the whole affair.

"You're promoted," snarled the Prince of Darkness, and he gave Darrow the premier spot in Hell, on the ninth level. Satan even added a fourth mouth to his clone (which, contrary to Dante, isn't actually the Devil himself) so that Clarence Darrow could join Cassius, Brutus and Judas Iscariot as a chewee.

But Darrow wasn't fazed. Right away he introduced himself to his neighbors.

"Boy, am I glad to see you," said Judas.

"It was temporary insanity!" cried Cassius. "Caused by eating junk food. Shakespeare's my witness. He said himself I had 'a lean and hungry look.'"

"I had a warped childhood," whined Brutus. "Too much privilege."

As for the thief, he had ten years to think over the course of his life. Ten *long* years, because Purgatory is a doctor's waiting room. And he never got any time off for good behavior because he screwed up. (Tried to steal a six-year-old copy of *Sports Illustrated*. Wasn't even the swimsuit issue.)

But eventually, he served the time, and was materialized back in Loretta's cellar.

And found that the cellar was now the TV room of a very large and muscular truck driver who immediately beat him to a pulp. Partly for trespassing, but mostly because he materialized in front of the TV set in the last ten seconds of the Super Bowl with the go-ahead field goal on its way. The truck driver had four friends with him, too. Raiders fans.

A few days later, when the thief got out of the hospital, he went looking for Loretta. It took him weeks, but eventually he tracked her down to a very fancy house in a very nice part of town.

His tongue was practically hanging out as he rang the doorbell. Ten years abstinence, you understand.

Loretta was there, all right. She even opened the door wearing her roller derby queen gear, all the way down to the knee and elbow pads. That had him salivating immediately. He'd always loved that outfit! I've got to tell the truth, now that we're getting to the end of the story. That thief was a warped, depraved, degenerate, kinky sicko.

Alas. She wasn't Loretta Minisci, stripper, would-be witch, anymore. She was still a roller derby queen—*the* roller derby queen, in fact—but she was also Mrs. Loretta White, Ph.D. (Harvard—*summa cum laude*, *Phi Beta Kappa*, the whole shot). It turns out that a week after she got back from Hell she met a chemist at the supermarket and while they were chatting in the cashier's line he explained to her that brimstone was just another word for sulfur, which, (hey, what do you know?) he happened to have a lot of in his laboratory and before they even got there she'd fallen in love with the mousy little guy and one thing led to another and ten years later she'd not only earned her Ph.D. in chemistry but had been able to apply her talent for witchcraft to revolutionize the entire science, and, no, she'd love to talk (*How have you been, anyway? Still stealing?*) but she had to catch a plane for the Olympics where she was going to win the gold medal—she'd gotten the sport internationally recognized just last year, *isn't that great?*—before she had to catch another plane to Stockholm to accept the Nobel Prize. *Bye.*

The thief went berserk at that point and tried to force his affections upon her. (As they say.) But that's really not the best seduction technique to use on a roller derby queen. A few knees and elbows later, Loretta was off to catch her plane and the thief went back into the hospital for a few more days.

✡

Things went downhill from there.

He started thieving again, but the truth is that it's a young man's game and he was over the hill. Ten years out of practice, too. So he got caught. Hubcaps, believe it or not. He tried to steal them off a slow-moving car in the inaugural parade—yeah; Limo One. Sent up for three years. (Would have been way more—assassination attempts get twenty, easy—except the psychiatrist informed the court that the thief didn't know the names of any presidents since Abraham Lincoln led the war of independence against George Washington III.)

After he got out, he lasted on the streets for six weeks before he was sent back to prison. Stealing hubcaps, again. In the pits, at the Daytona 500. Five years. No time off for good behavior because they caught him trying to steal—never mind. You wouldn't believe it.

The next time he got caught he was a three-time loser and so they sent him up for life in the toughest prison in the state. He survived six, count 'em, six hours. After finding himself with two cellmates wearing "Aryan Nation" tattoos, he got into a religious discussion in which he explained that he had met Satan personally and could assure them that the Devil was a white man.

✡

So there he was, back again, a thief in Hell. "I want Darrow!" he cried.

But the Devil just laughed at him. "Not this time, chump. You've already been convicted. No trial. No rights. No appeals. And I've been waiting for this day to come."

Satan rubbed his hands together with glee. It sounded like a rattlesnake. "Boy," snickered the Lord of Flies, "have I got plans for you!"

And he did, too. Grotesque plans. Horrible plans. Indescribable plans. The worst thing you could imagine.

He made the thief listen to one performance of Wagner's *Parsifal* (which, of course, lasts for eternity).

It all goes to show the importance in the modern world of getting a formal education.

Although, now that I think about it, maybe it wouldn't have made much difference in the thief's case. Ignorance can be fixed. Stupid is forever.

Copyright © 2000 by Eric Flint

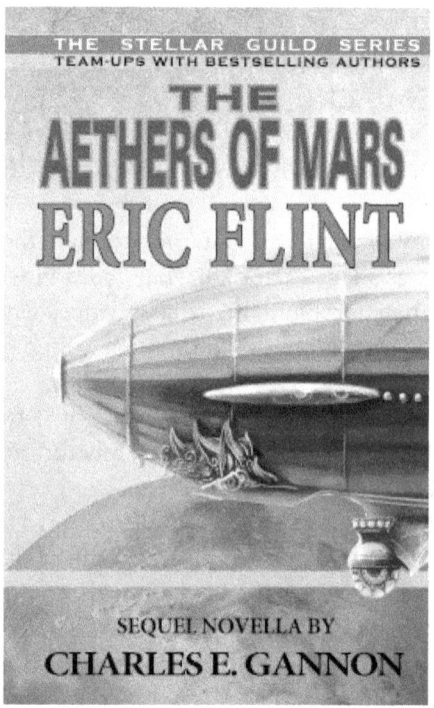

THE STELLAR GUILD SERIES
TEAM-UPS WITH BESTSELLING AUTHORS

THE AETHERS OF MARS
ERIC FLINT

SEQUEL NOVELLA BY
CHARLES E. GANNON

Welcome to Mars…circa 1900. Cecil Rhodes rules Mars and is on his way to transforming the British Empire into his vision of a powerful force, managed by the "right" type of people.

But what of Savinkov…presumably on board the British aethership Agincourt, *travelling from Earth to Mars? Savinkov is a legendary revolutionary and assassin and, with Russian secret agents hot on his heels, is reputedly planning something truly dramatic and Mars-shattering.*

Joy Ward is the author of one novel. She has several stories in print, at magazines and in anthologies, and has also done interviews, both written and video, for other publications.

George R. R. Martin is a four-time Hugo winner and former Worldcon Guest of Honor. He is also the best-selling author currently working in any field. As this issue goes to press, the television series A Game of Thrones, *based on his work, is up for a record 19 Emmy Awards.*

THE *GALAXY'S EDGE* INTERVIEW
✹ GEORGE R. R. MARTIN ✹

George R. R. Martin, one of the most prolific writers of our time and a man who is considered by many to be one of our greatest living writers, was kind enough to let me visit with him in his den, overseen by a full-size functional replica of Robby the Robot and numerous other fascinating models and collectible space toys, including his first set of spacemen.

Joy Ward: *How did you get started writing?*

Martin: I've always written. As far back as I can remember. When I was a little kid I used to make up stories about my toys and write them down. Give them all names. I had a collection of space men. I learned later they are called Miller Aliens. On the basis of where they were from like being from Mars or the dark side of the moon, but that was enough for me. I gave them all names and I decided they were a gang of space pirates. This guy was the brains of the operation and here was this lieutenant. This guy was in charge of torture. There's a little guy there who's holding a weird weapon that looked to me like a drill so I said "Oh, this guy must be in charge of torture," because he drills people with that little drill. They had weird guns and all that so I invented personalities for the whole thing and adventures of them, this gang of space pirates. I couldn't have been more than 9 or 10 at that time.

I would also write monster stories that I would sell to the other kids in the projects for a nickel and I could buy a Milky Way bar. Usually, the stories were two pages long handwritten. They had a werewolf and I would howl for them. I liked to frighten the other kids.

It was a short-lived career though, because one of the other kids was having nightmares. His mother came to my mother and said, "Stop frightening the other kids. You can't tell them these monster stories anymore." So it dried up my source of extra Milky Ways and comic books.

JW: *What did you do then?*

Martin: I just went back to not scaring the other kids for a few years. I read a lot. Books were my comic books.

At a certain formative age one of my mother's friends gave me a Scribner's hardcover copy of *Have Space Suit – Will Travel* by Robert A. Heinlein. That, of course, is still one of my favorite science fiction books; one of the great science fiction books of all time. Up there with the best of Heinlein, I think, even though it was part of his juvenile series. It works for adults too. I can still read that book with pleasure.

That got me into reading science fiction. I had my dollar a week allowance so I had to decide, because paper books were 35 cents, did I want to take the equivalent of 3 comic books and spend it on one paperback? It was a hard decision to make sometimes. You had to figure out these budgets here. Well, there's a new Spiderman and Fantastic Four but oh, look at this here's a Robert A. Heinlein I haven't seen or an Andre Norton or A. E. van Vogt. The Ace Doubles. I liked the Ace Doubles because you got, for 35 cents you got two stories. The Heinlein of *Have Space Suit – Will Travel*, which was actually a beautiful first edition Scribner's hardcover, I read that to pieces but for a decade it was the only hardcover book I owned because we didn't have much money.

JW: What other writers did you read?

Martin: Well, I mentioned a few of them. Andre Norton was the other big writer that was part of the Ace Doubles. I loved her stuff.

I liked Jerry Sohl. He wrote some good Ace Doubles. I read A. E. van Vogt but I didn't quite get into him. It was interesting but his stories were kind of confusing in some ways and they're still confusing. But he was certainly an original. Münster, Isaac Asimov, Jack Williamson, all of the people who were writing back then and from previous decades.

I discovered Doc Smith at one point and devoured the Skylark series, *The Skylark of Space* and its sequels.

Then at a certain point I discovered fantasy. The first discovery was a little book called *Swords and Sorcery* by L. Sprague de Camp and I picked that up off a spinner rack and it had a Conan story. I was hooked, particularly by Conan.

I got into horror, which I didn't call horror; I just called them monster stories. The same way, there was an anthology that I found on a spinner rack, Boris Karloff's favorite horror stories or something. In that book I encountered "The Whisperer in Darkness," my first H. P. Lovecraft story. I'd never read anything so terrifying as what Lovecraft did.

JW: What's the first thing you sold?

Martin: Before pro, I was a published fan. I wrote for fanzines initially.

I've been outspoken on the Internet and other places in not being in favor of fan fiction. Sometimes I get criticized by fans who don't understand and say, "You say you wrote fan fiction and now you're against fan fiction." What I wrote was not fan fiction like that term is used today. Today when people say fan fiction, they talk about taking my characters or Robin Hobb's characters or Robert Jordan's characters or Kirk or Spock or any characters from a television show or movie and writing stories about them. Writing stories about someone else's characters. I never did that and I never approved of that.

I did write what we called fan fiction. In the sixties it was simply fiction written by fans and published in fanzines. They were original stories about original characters. Yeah, some of them were pretty derivative. You could sort of look through the thin layer of cloth there and see, wow, this is Batman, even though they've changed his name to Kookaburraman.

I wrote stories about Manta Ray and Powerman and Doctor Weird and numerous other characters, some created by me, some created by other writers who then solicited me to write about their characters. They were published in the fanzines and I became pretty popular. I got a lot of praise, which encouraged me.

I was a very shy and introverted kid. I think the life of the imagination was a refuge for me; daydreams and books and comic books.

I was always a little hesitant to put myself out there. I don't know, fear of rejection or whatever. But actually having these things published in fanzines and having editors say, "This is great, one of the best stories we've ever gotten here," readers writing in and saying, "This George Martin is terrific," was really encouraging to me. I think it was a crucial step in my development.

JW: What did that say to you, that people were writing in saying you were a great writer?

Martin: It says to me they were high school kids who didn't know any better. So was I. I mean, comic fandom in those early days was 90% high school kids and younger. There was a 10% college kids and adults that were sort of in the leadership position that got things rolling but the guys I was dealing with were all high school kids. So you were in the little leagues. You weren't in the major leagues. You were a star in the little leagues. But that didn't mean you were able to play in the majors. I always dreamed of playing in the majors.

I knew that eventually I wanted to write comic books professionally. I wanted to write stories professionally. But I was hesitant even then to make that leap. What if they didn't like it? What if they rejected me? What if they said, "You're no good?" So

I always wanted to save it until I got better. A few years I'll be a little older, I'll be a little better.

By this time I was in college. In college at every opportunity I took courses that would allow me to write fiction. I took creative writing and short story writing.

Even in other courses I would say, "Instead of a term paper can I do fiction?" I made that offer, it was my sophomore year at Northwestern University in Evanston, Illinois, and I was taking a course in Scandinavian history of all things. History was my minor. We were supposed to do a term paper for a big part of our grade and I approached the professor and said, "Could I write, instead of a term paper, historical fiction?" He had never had this offer before but he was intrigued by it. He said, "Sure. See what you can do with the history that we've taught you."

So I wrote a story about the Russo-Finnish War of 1808 and the surrender of the Great Fortress of Sveaborg, the Gibraltar of the North. It's a great mystery of history in that part of the world. I wrote a story where I explained it. It was called "The Fortress." It got an "A," which was great. But not only did it get an "A," the professor liked it so much that he sent it to a professional magazine called *American-Scandinavian Review*. They liked it too but they didn't publish fiction. They sent a very nice rejection letter to the professor, which he passed on to me. That was my first professional rejection. I said, "Okay, this is a professional editor and he said it was good. Maybe I don't have to be afraid."

So the next year I took a creative writing course and I wrote some science fiction stories and some mainstream stories. For the first time I started sending them out myself to professional magazines. The mainstream stories I never got anything but straight rejection slips on those. But the two science fiction stories I wrote, both of them eventually sold, though one of them took a decade. But the other one sold within a couple of years. That was "The Hero."

That was my first professional sale. I wrote it, I think, in my junior year at Northwestern for the creative writing course. I started sending it out and I got a rejection letter from John W. Campbell Jr., which

was quite a feather in my cap. He wrote personal letters, too. Then I got an acceptance from *Galaxy Magazine*. It appeared in *Galaxy* in early 1971. I got $94 for it, which was real money back in those days.

I remember when it came out in February 1971. I was with my friends scouring all of Chicago to look for copies of it. Buying two copies at this news stand and two more at that news stand and oh, this doesn't have it and carrying it home. They didn't send you authors' copies in those days. You had to go out and hunt it down yourself.

It was pretty exciting. Your first time is always pretty exciting, whether it's publishing or sex. And you always remember it. Opening that envelope and seeing that check in there. It was pretty amazing seeing it on the news stand, seeing my name in print. This was my name in print attached to a story and that was pretty amazing.

I was very lucky. I know many people who have struggled for years, have collected a lot of rejection and certainly I did collect a lot of rejection. I wrote four stories in that creative writing course and the other three of them all got more than forty rejection slips. Some of them never sold.

Having had one story that broke through made the others not seem so bad. If all of the stories had gotten forty rejections I may have been so discouraged I might have stopped but instead it encouraged me to persevere. Then I wrote more stories and those started selling, too. Science fiction, fantasy. So all through the '70s I was publishing everywhere. There was one month in '73 I had three stories come out simultaneously in three different magazines—one in *Analog*, one in *Amazing* and one in *F&SF*.

It felt great. It felt like I was conquering the world.

I wrote short stories and published short stories all through the early and mid '70s. I was nominated for the Campbell Award. I didn't win. I was nominated for Hugos and Nebulas, although I didn't win. Finally I was nominated for a Hugo and I did win. "A Song for Lya" in 1975. Best Novella.

At that point I thought it was time for me to do my first novel. *Dying of the Light* was published in 1977. Once again, I was very, very lucky. All through the '70s new writers that I knew who breaking in were getting 3000 dollars for their first novel.

In 1977, just as I was completing my novel, and I had no confidence I could work in something that long because I had only worked in short ones so far. During the time that I was writing the book, the great science fiction boom of the late '70s hit. Science fiction books were beginning to hit the best-seller list for the first time. The great writers of the Golden Age and the '50s, Asimov and Heinlein, were having best sellers for the first time in their lives. The publishers that had them were happy but there were more publishers in those days. It wasn't the Big Five; it was the Big Thirty. The others were all looking around. Maybe that's the next Heinlein, the next Asimov. There were auctions going on, crazy auctions where people were bidding for a lot of money on first novels and second novels by younger writers.

I was in the right place at the right time. I got four publishers bidding on *Dying of the Light* so it went for a lot more money than I could have gotten even in a year. That made it possible for me to contemplate actually being a full-time writer.

Up to that point in my career I always worked other jobs. I'd been a chess tournament director. I'd done some journalism. I worked as a VISTA volunteer for two years. I'd done public relations. I was looking at the careers of other writers and saying there's Heinlein who has been a professional writer since the beginning. But there is also Clifford Simak, who was never a full-time writer. He always wrote his fiction on the side and I thought that's the kind of life I was heading toward until *Dying of the Light* sold for so much money.

After *Dying of the Light* I wrote *Windhaven* with Lisa Tuttle and *Fevre Dream*. It kind of brought me out from straight science fiction.

Then I wrote a novel called *The Armageddon Rag*. It provoked great enthusiasm among the people who had read it and it got me my first really big advance. Up to that point in my life I had led a charmed ca-

reer really. Unfortunately, nobody bought it. It was commercially a huge failure. I quickly discovered that a world like publishing is not a world with a lot of security. You're as hot as your latest book or your latest movie or TV show.

JW: How do you see that progression in yourself from probably television's best love story ever, Beauty and the Beast, *to* Game of Thrones, *which is very different?*

Martin: For me it was not that different. I've always been different. As a kid I fell in love with science fiction, with fantasy, with horror, and I wrote all three. You look at my earlier stuff, "The Hero," that story I sold to *Galaxy*. That was a hard-core science fiction story. The second story I sold to *Fantastic* was a ghost story set when people have stopped driving automobiles. That was a fantasy, a little bit of horror story and ghosts. Even in my first three stories I was hitting all three bases. I kept moving around. I never like to repeat myself. I always like to move around and change things and what should I do next?

I was a child of the spinner rack. We didn't have any bookstores in Bayonne, New Jersey, when I was growing up. I bought my paperbacks off the spinner rack next to comic books. There was no sorting there. Dumas was next to Vance and Norman Vincent Peale was on a shelf below. All the books were together. I've always read a lot of things and I like to write a lot of different things.

JW: How do you use death in your writing?

Martin: I don't think of it in those terms, that I'm using death for any purpose. I think a writer, even a fantasy writer, has an obligation to tell the truth and the truth is, as we say in *Game of Thrones*, all men must die. Particularly if you're writing about war, which is certainly a central subject in *Game of Thrones*. It has been in a lot of my fiction, not all of it by any means but certainly a lot of it, going all the way back to "The Hero," which was a story about a warrior. You can't write about war and violence without having death. If you want to be honest it should affect your main characters. We've all read this story a million times when a bunch of heroes set out on adventure and it's the hero and his best friend and his girlfriend and they go through amazing hair-raising adventures and none of them die. The only ones who die are extras.

That's such a cheat. It doesn't happen that way. They go into battle and their best friend dies or they get horribly wounded. They lose their leg or death comes at them unexpectedly.

Death is so arbitrary. It's always there. It's coming for all of us. We're all going to die. I'm going to die. You're going to die. Mortality is at the soul of all this stuff. You have to write about it if you're going to be honest, especially if you're writing a story high in conflict. Once you've accepted that you have to include death then you should be honest about death and indicate it can strike down anybody at any time. You don't get to live forever just because you are a cute kid or the hero's best friend or the hero. Sometimes the hero dies, at least in my books.

I love all my characters so it's always hard to kill them but I know it has to be done. I tend to think I don't kill them. The other characters kill 'em. I shift off all blame from myself.

JW: What kind of advice would you give the young George Martin?

Martin: Writing is a terrible career if you're looking at it as a way to have a career.

You should not choose writing as a way to make money, to make a name for yourself or any of these other external things. If you have to write, if the stories are in you, if you made up names and stories for your toy spacemen when you were little, if the stories come to you, ask yourself the question What if no one ever gives me a penny for my stories? Will I still write them? And if the answer is yes, then you're a writer. Then you have to be a writer. It's the only thing you can do. If the answer is No, I'm going to quit after a few years because I'm not selling, then maybe you should quit right now and learn computer science. I hear there's a real future in these computer things.

Everybody looks at the writer's lifestyle. There are a lot of cool things about it. The reason to write is you have stories to tell. You have people inside you clamoring to get out. That's what I'd tell the young kid.

JW: What do you want to do that you haven't done?

Martin: I want to be thirty years old again. I want to travel around the world. I want to keep going to amazing places and having adventures there. But I do want to work on that being thirty years old again.

Views expressed by guest or resident columnists are entirely their own.

Greg Benford is a Nebula winner and a former Worldcon Guest of Honor. He is the author of more than 30 novels and 6 books of non-fiction, and has edited 10 anthologies.

SUNSHINE TECHNOPOLIS: SOUTHERN CALIFORNIA'S UTOPIAN FUTURES

by Gregory Benford

At first glance, southern California seems an unlikely place to build a world-class technical-scientific complex. The weather promises sunny beaches and mild breezes, not the chilly, gloomy ambience of an MIT or Harvard.

Yet that is what drew me here in 1963, to get a doctorate in physics at UCSD. The dream was as obvious as the weather—and there was surfing. Mostly, though, an idea drew me—the future: the stuff of science fiction.

Writers have envisioned SoCal as a potential paradise, perhaps more than any other part of America. There were many pessimists such as Nathanael West in *Day of the Locust*, and hardboiled noir emerged from the Raymond Chandler decades of the 1930s-50s, but the optimists prevailed, as we shall see.

History matters here. The SoCal industrial behemoth millions dwell within had its origins written plainly across the late 19th century. Weather is not just a comfort—it shapes human enterprises. Mt. Wilson and then Mt. Palomar drew the Andrew Carnegie Foundation to build the biggest optical telescopes because they offered the best astronomical "seeing" conditions in North America.

Clarity and dependable sunlight led to Hollywood's dominance over New York. Being able to train troops out of doors drew Marines to Camp Pendleton and the Army Air Force to Edwards and other air bases.

"There is going to be a Detroit of the aircraft industry. Why not here in Los Angeles?" businessman E.J. Clapp wrote in 1926, pointing out the ease of building aircraft outdoors and flying them in clear skies. Allen Scott's study of techno-growth, *Technopolis*, shows that weather was less determining than was determination itself.

Immigrants here had already crossed many horizons; they were willing to venture on conceptually as well. Clapp's boosterism flowed into a rising tide of synergistic effects as each imported technical skill fed others. Optical trickery made better movies and bomb-sights alike. Machinists at lathes could turn out better oil drills or tank barrels or airplane exhausts. Switching talent from one field to another enabled skilled workers to navigate the ebb and flow of industrial currents.

But the Southland's new industries did not resemble William Blake's 19th century Satanic mills. They seldom gave us views like the Long Beach refineries, though oil played a major role in drawing wealth from and to the region. Many new methods of extraction were pioneered in the Long Beach fields. Raymond Chandler got himself fired from his oil company executive job in the early 1930s, partly because he was a drunk and partly because he could not keep up with the pace of change in the industry. This lucky failure gave us his classic wise-cracking skepticism about the mean streets that were spreading over the obliging land.

Spreading innovation was always crucial. SoCal offered not the old way but the freeway. Key to this culture was a new idea: tools open us to fresh possibility faster than theories. Through Mt. Wilson's clear air Edmund Hubble discovered that the universe was expanding. Einstein came to Caltech to confer with Hubble, who had directly shown what Einstein had not ventured to propose—a universe growing larger, not static.

The race for insight and new products alike came from mobile intellectual resources, not from highly fixed natural resources, the old form of wealth. Quick minds gathered in close clusters were the crucial elements, realized early by a state that built a new kind of bridging institution—the University of California, the greatest of public universities. Few now realize how revolutionary UC's close concert of university abstraction and business practicality was in the early decades of the 20th century.

From the beginning, UC was a driver of the economy. At UC Davis the system enshrined viniculture as a legitimate intellectual pursuit, fostering the nation's leading wine industry. Oceanographers at UCSD invented the wet suit, only to have a UC committee recommend not bothering to patent it because only scientists would use it. Medical radiation therapy got its momentum from high-energy physics at UC Berkeley, where Ernest Lawrence's cyclotron provided the particles. Orange grove yields grew using the lore discovered at an agricultural field station in Riverside, later the kernel of UCR.

Building our paradise, we Californians shamelessly mirrored the best of the Other Coast. Stanford was like Harvard, Caltech (CIT) like MIT, Scripps Institute of Oceanography in La Jolla like Woods Hole in the Massachusetts Cape.

If San Francisco was somewhat like Boston, though, LA was like nothing in the East. For a while it seemed more like brawling Chicago, its cultural currents making for tricky navigation, as the novel and film *LA Confidential* showed so well. LA's Old Money scarcely dated back more than a few generations, and usually kept its cash in real estate, where it grew fast. Hammett and Chandler wove their noir visions of the seamy underside in the 1930s and 1940s. Robert A. Heinlein briefly attended UCLA and lived in the LA area alongside such SF authors as Jack Williamson and L. Ron Hubbard. Their tech-centered SF was crucial to the Golden Age of the genre.

Such newcomers brought a sense of open horizons. Though the Other Coast had invented and first developed the airplane, their advantages yielded to our sheer energy. By the 1950s the aerospace-electronics complex bestrode the largest high-tech industrial region in the world, a rank it holds today. The Jet Propulsion Lab and Ramo-Wooldridge provided the first U.S. space satellite, Explorer, in 1958. A year later, Rocketdyne's Redstone engine drove the first Project Mercury flights. The Shuttle lifted off from Cape Canaveral, but it landed at Edwards Air Force Base. Meanwhile the U.S.'s most active spaceport is at Vandenberg, at SoCal's northern edge.

In aerospace and electronics especially, SoCal pioneered the new high-tech hierarchy: well-paid managers, scientists and engineers, underpinned by a vast stratum of laborers who assembled and built the molded plastics, aluminum cowlings, printed circuit boards, and, lately, personal computers. Growth was cutthroat and unregulated among this understory. Price gouging and lurching job growth brought their Darwinnowings of the small capital firms that came and went like vagrant, failed species in evolution's grand opera.

Californians did not stay put when firms went bust. They could cruise the mile-equals-a-minute freeways to new frontiers, where towns became mere off-ramps. A mobile cadre of people used to living by their wits made innovation paradoxically routine.

Today, nestled around my campus, UC Irvine, are brightly growing new-techs like medical device manufacture and biotechnology. Broadcom Corp is entirely on the campus itself, because UCI has ushered onto the campus the research labs owned by private companies, which will hand them over a few decades hence. Not that older industries will not recede as these advance. It seems unlikely that a Dickensian jungle of faltering assembly plants and techno-sweatshop sociology could grow.

So far SoCal has uniquely managed the handoff from one tired wonder-tech to the newest, unlike Massachusetts' Route 128, which is declining in clout and profits. Route 128 ceded its comparative advantages in computer design and manufacturing both to the Stanford-inspired Silicon Valley and to burgeoning assembly complexes in the San Gabriel Valley and San Diego.

California's secret seems to be its decentralized, experimental style, easy-going only in appearances. Technology workers learned to value collaboration and collective learning among a jostling, competitive crowd of hungry start-ups. Route 128 settled into its middle age with a complacent band of a few self-sufficient corporations who learned little from each other. They tried to innovate by pyramid management, rather than draw innovation up from the grunts laboring below. Think 1970s Detroit for a comparison.

Only slowly did a basic aspect of SoCal sink in— its great driver was no longer weather or agriculture. The pace was set by the Technopolis style SoCal has done more to invent than any other region on the planet. The complex gained great advantage from innovations developed locally, and thus applied most immediately here. After 1990, the decline of aerospace forced many engineers to find hot new jobs in Hollywood special effects teams. Heads-up pilot displays for real fighter planes led to great simulation games bought by twelve-year-olds.

Writers pondered this. It is no accident that much modern science fiction thinking has anchored in Southern California. Philip K. Dick, long-term resident of Orange County, gave us the remarkable future vision of *Blade Runner*, a noir LA where artificial human replicants struggle to live, and fail. This is a dark world indeed, its only oddity the constant rain in a dry land.

It is striking that older science fiction writers like Isaac Asimov and Arthur C. Clarke, both proselytizers for the beneficence of technological advance, depicted no actual American utopias. Unless, that is, they meant a future across the whole sprawling solar system, full of opportunities, as their version of as close to utopia as humanity could get.

The 1960s gave us many rural, back-to-the-earth visions, but more recently several Californians have realized that California cannot return to the land and keep its many millions. So they thought of more realistic themes.

A robustly libertarian line taken by Larry Niven and Jerry Pournelle in their quasi-utopian "arcology" or "keep" in *Oath of Fealty* dealt with the growing sense of insecurity and class division. The novel envisions a return to closed communities, basically a return to secure towns, in an arcology in south Los Angeles. Urban violence and crime force people into their own retreats, ignoring governmental attempts to interfere. The community instead defends its wealthy inhabitants from freaks and terrorists, and keeps on innovating.

Oath of Fealty explicitly shows ebooks and heightened, smart security—accurate forecasts. They also caught the feel of a future that may feel familiar. Consider today in Orange County and LA, from the viewpoint of prosperous citizen X. He gets up in the morning and leaves his guard-gated community (government's police fail to keep people safe at home), drops his children off at a private school (many government schools fail their students),

drives to work on a private toll road (government roads are jammed, since cities zone for this), goes to work in a building with a private security staff and ships his goods by private companies like FedEx (who outperform the USPS). We all know someone like X, or may be X ourselves. All this *Oath of Fealty* either describes or implies.

Added to this novel are those Niven and Pournelle wrote with black SF writer Steven Barnes, centered around social issues in future, high-tech LA vistas. These plus *Oath of Fealty* are the most extended discussions of future SoCal society ever done.

Kim Stanley Robinson's "Three Californias" sequence is set in three versions of Orange County, a small county that got its start after noting the triumphs and tragedies of LA. These novels are notable for ambition as his thought experiments unfold. All are technology-driven. *The Wild Shore* shows an American SF pastoral after a catastrophe. In *The Gold Coast*, Orange County several decades later is polluted, corrupt, desperately overcrowded—alas, much like our present. Ecological degradation proceeds in *Pacific Edge*, but Orange County has benefited from restrictions on corporate size and strict controls over land use and pollution. People play softball pretty constantly, an implausible centering sport that somehow controls the vagrant social forces. This, too, is nostalgic of Robinson's own past: he grew up in Orange. He seems to feel that humane Utopias can emerge from an increasingly disaster-prone real world. For him, the alternative to making the world better is allowing it to become fatally worse.

✧

SF writers still ask: Whither Technopolis?

I've set several novels and short stories in Orange County, where I live. I depicted dikes keeping the expanding ocean out of Huntington Beach; a cryonics firm that freezes the dead, with much opposition (*Chiller*); a black woman physicist who makes a big discovery at UC Irvine and can't fit into a future Orange County scene (*Cosm*). These all show future SoCals under pressures that mount steadily.

SoCal sees ahead an era of limits, if only because it cannot build 'burbs to the Arizona border. Our disjointed mosaic of seven counties and 200 cities is failing the world's biggest and best Technopolis at the most basic, seldom-mentioned level—infrastructure. Traffic now compels decisions about location and office hours. Air pollution limits what shops can set up in the region, so that some painting and finishing gets shipped to who-cares Nevada. Even the techno-triumph of our water system is straining to carry so much water to agriculture, which drinks 80% of the supply (yet adds less than 5% to its GDP). And the public schools woefully fail many students, leaving corporations to train them later—or maybe just leave for lower-tax states. Northern California has echoed SoCal's earlier techno patterns, outstandingly through computers. Stanford generated much of that, but many other industries blossomed—biotech, aircraft, and offshoots of the Lawrence Radiation Labs.

There are limited techno-solutions to such problems, and we Californians will probably try them all. SoCal could easily become the premier electric car complex for the world, not just the US—but we'd need a lot of expensive green electricity, and our anti-nuclear fear mongers are still powerful; opposition to the San Onofre nuclear plant was an element in its permanent closure in 2013. Biotech can find drought-resistant genes to tailor our commercial crops, while we landscape with drought-tolerant native plants. Tele-commuting of great power can keep more of us working at home. More computers might marginally help some schools.

I suspect Technopolis is about to realize that it must have a regional government with imagination comparable to its own, private visions. No more municipal workers hired to fill out ethnic quotas or just provide jobs, jobs, jobs. No more constant bickering over local traffic and managerial levels. No streets jackhammered up again and again because utilities do not cooperate on timing.

When the Technopolis glimpses such a possibility, politics-as-usual had better clear out of the way.

The last year has seen the sixth straight year of recession for California. Seldom since the Great Depression has the state seen such chaos. The voter revolt of 2003 onward, bringing about the first recall vote on a governor, seems to be in part anger over the breakdown of infrastructure—roads, health care, and schools, particularly. These are over-stretched by the added burden of a huge illegal immigration. (The left's latest response seems to be to try to ban the term, an Orwellian language-managing tactic.)

No one seems willing to stem the tide of population, not even environmentalists. A recent census analysis of emigration showed that the top-end Californians in both education and income are leaving, mostly for other western states, while many unskilled flock in. California has 12% of the US population and 32% of its welfare recipients. It also has the highest income tax in the USA, 13% at the top. This further weakens the foundation for a further flowering of technoculture.

None of this promises a new burgeoning of technical industrial growth. Yet that is how California has won its image as a golden state, above the flowing tides of commerce, always nose-to-the-grindstone. So we may be seeing a sea change, in the state with so much coastline. With nearby ally Silicon Valley, innovation may yet find its way to solid political power.

Plainly the state has exceeded its political ability to organize for prosperity. It has the ninth largest economy in the world, yet none of the vital controls that nation-states enjoy. It cannot manage its borders, design all its taxes, or make most of the laws that govern it. It could well be that California is approaching the limits of the Federal Republic model and will have to become an independent country to maintain its founding dream.

We are witnessing the over-stressed crumpling of a system that worked for most of the 20th century. Whether the establishment can form a new political coalition, capable of using ideas from the right (private investment) and the left (wise state investment), plus greater regional control (generally a left position, as described above)—is an open question. Certainly one of the best ways to chart the region's course could be through SF works that envision in detail how its changing society can deal with the 50 million population the US Census projects for California in 2050.

Copyright © 2013 (revised 2014) by Gregory Benford

Views expressed by guest or resident columnists are entirely their own.

FROM THE HEART'S BASEMENT

by Barry Malzberg

Barry N. Malzberg won the very first Campbell Memorial Award, and is a multiple Hugo and Nebula nominee. He is the author or co-author of more than 90 books.

COUNTING COUP

A reader (comprising in his authority perhaps a full third of my audience) suggests a column on the early seventies of science fiction. "What you don't realize," Robert Silverberg (not the reader at issue) said to me a few years ago, "is that we were living in a goddammed Renaissance." Well, maybe we were. The society was moving and shaking, *Dangerous Visions* was a central, not a fringe project, Ballard and Moorcock were lighting up the sky. The novels were tumbling from the mass-market publishers and the editors were not even questioning their provenance as science fiction. *Camp Concentration, Behold the Man, A Time of Changes, Do Androids Dream of Electric Sheep?*, and one could go on and on. A torrent of ambitious, literary and sophisticated short stories, a conviction that amidst the chaos, the societal shaking, the bloody schism of Vietnam and the indignity of Nixon, the polity with our little category as a beacon, was being dragged through Woodstock and convulsion to deep and abiding change.

Richard Lupoff, in his introduction to "With the Bentfin Boomer Boys on Little Old New Alabama" in *Again, Dangerous Visions*, described an earlier draft which humility had led him to discard: "Science fiction changing the world with me at the head of it". Grandiose, he decided, but the sentiment was shared (not always silently) by a hundred of us. Anything seemed possible. Campbell died, Bova replaced him, that old tiger Fred Pohl returned to writing in 1972 with "The Gold at the Starbow's End" (in *Analog*!) and Asimov imported enough graphic sex into the middle third of *The Gods Themselves* to give some of his older fans the vapors. Joe Haldeman's anti-war allegory *The Forever War* won the Hugo and Nebula in the novel category, and Avon, blushing, paid six figures for the paperback rights to his next novel. Brave new world with such creatures in it.

Well, my fan and I (and of course Robert Silverberg) know how all that turned out. That rough beast had been slouching toward Bethlehem all the time. The mid-sixties republication of the four Tolkien novels. Lin Carter's Ballantine "Adult Fantasy" series lit the fuse and set all of the traps for the coming marginalization of science fiction only a little more than a decade later as an appendage of fantasy. And then of course, in 1976, *Star Wars* premiered, that magnificent tangle of special effects and *Foundation* echoes which synchronously brought science fiction to the mass audience and assured that this overtaking would be in the form of the 1930s. The mass market held on to remnants of extensions of that early '70s revival for a while but that renaissance of the early 1970s terminated in a *cul de sac*. Very sad for some of us and good riddance to the majority. Fun until Daddy (in the personae of Lucas or Ridley Scott) took our T-Bird away.

To read *Locus* or the online sources today is to hear that great gong in the heavens from Silverberg's *Tower of Glass*, it is to attend over and again to that Spinrad remark I have been quoting for thirty years. Science fiction as a literary medium has become a small special interest at science fiction conventions, within the dialectic of the field. The genre as hermetic and self-sustaining phenomenon is finished. George Saunders and James Patterson and a hundred films have shown its migration in altered or debased or surreal or contrived form to what Judith Merril liked to call "the mainstream" for Samuel R. Delany's "mundanes" but the architecture of Gold's *Galaxy*, of Walter Miller Jr.'s dumbwaiter, has crumbled. I suppose Horace would shudder at the word … but the fifties *Galaxy* to any modern audience would be as quaint as any product of Gissing's Grub Street.

Well, there again in lyrical and elegiac mood, a default mode for well over 30 years now. *Engines of the Night* is written in that voice and 25 years later it was republished with later essays and was even more elegiac and despairing, an act which by the late eighties had already become wearying to all. "The trouble with Malzberg," Gregory Feeley said to a friend (who happily carried the news from Ghent to Aix) "is that he has only one story to tell and he tells it over and again." This is very possibly true although the temptation is to whimper, "Well, yes, but couldn't you say the same of Nabokov or Wagner or Henry Miller?" How many stories do any of us have to tell? Mine is of the transition from the fifties to the seventies in science fiction which I was able to make, and that from the seventies to the nineties which I was clearly not, and the situation although rather narrow, is certainly exemplary. Most of us have only one story to tell (which comes from the one story of our lives) and as Big Ernie might note, it can at least be true. The truth is this as in Eliot's East Coker: In our beginning is our end and we must always find ourselves come to the same place again. To be confronted by Larkin's "One enormous thing," which was always waiting for us.

So there you are, my fan and third of my readership. There is my word on the early seventies in science fiction. All we ever wanted was a room somewhere. On the street where the rest of you live. Wouldn't it have been loverly?

I ended the last column with a promise: "Next time we will review some books." I will not fail in the breach to make good on that promise. Here is a review of my science fiction novels, from *The Empty People* (1969) to *The Remaking of Sigmund Freud* (1985): they failed. Sort of.

11 July 2014: New Jersey

Copyright © 2014 by Barry N. Malzberg

Paul Cook is the author of 8 books of science fiction, and is currently both a college instructor and the editor of the Phoenix Pick Science Fiction Classics line.

BOOK REVIEWS

by Paul Cook

The Year's Best Science Fiction: Thirtieth Annual Collection
Edited by Gardner Dozois
St. Martin's Griffin - 2013
ISBN-13: 978-1250029133 (Trade Paperback)

It goes without saying that these *Year's Best* anthologies edited by Gardner Dozois are the 800-pound gorillas of the industry. No one even comes close to matching either the quality or quantity of fiction Mr. Dozois anthologizes. Besides 654 pages of fiction by a wide range of authors, both old and new, you also get an in-depth summary of the year's publishing events, market developments, obituaries, etc., that you won't find anywhere else. Dozois is also on the forefront in finding stories from online sources that most readers would have missed. As publishing has changed, so too has Mr. Dozois.

Dozois of course does his best to collect what he imagines as the best of the year, in any given year; the results in the past have been iffy, at best. This isn't the editor's fault (it isn't any editor's fault). Science fiction these last twenty years or so has relied so much on old tropes and familiar conceits that it really does give the impression that there's nothing new out there. But the Old Masters seem to have a bit more to say and the younger, newer writers do show promise. The good news is that a lot of this promise—as well as some very fine writing—is in this year's anthology. So let's get to it.

Dozois has always favored the long story, especially the novella and the novelette. Even when he edited *Isaac Asimov's Science Fiction Magazine* starting in 1986, he always had a keen eye for a story that needed a bit more room to roam. This year's anthology has a good half-dozen longer works that make the whole collection sparkle. Among the best of these are Andy Duncan's award-winning "Close Encounters," a coy throwback to the alien-contact stories of the 1950s; Michael Bishop's quaintly cheerful Dalai Lama-in–space story, "Twenty Lights to 'The Land of Snow'"; Pat Cadigan's Hugo Award-winning "The Girl-Thing Who Went Out For Sushi"; and two novellas by Robert Reed, "Katabasis" and "Eater-of-Bone," both of which are part of Reed's "Great Ship" series about a galaxy-wandering, Jupiter-sized Ship of unknown origin but now inhabited by millions of humans and aliens trying to get along.

What I found impressive about these works was their clarity of story-telling, and how efficiently they ground the reader in their various tropes and conceits while keeping the narrative flow unencumbered with literary obfuscation or sheer info-dumping. (In other words, they were fun to read and didn't call attention to themselves as fictional documents trying to out-clever themselves, to quote John Cleese.)

This is also true of the short stories collected here. Among the best of the them are Lavie Tidhar's "The Memcordist"; "Steamgothic" by Sean McMullen; "The Water Thief" by Alastair Reynolds; Paul McAuley's touching "Macy Minnot's Last Christmas on Dione, Ring Racing, Fiddler's Green, The Potter's Garden"; and "Old Paint" by Megan Lindholm. The two best short stories in this year's collection are "Tyche and the Ants" by Hannu Rajaniemi and "The Wreck of the 'Charles Dexter Ward'" by Sarah Monette and Elizabeth Bear (who wrote the grimly charming "Mongoose" a couple of years ago, a story that still gives me shivers).

The stories mentioned above have several things in common: They quickly and cleanly establish their conflicts and are written in an openly readable prose quite like science fiction stories in the days of yore. The others do not have these qualities, and this is a widespread problem in the field, at least in the short form; novels are largely immune from this.

There are a few stories in this *Year's Best* that succumb to this sense of intentional obfuscation, stories that take several pages to get going or that simply make no sense at all. But Dozois saw something in them and chose to include them here. Among them are Jay Lake's "The Stars Do Not Lie"; "The Finite Canvas" by Brit Mandelo; "Astrophilia" by Carrie Vaughn; "What Did Tessimond Tell You?" by Adam Roberts; "Sudden, Broken, and Unexpected" by Steven Popkes; and "Ruminations in an Alien Tongue" by Vandana Singh. These stories variously take their time in getting going (the Lake story) or are just no fun at all (the Singh story). When you compare them to the stories that *do* work in this collection, the differences are startling.

Editors, however, are allowed their quirks, and I grant Dozois his because I know that he can deliver excellent stories in the long form, and good stories in the shorter form, when they appear. This year's collection is better than most. Despite my complaints above about particular stories, I do recommend this *Year's Best Science Fiction*.

The Year's Best SF 18
Edited by David G. Hartwell
Tor - 2013
ISBN: 978-0765338204 (Trade paperback)

If Gardner Dozois is the master at collecting longer science fiction stories for his year's best anthologies, David G. Hartwell is the master at finding the best *short* stories in the field. As mentioned in the above review of Gardner Dozois' anthology, the same problem afflicting a lot of science fiction published today (such as the use of overly familiar tropes and conceits and, I would add, a profound lack of metaphor) can be found in a handful of stories in Hartwell's collection. These, thankfully, are simply overwhelmed by the number of excellent science fiction stories that Hartwell does collect here.

The stories that truly impressed me were Robert Reed's intelligent railgun tale, "Prayer"; Gene Wolfe's endearing story of a little girl and an alien emissary, "Dormanna"; Lewis Shiner's revenge-of-the-computer-screen-wallpaper story, "Application"; Andy Duncan's award-winning "Close Encounters," a story of a contactee and a persistent reporter who isn't all she seems; "The North Revena Ladies Literary Society" by Catherine H. Shaffer, a homage to the conceit behind Asimov's Foundation stories; "The Woman Who Shook the World Tree" by Michael Swanwick, a story that could become a classic; and Bruce Sterling's very, very strange story about marriage on Mercury, "The Peak of Eternal Light."

These are the stories that really stood out for me. I read them all twice out of sheer pleasure. The other stories that helped strengthen this anthology were: Eleanor Arnason's "Holmes Sherlock: A Hwarhath Mystery"; Sean McMullen's "Electrica"; Paul McAuley's "Antarctica Starts Here"; Tony Ballantyne's "If Only . . ."; and Linda Nagata's "Nahiku West" (which suggests either a series of stories or a novel, as the main character does emerge as an interesting protagonist we could see more of).

Only three stories didn't work for me (and I'm not too sure why they were collected here): John Barnes' "Swift as a Dream and Fleeting as a Sigh," Gregory Benford's "The Sigma Structure Symphony," and "Bricks, Sticks, Straw" by Gwyneth Jones. Each of these stories suffers from an effort to keep the reader guessing as to what they are about for much too long. The Barnes story, for example, makes no sense for several pages and it was only when I went back to read Hartwell's introduction to the story that it made perfect sense. A good story does not need a heads-up from an editor, but somehow many science fiction writers have come to believe that being obscure and evasive is a good way to tell a story. Bradbury did not write this way, nor did Heinlein—nor Ernest Hemingway, for that matter; the same for William Faulkner, Flannery O'Connor, or John Cheever. Their stories began clearly and cleanly. There's no reason stories in our field shouldn't do the same. (And I don't accept the notion that science fiction is trying to do something differently so our writers have to write differently. They didn't used to, even as "far" back as the Sixties and the Seventies. Go back and reread Harlan Ellison's *Dangerous Visions*. As bizarre as some of those stories were, none began or conducted themselves obscurely.)

Don't misunderstand me here. That *The Year's Best SF 18* anthology—like all of the other Year's Best anthologies—comes with a couple of weak entries shouldn't deter you from purchasing it. In fact, I'd say that this is one of Hartwell's best collections and it confirms my long-time conviction that he is our finest anthologist of short fiction. At the very least, I have to thank him for reprinting Gene Wolfe's "Dormanna." I don't think I've ever read a more beautiful story within the field or without.

Nebula Awards Showcase 2014
Edited by Kij Johnson
Pyr - 2014
ISBN: 978-1616149017 (Trade paperback)

Gathered here are the Nebula Award winners in the short fiction categories for works published in 2012 and handed out at the Nebula Awards banquet in

2013. Also here are excerpts from the winner in the novel category as well as an excerpt from the Andre Norton Award winner for best novel in the Young Adult category. There are also two essays saluting Gene Wolfe, the year's Damon Knight Grand Master, and one of his stories. The collection is rounded out with stories by Ken Liu and Cat Rambo, who were finalists in the short story category.

The Nebulas are chosen by the members of the Science Fiction and Fantasy Writers of America ("SFWA") and their award winners frequently diverge from those chosen for the Hugo Awards which are given out during the World Science Fiction convention over Labor Day weekend. One is chosen by professionals in the field–editors, publishers, and authors–and the other is chosen by fans—which are made up of anyone attending the WorldCon. What fans prefer often varies widely from what writer and editors prefer. The differences are telling.

This year's Nebula winners are: For the Short Story, "Immersion" by Aliette de Bodard; the Novelette, "Close Encounters" by Andy Duncan; the Novella, "After the Fall, Before the Fall, During the Fall" by Nancy Kress. Kim Stanley Robinson's *2312* won the award in the Novel category. The Andre Norton Award for best young adult science fiction novel went to E.C. Myers' *Fair Coin*.

I said the differences between the Hugos and the Nebulas are telling. That's an understatement. For example, the Hugo winners for 2013 were: John Scalzi's *Redshirts* won the Novel category; "The Emperor's Soul" by Brandon Sanderson won the Novella category; "The Girl-Thing Who Went Out for Sushi" by Pat Cadigan won the Novelette category; and "Mono no Aware" by Ken Liu took the Short Story award. No overlap at all. This is rare, but the fact that it happens at all suggests that there is little consensus regarding what is good during any given year. Even our Year's Best SF anthologies have little overlap.

This is typical, however. Fans and authors often have different tastes, but in the case of the Nebula, some authors win because it is their "time" or they're the flavor of the month or because fewer and fewer members of SFWA deign to vote. It's also the case that so much is published that members of SFWA usually vote for what they've had the time to read

and let the rest go. After all, something like 600 stories are published each year and hundreds of novels. Fans, on the other hand, can be voracious readers.

Regarding the works assembled here, only Andy Duncan's story "Close Encounters" was a true winner. It was clever and fun and holds up on several readings. "Immersion" by Aliette de Bodard is not one of her best. It seems to have been written in the *au courant* mode of believing that truly great stories are obscure stories; that keeping readers confused or puzzled for as long as possible is a virtue, not a vice. Even now, I couldn't tell you what this story was about and I wouldn't have finished it if I didn't have to review this book–though it probably was the best among those that were nominated. She has written better and I'm sure will continue to do so.

I've already commented on Nancy Kress' "After the Fall, Before the Fall, During the Fall" in an earlier issue of *Galaxy's Edge*. It's up to Kress' usual standards in terms of her ability to create believable characters, including their familial interactions. Its only fault is that it is one of literally hundreds of stories published in the last decade based on global warming. The trope of global warming is the lowest-hanging fruit in the field today. (That and everything nanotech.) I would have wanted a more interesting catastrophe. The story itself is quite compelling.

The excerpts from Kim Stanley Robinson's *2312* and E.C. Myers' *Fair Coin* are just brief enough to give the reader a taste of what each novel is about (I found the snippet from *Fair Coin* to be much more engaging than the one from *2312*.) Gene Wolfe was the year's Damon Knight Memorial Grand Master award winner, and deservedly so. There are two short essays about him, plus a story called "Christmas Inn" which shows Wolfe's skills in the shorter form–as well as his ability to tell a great ghost story.

Lastly, the editor decided to include three poems: the two winners of the Rhysling Award, and the Dwarf Stars Award winner. I don't know why they're included. I've written about this elsewhere: What passes for SF poetry these days is just sentences broken down into short lines (or bunched into paragraphs for so-called "prose" poems). These poems, like their kindred, have no sense of the lyric, no sense of the natural cadences the English language brings, nor do any resonate with any kind of metaphorical suggestiveness. They get the tropes right—the science fiction stuff—but they are totally without invention or surprise. When someone in the Rhysling club writes the equivalent of Randall Jarrell's "The Death of the Ball Turret Gunner" or Wallace Stevens' "The Auroras of Autumn," I'll sit up take notice. Since the poems here take up such little space, they do little actual harm.

The Nebula Awards anthologies are worth purchasing each year if only to measure the mood of SFWA. Anyone who reads a lot of science fiction will always disagree with some choices over others, but there is enough good fiction here to make it worth your while. Just ignore the poems.

✡

Shovel Ready
by Adam Sternbergh
Crown - 2014
ISBN-13: 978-0385348997 (Hardbound)

For some time now, writers in what we would call the "mainstream" have been cranking out full-blown, dead-on science fiction. We know that Margaret Atwood has done this for decades. So did Doris Lessing when she was alive. Thomas Pynchon has done it (especially in *Gravity's Rainbow* and *Against the Day*); so has Kazuo Ishiguro in *Never Let Me Go*. Most recently we've had *Jennifer Government* by Max Barry and I've reviewed in these pages the wonderful and hilarious *The Teleportation Accident* by Ned Beauman. None of these writers are in any way considered science fiction writers nor are their novels marketed as science fiction. (Heaven forbid that Margaret Atwood would cop to being called a

science fiction writer, even if Doris Lessing—winner of the Nobel Prize in Literature—didn't mind at all and Pynchon fairly wallows in the label. But that's Pynchon for you.)

But, you know, there's an old expression that is pertinent here: If it looks like a duck, walks like a duck, and quacks like a duck, it's a *duck*.

Shovel Ready is a duck. And a great one, too.

The novel follows Spademan, a garbage man who cleans up the "human" garbage of a futuristic, bombed-out New York in a truly cyber-noir world. In other words, he's a hitman.

Before the novel's opening, Times Square was struck with a dirty bomb and had to be largely evacuated. Those who remain are the super-rich who live in the high penthouses and lose themselves in the "limnosphere," a virtual reality getaway zone where they don't have to face reality. The others, including Spademan, were unable to leave Manhattan and have to scrounge for a living on its plutonium-dusted streets. Little else of America is mentioned in the novel. Mostly, the world has changed (Wall Street, or what's left of it, has moved elsewhere.) Thus, it's every man and woman for themselves. One takes what work one can get and killing people for a fee is all right for the likes of Spademan. (Had this been a straightforward science fiction novel, he'd be called an "assassin"—because in science fiction we don't tolerate the idea of hired killers. By calling them "assassins" we avoid the questions of their moral choices in sacrifice to the prurient excitement their actions evoke.)

Spademan has been hired to kill the runaway daughter of a televangelist named T.K. Harrow. The novel centers around what happens when Spademan finds this man's daughter and realizes that all is not what it seems.

The novel is told in a first-person present-tense voice without the use of quotation marks to set aside dialogue. The narrative is fast-paced, deeply observant of human nature, and vividly evokes a credible New York post-apocalyptic future . . . and is virtually indistinguishable from the kind of science fiction that's appeared in our field over the last 25 years. It could easily have been serialized in *Asimov's Science Fiction* or comfortably published by Tor and no one would have known the difference: Sternbergh's story-telling voice is *that* familiar. It's also a damn fine book. Had Mr. Sternbergh published *Shovel Ready* within the field, I have no doubt that it would have made the preliminary ballots of both the Nebula and Hugo awards. It should be recognized for what it is: pure science fiction. I couldn't put it down.

✿

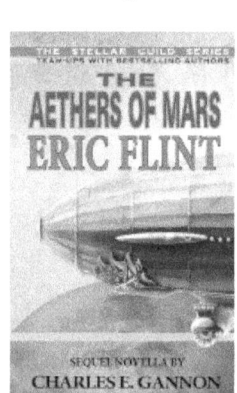

The Aethers of Mars: Two Novellas
by Eric Flint and Charles E. Gannon
(The Stellar Guild Series)
Phoenix Pick - 2014
ISBN 978-1612421308 (Trade paperback)

The Aethers of Mars is the latest installment in Phoenix Pick's Stellar Guild Series, which combines a story by a best-selling author with a follow-up tale by a newer author. In this case we have Eric Flint teaming up with Charles E. Gannon. *The Aethers of Mars* is the umbrella title for two novellas: "In the Matter of Savinkov," by Flint, and "White Sand, Red Dust" written by Gannon. The first centers around a Russian assassin in 1900 on his way to Mars via a space-traveling aethership to kill Cecil Rhodes, a dictator who has lifted the British Empire into the 20th century after a successful war in South Africa and an equally successful takeover of Mars and its various indigines. Gannon's story follows (to Mars) one of the soldiers in the South Africa campaign who needs to find a cure for a murderous insect that was given to him in some bad opium and is slowly killing him from the inside out. While there, Conrad Von Harrer sees first-hand what Rhodes has done to the Martians (which is an analog to what the English, Germans, Portuguese, Spanish, and Dutch did to the black Africans in sub-Saharan Africa).

Both stories are extremely well-written and immediately engaging, and the alternate-history scenario that Flint created and Gannon embellished is very well imagined by both men. (Flint gets the politics and intense characterization; Gannon gets the grittiness of a single man's desperation after having been on the losing side of a very bad war.) Both men seem to understand well how imperialism affects everyone on both sides of the equation, including the hapless Martians. Gannon also takes a few refreshing stabs at monopolistic capitalism that wages its own kind of war on the Martians in this tale. Gannon does this so effortlessly that by the end of the novella, he generates quite a lot of sympathy for the Martians.

This is adventure science fiction (and world-building) at its best. I highly recommend *The Aethers of Mars* to you.

✿

FROM THE VAULT:
Reprints, Reissues and Re-releases of Note

The Time Trap by Henry Kuttner and *The Lunar Lichen* by Hal Clement
Armchair Fiction - 2013
ISBN: 978-1612871424 (Trade paperback)

I stumbled on this book by trolling amazon.com's science fiction section and would like to bring it—or at least the series that it's part of—to your attention. Armchair Fiction (www.armchairfiction.com) has begun a reprint program of pulp science fiction novellas and novelettes (some of them classics, many of them not) emulating the look of the old Ace Science Fiction Doubles. Each book contains two long stories (or short novels), but they are back-to-back rather than the second novel being upside down. The spine, in red and blue like the Ace Doubles, is also printed normally.

The stories are taken variously from the pulp science fiction magazines that were "secondary" to the primary science fiction publication of the era, *Astounding Science Fiction*. These stories come from *Super Science Fiction*, *Planet Stories*, *Fantastic Adventures*, *Space Stories* and others. Some originally came out in paperback but have long been out of print. What you get in this series are stories by some familiar names and some not-so-familiar; but all of the authors in this series formed the backbone of early modern science fiction from the late 1930s to the 1960s.

Rather randomly, I ordered *The Time Trap* by Henry Kuttner and Hal Clement's *The Lunar Lichen*. *The Time Trap* was published in *Marvel Science Fiction* in 1938, at the beginning of Kuttner's career. Hal Clement's *The Lunar Lichen* was published in *Future Science Stories* in February of 1960, about a decade into Clement's career. The Kuttner is, of course, not of the quality of the Kuttner we've come to know, nor is the Clement. The Kuttner story is variously influenced by the "super science" stories of the Twenties and Thirties (with a lot of A. Merritt thrown in) and the Clement is more in the line of an Arthur C. Clarke-inspired tale about a murder mystery on the moon and a substance that may or may not be actual lichen on moon rocks.

I recommend this series, if only that it reminds us of the pulp (and pulpish) origins of science fiction. (The covers are taken from the original magazines or paperbacks.) My only criticism of the series is a technical one: few of these books list their original magazine publication history–the specific issue, the month, the year, etc. I had to look up the publishing history for the two novellas in this collection. (It would also help to know who the cover artists were–even the covers designed specifically for individual titles.)

Beyond that, I plan on reading as many of these books as possible.

Copyright © 2014 by Paul Cook

Subscribe Today

www.GalaxysEdge.com

SERIALIZATION
Lest Darkness Fall

Part 4

**LEST DARKNESS FALL &
RELATED STORIES**

(only Lest Darkness Fall is being serialized)
by L. Sprague de Camp
Phoenix Pick, 2011
Trade Paperback: 290 pages.
ISBN: 978-1-61242-015-8

L. Sprague de Camp came pretty close to being the compleat science fiction writer. His work included novels, short stories, science fiction, fantasy, poetry, criticism, history, you name it. He won the Hugo and the International Fantasy Award, was the Guest of Honor at the 1966 Worldcon, won the World Fantasy Lifetime Achievement Award in 1984, became a Nebula Grand Master (the fourth ever) in 1979, and was given a Special Achievement Sidewise Award for Alternate History in 1996. He also edited and continued Robert E. Howard's Conan saga.

De Camp's career lasted for more than 60 years, and he authored more than 100 books, alone and in collaboration with his wife Catherine, and also with Fletcher Pratt (the Incomplete Enchanter and Gavagan's Bar series) and Lin Carter (the Conan series). His other series include the Viagens Interplanetarias, Reginald Rivers, Pusadian, Novaria, Marko Prokopiu, and The Incorporated Knight.

LEST DARKNESS FALL
L. Sprague de Camp
(continued from issue 9)

CHAPTER XII

Little by little Ravenna's nonce population flowed away, like trickles of water from a wet sponge on a tile floor. A big trickle flowed north, as fifty thousand Goths marched back toward Dalmatia. Padway prayed that Asinar, who seemed to have little more glimmering of intelligence than Grippas, would not have another brainstorm and come rushing back to Italy before he'd accomplished anything.

Padway did not dare leave Italy long enough to take command of the campaign himself. He did what he could by sending some of his personal guard along to teach the Goths horse-archery tactics. Asinar might decide to ignore this newfangled nonsense as soon as he was out of sight. Or the cuirassiers might desert to Count Constantianus. Or—but there was no point in anticipating calamities.

Padway finally found time to pay his respects to Mathaswentha. He told himself that he was merely being polite and making a useful contact. But he knew that actually he didn't want to leave Ravenna without another look at the luscious wench.

The Gothic princess received him graciously. She spoke excellent Latin, in a rich contralto vibrant with good health. "I thank you, excellent Martinus, for saving me from that beast. I shall never be able to repay you properly."

They walked into her living room. Padway found that it was no effort at all to keep in step with her. But then; she was almost as tall as he was.

"It was very little, my lady," he said. "We just happened to arrive at an opportune time."

"Don't deprecate yourself, Martinus. I know a lot about you. It takes a real man to accomplish all you have. Especially when one considers that you arrived in Italy, a stranger, only a little over a year ago."

"I do what I must, princess. It may seem impressive to others, but to me it's more as if I had been forced into each action by circumstances, regardless of my intentions."

"A fatalistic doctrine, Martinus. I could almost believe that you're a pagan. Not that I'd mind."

Padway laughed. "Hardly. I understand that you can still find pagans if you hunt around the Italian hills."

"No doubt. I should like to visit some of the little villages some day. With a good guide, of course."

"I ought to be a pretty good guide, after the amount of running around I've done in the last couple of months."

"Would you take me? Be careful; I'll hold you to it, you know."

"That doesn't worry me any, princess. But it would have to be some day. At the present rate, God knows when I'll get time for anything but war and politics, neither of which is my proper trade."

"What is, then?"

"I was a gatherer of facts; a kind of historian of periods that had no history. I suppose you could call me a historical philosopher."

"You're a fascinating person, Martinus. I can see why they call you Mysterious. But if you don't like war and politics, why do you engage in them?"

"That would be hard to explain, my lady. In the course of my work in my own country, I had occasion to study the rise and fall of many civilizations. In looking around me here, I see many symptoms of a fall."

"Really? That's a strange thing to say. Of course, my own people, and barbarians like the Franks, have occupied most of the Western Empire. But they're not a danger to civilization. They protect it from the real wild men like the Bulgarian Huns and the Slavs. I can't think of a time when our western culture was more secure."

"You're entitled to your opinion, my lady," said Padway. "I merely put together such facts as I have, and draw what conclusions I can. Facts such as the decline in the population of Italy, despite the Gothic immigrations. And such things as the volume of shipping."

"Shipping? I never thought of measuring civilization *that* way. But in any event, that doesn't answer my question."

"*Triggws*, to use one of your own Gothic words. Well, I want to prevent the darkness of barbarism from falling over western Europe. It sounds conceited, the idea that one man could do anything like that. But I can try. One of the weaknesses of our present set-up is slow communication. So I promote the telegraph company. And because my backers are Roman patricians suspected of Graecophile leanings, I find myself in politics up to my neck. One thing leads to another, until today I'm practically running Italy."

Mathaswentha looked thoughtful. "I suppose the trouble with slow communication is that a general can revolt or an invader overrun the border weeks before the central government hears about it."

"Right. I can see you're your mother's daughter. If I wanted to patronize you, I should say that you had a man's mind."

She smiled. "On the contrary, I should be very much pleased. At least, if you mean a man like yourself. Most of the men around here—*bah!* Squalling infants, without one idea among them. When

I marry, it must be to a man—shall we say both of thought and action?"

Padway met her eyes, and was aware that his heart had stepped up several beats per minute. "I hope you find him, princess."

"I may yet." She sat up straight and looked at him directly, almost defiantly, quite unconcerned with the inner confusion she was causing him. He noticed that sitting up straight didn't make her look any less desirable. On the contrary.

She continued: "That's one reason I'm so grateful to you for saving me from the beast. Of all these thick-headed ninnies he had the thickest head. What became of him, by the way? Don't pretend innocence, Martinus. Everybody knows your guards took him into the vestibule of the church, and then he apparently vanished."

"He's safe, I hope, both from our point of view and his."

"You mean you hid him? Death would have been safer yet."

"I had reasons for not wanting him killed."

"You did? I give you fair warning that if he ever falls into my hands, I shall not have such reasons."

"Aren't you a bit hard on poor old Wittigis? He was merely trying, in his own muddle-headed way, to defend the kingdom."

"Perhaps. But after that performance in the church I hate him." The gray eyes were cold as ice. "And when I hate, I don't do it halfway."

"So I see," said Padway dryly, jarred out of the pink fog for the moment. But then Mathaswentha smiled again, all curvesome and desirable woman. "You'll stay to dinner, of course? There will only be a few people, and they'll leave early."

"Why—" There were piles of work to be done that evening. And he needed to catch up on his sleep—a chronic condition with him. "Thank you, my lady, I shall be delighted."

✿

By the third visit to Mathaswentha, Padway was saying to himself: There's a real woman. Ravishing good looks, forceful character, keen brain. The man who gets her will have one in a million. Why shouldn't I be the one? She seems to like me. With her to back me up, there's nothing I couldn't accomplish. Of course, she *is* a bit bloodthirsty. You wouldn't exactly describe her as a "sweet" girl. But that's the fault of the times, not of her. She'll settle down when she has a man of her own to do her fighting for her.

In other words, Padway was as thoroughly in love as such a rational and prudent man can ever be.

But how did one go about marrying a Gothic princess? You certainly didn't take her out in an automobile and kiss her lipstick off by way of a starter. Nor did you begin by knowing her in high school, the way he had known Betty. She was an orphan, so you couldn't approach her old man.

He supposed that the only thing to do was to bring the subject up a little at a time and see how she reacted.

He asked: "Mathaswentha, my dear, when you spoke of the kind of man you'd like to marry, did you have any other specifications in mind?"

She smiled at him, whereat the room swam slightly. "Curious, Martinus? I didn't have many, aside from those I mentioned. Of course he shouldn't be *too* much older than I, as Wittigis was."

"You wouldn't mind if he wasn't much taller than you?"

"No, unless he were a mere shrimp."

"You haven't any objections to large noses?"

She laughed a rich, throaty laugh. "Martinus, you *are* the funniest man. I suppose it's that you and I are different. I go directly for what I want, whether it's love, or revenge, or anything else."

"What do I do?"

"You walk all around it, and peer at it from every angle, and spend a week figuring out whether you want it badly enough to risk taking it." She added quickly. "Don't think I mind. I like you for it."

"I'm glad of that. But about noses—"

"Of *course* I don't mind! I think yours, for instance, is aristocratic-looking. Nor do I mind little red beards or wavy brown hair or any of the other features of an amazing young man named Martinus Paduei. That's what you were getting at, wasn't it?"

Padway knew a great relief. This marvelous woman went out of her way to ease your difficulties! "As a matter of fact it was, princess."

"You needn't be so frightfully respectful, Martinus. Anybody would know you are a foreigner, the way you meticulously use all the proper titles and epithets."

Padway grinned. "I don't like to take chances, as you know. Well, you see, now, it's this way. I—uh—was wondering—uh—if you don't dislike these—uh—characteristics, whether you couldn't learn to—uh—uh—"

"You don't by any chance mean love, do you?"

"Yes!" said Padway loudly.

"With practice I might."

"*Whew!*" said Padway mopping his forehead.

"I'd need teaching," said Mathaswentha, "I've lived a sheltered life, and know little of the world."

"I looked up the law," said Padway quickly, "and while there's an ordinance against marriage of Goths to Italians, there's nothing about Americans. So—"

Mathaswentha interrupted: "I could hear you better, dear Martinus, if you came closer."

Padway went over and sat down beside her. He began again: "The Edicts of Theoderik—"

She said softly: "I know the laws, Martinus. That is not what I need instruction in."

Padway suppressed his tendency to talk frantically of impersonal matters to cover emotional turmoil. He said, "My love, your first lesson will be this." He kissed her hand.

Her eyes were half closed, her mouth slightly open, and her breath was quick and shallow. She whispered: "Do the Americans, then, practice the art of kissing as we do?"

He gathered her in and applied the second lesson.

Mathaswentha opened her eyes, blinked, and shook her head. "That was a foolish question, my dear Martinus. The Americans are way ahead of us. What ideas you put in an innocent girl's head!" She laughed joyfully. Padway laughed too.

Padway said: "You've made me very happy, princess."

"You've made me happy, too, my prince. I thought I should never find anyone like you." She swayed into his arms again.

Mathaswentha sat up and straightened her hair. She said in a brisk, businesslike manner: "There are a lot of questions to settle before we decide anything finally. Wittigis, for instance."

"What about him?" Padway's happiness suddenly wasn't quite so complete.

"He'll have to be killed, naturally."

"Oh?"

"Don't 'oh' me, my dear. I warned you that I am no halfhearted hater. And Thiudahad, too."

"Why him?"

She straightened up, frowning. "He murdered my mother, didn't he? What more reason do you want? And eventually you will want to become king yourself—"

"No, I won't," said Padway.

"Not want to be king? Why, Martinus!"

"Not for me, my dear. Anyhow, I'm not an Amaling."

"As my husband you will be considered one."

"I still don't want—"

"Now, darling, you just *think* you don't. You will change your mind. While we are about it, there is that former serving-wench of yours, Julia I think her name is—"

"What about—what do you know about her?"

"Enough. We women hear everything sooner or later."

The little cold spot in Padway's stomach spread and spread. "But—but—"

"Now, Martinus, it's a small favor that your betrothed is asking. And don't think that a person like me would be jealous of a mere house-servant. But it would be a humiliation to me if she were living after our marriage. It needn't be a painful death—some quick poison …"

Padway's face was as blank as that of a renting agent at the mention of cockroaches. His mind was whirling. There seemed to be no end to Mathaswentha's lethal little plans. His underwear was damp with cold sweat.

He knew now that he was not in the least in love with Mathaswentha. Let some roaring Goth have this fierce blond Valkyr! He preferred a girl with less direct ideas of getting what she wanted. And no insurance man would give a policy on a member of the Amal clan, considering their dark and bloody past.

"Well?" said Mathaswentha.

"I was thinking," replied Padway. He did not say that he was thinking, frantically, how to get out of this fix.

"I just remembered," he said slowly, "I have a wife back in America."

"Oh. This is a fine time to think of *that*," she answered coldly.

"I haven't seen her for a long time."

"Well, then, there's a divorce, isn't there?"

"Not in my religion. We congregationalists believe there's a special compartment in hell for frying divorced persons."

"Martinus!" Her eyes were a pair of gray blowtorches. "You're afraid. You're trying to back out. No man shall ever do that to me and live to tell—"

"No, no, not at all!" cried Padway. "Nothing of the sort, my dear! I'd wade through rivers of blood to reach your side."

"*Hmmm.* A very pretty speech, Martinus Paduei. Do you use it on all the girls?"

"I mean it. I'm mad about you."

"Then why don't you act as if—"

"I'm devoted to you. It was stupid of me not to think of this obstacle sooner."

"Do you really love me?" She softened a little.

"Of course I do! I've never known anyone like you." The last sentence was truthful. "But facts are facts."

Mathaswentha rubbed her forehead, obviously struggling with conflicting emotions. She asked: "If you haven't seen her for so long, how do you know she's alive?"

"I don't. But I don't know that she isn't. You know how strict your laws are about bigamy. Edicts of Athalarik, Paragraph Six, I looked it up."

"You would," she said with some bitterness. "Does anyone else in Italy know about this American bitch of yours?"

"N-no—but—"

"Then aren't you being a bit silly, Martinus? What difference does it make, if she's on the other side of the earth?"

"Religion."

"Oh, the devil fly away with the priests! I'll handle the Arians when we're in power. For the Catholics, you have influence with the Bishop of Bologna, I hear, and that means with the Pope."

"I don't mean the churches. I mean my personal convictions."

"A practical fellow like you? Nonsense. You're using them as an excuse—"

Padway, seeing the fires about to flare up again, interrupted: "Now, Mathaswentha, you don't want to start a religious argument, do you? You let my creed alone and I'll say nothing against yours. Oh, I just thought of a solution."

"What?"

"I'll send a messenger to America to find out whether my wife is still alive."

"How long will that take?"

"Weeks. Months, perhaps. If you really love me you won't mind waiting."

"I'd wait," she said without enthusiasm. She looked up sharply. "Suppose your messenger finds the woman alive?"

"We'll worry about that when the time comes."

"Oh, no, we won't. We'll settle this now."

"Look, darling, don't you trust your future husband? Then—"

"Don't evade, Martinus. You're as slippery as a Byzantine lawyer."

"In that case, I suppose I'd take a chance on my immortal—"

"Oh, but, Martinus!" she cried cheerfully. "How stupid of me not to see the answer before! You shall instruct your messenger, if he finds her alive, to poison her! Such things can always be managed discreetly."

"That *is* an idea."

"It's the obvious idea! I'd prefer it to a mere divorce anyway, for the sake of my good name. Now all our worries are over." She hugged him with disconcerting violence.

"I suppose they are," said Padway with an utter lack of conviction. "Let's continue our lessons, dearest." He kissed her again, trying for a record this time.

She smiled up at him and sighed happily. "You shall never kiss anyone else, my love."

"I wouldn't think of it, princess."

"You'd better not," she said. "You will forgive me, dear boy, for getting a little upset just now. I am but an innocent young girl, with no knowledge of the world and no will of her own."

At least, thought Padway, he was not the only liar present. He stood up and pulled her to her feet. "I must go now. I'll send the messenger off the first thing. And tomorrow I leave for Rome."

"Oh, Martinus! You surely don't have to go. You just *think* you do—"

"No, really. State business, you know. I'll think of you all the way." He kissed her again. "Be brave, my dear. Smile, now."

She smiled a trifle tearfully and squeezed the breath out of him.

When Padway got back to his quarters, he hauled his orderly, an Armenian cuirassier, out of bed. "Put on your right boot," he ordered.

The man rubbed his eyes. "My *right* boot? Do I understand you, noble sir?"

"You do. Quickly, now." When the yellow rawhide boot was on, Padway turned his back to the orderly and bent over. He said over his shoulder, "You will give me a swift kick in the fundament, my good Tirdat."

Tirdat's mouth fell open. "*Kick my commander?*"

"You heard me the first time. Go ahead. Now."

Tirdat shuffled uneasily, but at Padway's glare he finally hauled off and let fly. The kick almost sent Padway sprawling. He straightened up, rubbing the spot. "Thank you, Tirdat. You may go back to bed." He started for the wash bowl to brush his teeth with a willow twig. (Must start the manufacture of real toothbrushes one of these days, he thought.) He felt much better.

But Padway did not get off to Rome the next day, or even the day after that. He began to learn that the position of king's quaestor was not just a nice well-paying job that let you order people around and do as you pleased. First Wakkis Thurumund's son, a Gothic noble of the Royal Council, came around with a rough draft of a proposed amendment to the law against horse stealing.

He explained: "Wittigis agreed to this revision of the law, but the counter-revolution took place before he had a chance to change it. So, excellent Martinus, it's up to you to discuss the matter with Thiudahad, put the amendment in proper legal language, and *try* to hold the king's attention long enough to get his signature." Wakkis grinned. "And may the saints help you if he's in a stubborn mood, my lad!"

Padway wondered what the devil to do; then he dug up Cassiodorus, who as head of the Italian Civil Service ought to know the ropes. The old scholar proved a great help, though Padway saw fit to edit some of the unnecessarily flowery phrases of the prefect's draft.

He asked Urias around for lunch. Urias came and was friendly enough, though still somewhat bitter about the treatment of his uncle Wittigis. Padway liked him. He thought, I can't hold out on Mathaswentha indefinitely. And I shan't dare take up with another girl while she looks on me as a suitor. But this fellow is big and good-looking, and he seems intelligent. If I could engineer a match—

He asked Urias whether he was married. Urias raised eyebrows. "No. Why?"

"I just wondered. What do you intend to do with yourself now?"

"I don't know. Go rusticate on my land in Picenum, I suppose. It'll be a dull life, after the soldiering I've been doing the past few years."

Padway asked casually: "Have you ever met the Princess Mathaswentha?"

"Not formally. I arrived in Ravenna only a few days ago for the wedding. I saw her in the church, of course, when you barged in. She's attractive, isn't she?"

"Quite so. She's a person worth knowing. If you like, I'll try to arrange a meeting."

Padway, as soon as Urias had gone, rushed around to Mathaswentha's house. He contrived to make his arrival look as unpremeditated as possible. He started to explain: "I've been delayed, my dear. I may not get off to Rome *ubb*—" Mathaswentha had slid her arms around his neck and stopped his little speech in the most effective manner. Padway didn't dare seem tepid, but that wasn't at all difficult. The only trouble was that it made coherent thought impossible at a time when he wanted all his craft. And the passionate wench seemed satisfied to stand in the vestibule and kiss him all afternoon.

She finally said: "Now, what were you saying, my dearest?"

Padway finished his statement. "So I thought I'd drop in for a moment." He laughed. "It's just as well I'm going to Rome; I shall never get any work done as long as I'm in the city with you. Do you know Wittigis' nephew Urias by the way?"

"No. And I'm not sure I want to. When we kill Wittigis, we shall naturally have to consider killing his nephews, too. I have a silly prejudice against murdering people I know socially."

"Oh, my dear, I think that's a mistake. He's a splendid young man; you'd really like him. He's one Goth with both brains and character; probably the only one."

"Well, I don't know—"

"And I need him in my business, only he's got scruples against working for me. I thought maybe you could work your flashing smile on him, to soften him up a bit."

"If you think I could really help you, perhaps—"

Thus the Gothic princess had Padway and Urias for company at dinner that night. Mathaswentha was pretty cool to Urias at first. But they drank a good deal of wine, and she unbent. Urias was good company. Presently they were all laughing uproariously at his imitation of a drunken Hun, and at Padway's hastily translated off-color stories. Padway taught the other two a Greek popular song that Tirdat, his orderly, had brought from Constantinople. If Padway hadn't been conscious of a small gnawing anxiety for the success of his various plots, he'd have said he was having the best time of his life.

CHAPTER XIII

Back in Rome, Padway went to see his captive Imperial generals. They were comfortably housed and seemed well enough pleased with their situation, though Belisarius was moody and abstracted. Enforced inactivity didn't sit well with the former commander-in-chief.

Padway asked him: "As you can learn easily enough, we shall soon have a powerful state here. Have you changed your mind about joining us?"

"No, my lord quaestor, I have not. An oath is an oath."

"Have you ever broken an oath in your life?"

"Not to my knowledge."

"If for any reason you should swear an oath to me, I suppose, you'd consider yourself as firmly bound by it as by the others, wouldn't you?"

"Naturally. But that's a ridiculous supposition."

"Perhaps. How would it be if I offered you parole and transportation back to Constantinople, on condition that you would never again bear arms against the kingdom of the Goths and Italians?"

"You're a crafty and resourceful man, Martinus. I thank you for the offer, but I couldn't square it with my oath to Justinian. Therefore I must decline."

Padway repeated his offer to the other generals. Constantianus, Perianus, and Bessas accepted at once. Padway's reasoning was as follows: These three were just fair-to-middling commanders. Justinian could get plenty more of this kind, so there was not much point in keeping them. Of course they'd violate their oaths as soon as they were out of his reach. But Belisarius was a real military genius; he mustn't be allowed to fight against the kingdom again. Either he'd have to come over, or give his parole—which he alone would keep—or be kept in detention.

On the other hand, Justinian's clever but slightly warped mind was unreasonably jealous of Belisarius' success and his somewhat stuffy virtue. When he learned that Belisarius had stayed behind in Rome rather than give a parole that he'd be expected to break, the emperor *might* be sufficiently annoyed to do something interesting.

Padway wrote:

✧

King Thiudahad to the Emperor Justinian, Greetings.

Your serene highness: We send you with this letter the persons of your generals Constantianus, Perianus, and Bessas, under parole not to bear arms against us again. A similar parole was offered your general Belisarius, but he declined to accept it on grounds of his personal honor.

As continuation of this war seems unlikely to achieve any constructive result, we take the opportunity of stating the terms that we should consider reasonable for the establishment of enduring peace between us.

1. Imperial troops shall evacuate Sicily and Dalmatia forthwith.

2. An indemnity of one hundred thousand solidi in gold shall be paid us for damages done by your invading armies.

3. We shall agree never again to make war, one upon the other, without mutual consultation in advance. Details can be settled in due course.

4. We shall agree not to assist any third parties, by men, money, or munitions, which hereafter shall make war upon either of us.

5. We shall agree upon a commercial treaty to facilitate the exchange of goods between our respective realms.

This is of course a very rough outline, details of which would have to be settled by conference between our representatives. We think you will agree that these terms, or others very similar in intent, are the least that we could reasonably ask under the circumstances.

We shall anticipate the gracious favor of a reply at your serenity's earliest convenience.

By

Martinus Paduei, Quaestor.

When he saw who his visitor was, Thomasus got up with a grunt and waddled toward him, good eye sparkling and hand outstretched. "Martinus! It's good to see you again. How does it feel to be important?"

"Wearisome," said Padway, shaking hands vigorously. "What's the news?"

"News? News? Listen to that! He's been making most of the news in Italy for the past two months, and he wants to know what the news is!"

"I mean about our little bird in a cage."

"Huh? Oh, you mean"—Thomasus looked around cautiously—"ex-King Wittigis? He was doing fine at last reports, though nobody's been able to get a civil word out of him. Listen, Martinus, of all the lousy tricks I ever heard of, springing the job of hiding him on me without warning was the worst. I'm sure God agrees with me, too. Those soldiers dragged me out of bed, and then I had them and their prisoner around the house for several days."

"I'm sorry, Thomasus. But you were the only man in Rome I felt I could trust absolutely."

"Oh, well, if you put it that way. But Wittigis was the worst grouch I ever saw. Nothing suited him."

"How's the telegraph company coming?"

"That's another thing. The Naples line is working regularly. But the lines to Ravenna and Florence won't be finished for a month, and until they are there's no chance of a profit. *And* the minority stockholders have discovered that they're a minority. You should have heard them howl! They're after your blood. At first Count Honorius was with them. He threatened to jail Vardan and Ebenezer and me if we didn't sell him—give him, practically—a controlling interest. But we learned he needed money worse than he needed the stock, and bought his from him. So the other patricians have to be satisfied with snubbing us when they pass us in the street."

"I'm going to start another paper as soon as I get time," said Padway. "There'll be two, one in Rome and one in Florence."

"Why one in Florence?"

"That's where our new capital's going to be."

"*What?*"

"Yes. It's better located than Rome with regard to roads and such, and it has a much better climate than Ravenna. In fact I can't think of a place that *hasn't* a better climate than Ravenna, hell included. I sold the idea to Cassiodorus, and between us we got Thiudahad to agree to move the administrative offices thither. If Thiudahad wants to hold court in the City of Fogs, Bogs and Frogs, that's his lookout. I'll be just as glad not to have him in my hair."

"In your hair? Oh, ho-ho-ho, you *are the* funniest fellow, Martinus. I wish I could say things the way you do. But all this activity takes my breath away. What else of revolutionary nature are you planning?"

"I'm going to try to start a school. We have a flock of teachers on the public payroll now, but all they know is grammar and rhetoric. I'm going to have things taught that really matter: mathematics, and the sciences, and medicine. I see where I shall have to write all the textbooks myself."

"Just one question, Martinus. When do you find time to sleep?"

Padway grinned wanly. "Mostly I don't. But if I can ever get out of all this political and military activity I hope to catch up. I don't really like it, but it's a necessary means to an end. The end is things like the telegraph and the presses. My politicking and soldiering may not make any difference a hundred years from now, but the other things will, I hope."

Padway started to go, then said: "Is Julia from Apulia still working for Ebenezer the Jew?"

"The last I heard she was. Why? Do you want her back?"

"God forbid. She's got to disappear from Rome."

"Why?"

"For her own safety. I can't tell you about it yet."

"But I thought you disliked her—"

'That doesn't mean I want her murdered. And my own hide may be in danger, too, unless we get her out of town."

"Oh, God, why didst Thou let me get involved with a politician? I don't know, Martinus; she's a free citizen …"

"How about your cousin in Naples, Antiochus? I'd made it worth his while to hire her at higher wages."

"Well, I—"

"Have her go to work for Antiochus under another name. Fix it up quietly, old man. If the news leaks out, we'll all be in the soup."

"Soup? Ha, ha. Very funny. I'll do what I can. Now, about that old six-month note of yours …"

Oh, dear, thought Padway, now it would begin again, Thomasus was easy enough to get on with most of the time. But he could not or would not conduct the simplest financial transactions without three hours of frantic haggling. Perhaps he enjoyed it. Padway did not.

✿

Jogging along the road to Florence again, Padway regretted that he had not seen Dorothea while he was in Rome. He had not dared. That was one more reason for getting Mathaswentha married off quickly. Dorothea would be a much more suitable if less spectacular girl for *him*. Not that he was in love with her. But he probably would be if he saw enough of her, he thought somewhat cold-bloodedly.

But he had too much else to do now. If he could only get time to relax, to catch up on his sleep, to investigate the things that really interested him, to have a little fun! He liked fun as much as the next man, even if the next man would consider his ideas of fun peculiar.

But his sharp, conscientious mind goaded him on. He knew that his job rested on the unstable foundation of his influence over a senile, unpopular king. As long as Padway pleased them the Goths would not interfere, as they were accustomed to leaving civil administration in the hands of non-Goths. But when Thiudahad went? Padway had lots of hay to gather, and there were plenty of thunderheads sticking up over the barn.

In Florence Padway leased office space in the name of the government, and looked in on his own business. This time there were no irregularities in the accounts. Either there had been no more stealing, or the boys were getting cleverer at concealing it.

Fritharik renewed his plea to be allowed to come along, showing with much pride his jeweled sword, which he had redeemed and had sent up from Rome. The sword disappointed Padway, though he did not say so. The gems were merely polished, not cut; faceting had not been invented. But wearing it seemed to add inches to Fritharik's already imposing stature. Padway, somewhat against his better judgment, gave in. He appointed the competent and apparently honest Nerva his general manager.

They were snowed in by a late storm for two days crossing the mountains, and arrived in Ravenna still shivering. The town with its clammy atmosphere and its currents of intrigue depressed him, and the Mathaswentha problem made him nervous. He called on her and made some insincere love to her, which made him all the more anxious to get away. But there was lots of public business to be handled.

Urias announced that he was ready and willing to enter Padway's service. "Mathaswentha talked me into it," he said. "She's a wonderful woman, isn't she?"

"Certainly is," replied Padway. He thought he detected a faintly guilty and furtive air about the straightforward Urias when he spoke of the princess. He smiled to himself. "What I had in mind was setting up a regular military school for the Gothic officers, somewhat on the Byzantine model, with you in charge."

"What? Oh, my word, I hoped you'd have a command on the frontiers for me."

So, thought Padway, he wasn't the only one who disliked Ravenna. "No, my dear sir. This job has to be done for the sake of the kingdom. And I can't do it myself, because the Goths don't think any non-Goth knows anything about soldiering. On the other hand I need a literate and intelligent man to run the thing, and you're the only one in sight."

"But, most excellent Martinus, have you ever tried to teach a Gothic officer anything? I admit that an academy is needed, but—"

"I know. I know. Most of them can't read or write and look down on those who do. That's why I picked *you* for the job. You're respected, and if anybody can put sense into their heads you can." He grinned sympathetically. "I wouldn't have tried so hard to enlist your services if I'd had just an easy, everyday job in mind."

"Thanks. I see you know how to get people to do things for you."

Padway went on to tell Urias some of his ideas. How the Goths' great weakness was the lack of co-ordination between their mounted lancers and their foot archers; how they needed both reliable foot spearmen and mounted archers to have a well-rounded force. He also described the crossbow, the calthorp, and other military devices.

He said: "It takes five years to make a good long-bowman, whereas a recruit can learn to handle a crossbow in a few weeks.

"And if I can get some good steel workers, I'll show you a suit of plate armor that weighs only half as much as one of those scale-mail shirts, but gives better protection and allows fully as much freedom of action." He grinned. "You may expect grumbling at all these newfangled ideas from the more conservative Goths. So you'd better introduce them gradually. And remember, they're your ideas; I won't try to deprive you of the credit for them."

"I understand," grinned Urias. "So if anybody gets hanged for them, it'll be me and not you. Like that book on astronomy that came out in Thiudahad's name. It has every churchman from here to Persia sizzling. Poor old Thiudahad gets the blame, but I know you furnished the ideas and put him up to it. Very well, my mysterious friend, I'm game."

Padway himself was surprised when Urias appeared with a very respectable crossbow a few days later. Although the device was simple enough, and he'd furnished an adequate set of drawings for it, he knew from sad experience that to get a sixth-century artisan to make something he'd never seen before, you had to stand over him while he botched six attempts, and then make it yourself.

They spent an afternoon in the great pine wood east of the city shooting at marks. Fritharik proved uncannily accurate, though he affected to despise missile weapons as unworthy of a noble Vandal knight. "But," he said, "it is a remarkably easy thing to aim."

"Yes," replied Padway. "Among my people there's a legend about a crossbowman who offended a government official, and was compelled as punishment to shoot an apple off his son's head. He did so, without harming the boy."

When he got back, Padway learned that he had an appointment the next day with an envoy from the Franks. The envoy, one Count Hlodovik, was a tall, lantern-jawed man. Like most Franks he was clean-shaven except for the mustache. He was quite gorgeous in a red silk tunic, gold chains and bracelets, and a jeweled baldric. Padway privately thought that the knobby bare legs below his short pants detracted from his impressiveness. Moreover, Hlodovik was rather obviously suffering from a hangover.

"Mother of God, I'm thirsty," he said. "Will you please do something about that, friend quaestor, before we discuss business?" So Padway had some wine sent in. Hlodovik drank in deep gulps, "Ah! That's better. Now, friend quaestor, I may say that I don't think I've been very well treated here. The king would only see me for a wink of the eye; said you handle the business. Is that the proper reception for the envoy of King Theudebert, King Hildebert, and King Hlotokar? Not just *one* king, mind you; *three*."

"That's a lot of kings," said Padway, smiling pleasantly. "I am greatly impressed. But you mustn't take offense, my lord count. Our king is an old man, and he finds the press of public business hard to bear."

"So, *hrrmp*. We'll forget about it, then. But we shall not find the reason for my coming hither so easy to forget. Briefly, what became of that hundred and fifty thousand solidi that Wittigis promised my masters, King Theudebert, King Hildebert, and King Hlotokar if they wouldn't attack him while he was involved with the Greeks? Moreover, he ceded Provence to my masters, King Theudebert, King Hildebert, and King Hlotokar. Yet your general Sisigis has not evacuated Provence. When my masters sent a force to occupy it a few weeks ago, they were driven back and several were killed. You should know that the Franks, who are the bravest and proudest people on earth, will never submit to such treatment. What are you going to do about it?"

Padway answered: "*You*, my lord Hlodovik, should know that the acts of an unsuccessful usurper cannot bind the legitimate government. We intend to hold what we have. So you may inform your masters, King Theudebert, King Hildebert, and King Hlotokar, that there will be no payment and no evacuation."

"Do you really mean that?" Hlodovik seemed astonished. "Don't you know, young man, that the armies of the Franks could sweep the length of Italy, burning and ravaging, any time they wished? My masters, King Theudebert, King Hildebert, and King Hlotokar, are showing great forbearance and humanity by offering you a way out. Think carefully before you invite disaster."

"I have thought, my lord," replied Padway. "And I respectfully suggest that you and your masters do the same. Especially about a little military device that we are introducing. Would you like to see it demonstrated? The parade ground is only a step from here."

Padway had made the proper preparations in advance. When they arrived at the parade ground, Hlodovik weaving slightly all the way, they found Urias, Fritharik, the crossbow, and a supply of bolts. Padway's idea was to have Fritharik take a few demonstration shots at a target. But Fritharik and Urias had other ideas. The latter walked off fifty feet, turned, and placed an apple on his head. Fritharik cocked the crossbow, put a bolt in the groove, and raised the bow to his shoulder.

Padway was frozen speechless with horror. He didn't dare shout at the two idiots to desist for fear of losing face before the Frank. And if Urias was killed, he hated to think of the damage that would be done to his plans.

The crossbow snapped. There was a short *splash*, and fragments of apple flew about. Urias, grinning, picked pieces of apple out of his hair and walked back.

"Do you find the demonstration impressive, my lord?" Padway asked.

"Yes, quite," said Hlodovik. "Let's see that device. *Hm-m-m.* Of course, the brave Franks don't believe that any battle was ever won by a lot of silly arrows. But for hunting, now, this mightn't be bad. How does it work? I see; you pull the string back to here—"

While Fritharik was demonstrating the crossbow, Padway took Urias aside and told him, in a low tone, just what he thought of such a fool stunt. Urias tried to look serious, but couldn't help a faint, small-boy grin. Then there was another snap, and something whizzed between them, not a foot from Padway's face. They jumped and spun around. Hlodovik was holding the crossbow, a foolish look on his long face. "I didn't know it went off so easily," he said.

Fritharik lost his temper. "What are you trying to do, you drunken fool? Kill somebody—"

"What's that? *You* call me a fool? Why—" and the Frank's sword came halfway out of the scabbard.

Fritharik jumped back and grabbed his own sword hilt. Padway and Urias pounced on the two and grabbed their elbows.

"Calm yourself, my lord!" cried Padway. "It's nothing to start a fight over. I'll apologize personally."

The Frank merely got madder and tried to shake off Padway. "I'll teach that low-born bastard! My honor is insulted!" he shouted. Several Gothic soldiers loafing around the field looked up and trotted over. Hlodovik saw them coming and put his sword back, growling: "This is fine treatment for the representative of King Theudebert, King Hildebert, and King Hlotokar. Just wait till they hear of this."

Padway tried to mollify him, but Hlodovik merely grumped, and soon left Ravenna. Padway dispatched a warning to Sisigis to be on the lookout for a Frankish attack. His conscience bothered him a good deal. In a way he thought he ought to have tried to appease the Franks, as he hated the idea of being responsible for war. But he knew that that fierce and treacherous tribe would only take each concession as a sign of weakness. The time to stop the Franks was the first time.

✧

Then another envoy arrived, this time from the Kutrigurs or Bulgarian Huns. The usher told Padway: "He's very dignified; doesn't speak any Latin or

Gothic, so he uses an interpreter. Says he's a boyar, whatever that is."

"Show him in."

The Bulgarian envoy was a stocky, bowlegged man with high cheek bones, a fiercely upswept mustache, and a nose even bigger than Padway's. He wore a handsome furlined coat, baggy trousers, and a silk turban wound about his shaven skull, from the rear of which two black pigtails jutted absurdly. Despite the finery, Padway found reason to suspect that the man had never had a bath in his life. The interpreter was a small, nervous Thracian who hovered a pace to the Bulgar's left and rear.

The Bulgar clumped in, bowed stiffly, and did not offer to shake hands. Probably not done among the Huns, thought Padway. He bowed back and indicated a chair. He regretted having done so a moment later, when the Bulgar hiked his boots up on the upholstery and sat cross-legged. Then he began to speak, in a strangely musical tongue which Padway surmised was related to Turkish. He stopped every three or four words for the interpreter to translate. It ran something like this:

Envoy: (Twitter, twitter.)
Interpreter: I am the Boyar Karojan—
Envoy: (Twitter, twitter.)
Interpreter: The son of Chakir—
Envoy: (Twitter, twitter.)
Interpreter. Who was the son of Tardu—
Envoy: (Twitter, twitter.)
Interpreter: Envoy of Kardam—
Envoy: (Twitter, twitter.)
Interpreter: The son of Kapagan—
Envoy: (Twitter, twitter.)
Interpreter: And Great Khan of the Kutrigurs.

It was distracting to listen to, but not without a certain poetic grandeur. The Bulgar paused impassively at that point. Padway identified himself, and the duo began again:

"My master, the Great Khan—"
"Has received an offer from Justinian, Emperor of the Romans—"
"Of fifty thousand solidi—"
"To refrain from invading his dominions."

"If Thiudahad, King of the Goths—"
"Will make us a better offer—"
"We will ravage Thrace—"
"And leave the Gothic realm alone."
"If he does not—"
"We will take Justinian's gold—"
"And invade the Gothic territories—"
"Of Pannonia and Noricum."

Padway cleared this throat and began his reply, pausing for translation. This method had its advantages, he found. It gave him time to think.

"My master, Thiudahad, King of the Goths and Italians—"
"Authorizes me to say—"
'That he has better use for his money—"
"Than to bribe people not to attack him—"
"And that if the Kutrigurs think—"
"That they can invade our territory—"
"They are welcome to try—"
"But that we cannot guarantee them—"
"A very hospitable reception."
The envoy replied:
"Think man, on what you say."
"For the armies of the Kutrigurs—"
"Cover the Sarmatian steppe like locusts."
"The hoofbeats of their horses—"
"Are a mighty thunder."
"The flight of their arrows—"
"Darkens the sun."
"Where they have passed—"
"Not even grass will grow."
Padway replied:
"Most excellent Karojan—"
"What you say may be true."
"But in spite of their thundering and sun-darkening—"
"The last time the Kutrigurs—"
"Assailed our land, a few years ago—"
"They got the pants beat off them."

As this was translated, the Bulgar looked puzzled for a moment. Then he turned red. Padway thought he was angry, but it soon appeared that he was trying to keep from laughing. He said between sputters:

"This time, man, it will be different."

"If any pants are lost—"

"They will be yours."

"How would this be?"

"You pay us sixty thousand—"

"In three installments—"

"Of twenty thousand each?"

But Padway was immovable. The Bulgar finished:

"I shall inform my master—"

"Kardam, the Great Khan of the Kutrigurs—"

"Of your obduracy."

"For a reasonable bribe—"

"I am prepared to tell him—"

"Of the might of the Gothic arms—"

"In terms that shall dissuade him—"

"From his projected invasion."

Padway beat the Bulgar down to half the bribe he originally asked, and they parted on the best of terms. When he went around to his quarters he found Fritharik trying to wind a towel around his head.

The Vandal looked up with guilty embarrassment. "I was trying, excellent boss, to make a headgear like that of the Hunnish gentleman. It has style."

Padway had long since decided that Thiudahad was a pathological case. But lately the little king was showing more definite signs of mental failure. For instance, when Padway went to see about a new inheritance law, Thiudahad gravely listened to him explain the reasons that the Royal Council and Cassiodorus had agreed upon bringing the Gothic law more into line with the Roman.

Then he said: "When are you going to put out another book in my name, Martinus? Your name is Martinus, isn't it? Martinus Paduei, Martinus Paduei. Didn't I appoint you prefect or something? Dear me, I can't seem to remember anything. Now, what's this you want to see me about? Always business, business, business. I hate business. Scholarship is more important. Silly state papers. What is it, an order for an execution? I hope you're going to torture the rascal as he deserves. I can't understand this absurd prejudice of yours against torture. The people aren't happy unless they're terrified of their government. Let's see, what was I talking about?"

It was convenient in one way, as Thiudahad didn't bother him much. But it was awkward when the king simply refused to listen to him or to sign anything for a day at a time.

Then he found himself in a hot dispute with the paymaster-general of the Gothic army. The latter refused to put the Imperialist mercenaries whom Padway had captured on the rolls. Padway argued that the men were first-rate soldiers who seemed glad enough to serve the Italo-Gothic state, and that it would cost little more to enlist them than to continue to feed them as prisoners. The paymaster-general replied that national defense had been a prerogative of the Goths since the time of Theoderik, and the men in question were not, with some few exceptions, Goths. Q.E.D.

Each stubbornly maintained his point, so the dispute was carried to Thiudahad. The king listened to the argument with a specious air of wisdom.

Then he sent the paymaster-general away and told Padway: "Lots to be said on both sides, dear sir, lots to be said on both sides: Now, if I decide in your favor, I shall expect a suitable command for my son, Thiudegiskel."

Padway was horrified, though he tried not to show it. "But, my lord king, what military experience has Thiudegiskel had?"

"None; that's just the trouble. Spends all his time drinking and wenching with his wild young friends. He needs a bit of responsibility. Something good, consistent with the dignity of his birth."

Padway argued some more. But he didn't say that he couldn't imagine a worse commander than this self-conceited and arrogant puppy. Thiudahad was obstinate. "After all, Martinus, I'm king, am I not? You can't browbeat me and you can't frighten me with your Wittigis. Heh, heh I'll have a surprise for you one of these days. What was I talking about? Oh, yes. You do, I think, owe Thiudegiskel something for putting him in that horrid prison camp—"

"But I didn't put him in jail—"

"Don't interrupt, Martinus. It isn't considerate. Either you give him a command, or I decide in favor of the other man, what's-his-name. That is my final royal word."

So Padway gave in. Thiudegiskel was put in command of the Gothic forces in Calabria, where, Padway hoped, he wouldn't be able to do much harm. Later he had occasion to remember that hope.

Padway may seem rash to have incorporated such an alien element as the ex-Imperialists in the Italo-Gothic army. But in this age there was no such thing as nationalism in the modern sense. The ties that counted were those of religion and personal loyalty to a commander. Many of the Imperialists were Thracian Goths who had remained in the Balkans at that time of the migration under Theoderik. And some Italian Goths had served the Empire as mercenaries. They mixed with little prejudice on either side.

Then three things happened. General Sisigis sent word of suspicious activity among the Franks.

Padway got a letter from Thomasus, which told of an attempt on the life of ex-King Wittigis. The assassin had inexplicably sneaked into the dugout, where Wittigis, though slightly wounded in the process, had killed him with his bare hands. Nobody knew who the assassin was until Wittigis had declared, with many a bloodcurdling curse, that he recognized the man as an old-time secret agent of Thiudahad. Padway knew what that meant. Thiudahad had discovered Wittigis' whereabouts, and meant to put his rival out of the way. If he succeeded, he'd be prepared to defy Padway's management, or even to heave him out of his office. Or worse.

Finally Padway got a letter from Justinian. It read:

Flavius Anicius Justinian, Emperor of the Romans, to King Thiudahad, Greetings.

Our serenity's attention has been called to the terms which you propose for termination of the war between us.

We find these terms so absurd and unreasonable that our deigning to reply at all is an act of great condescension on our part. Our holy endeavor to recover for the Empire the provinces of western Europe, which belonged to our forebears and rightfully belong to us, will be carried through to a victorious conclusion.

As for our former general, Flavius Belisarius, his refusal of parole is an act of gross disloyalty, which we shall fittingly punish in due course. Meanwhile the illustrious Belisarius may consider himself free of all obligations to us. Nay more, we order him to place himself unreservedly under the orders of that infamous heretic and agent of the Evil One who calls himself Martinus of Padua, of whom we have heard.

We are confident that, between the incompetence and cowardice of Belisarius and the heavenly wrath that will attach to those who submit to the unclean touch of the diabolical Martinus, the doom of the Gothic kingdom will not be long delayed.

✧

Padway realized, with a slightly sick feeling, that he had a lot to learn about diplomacy. His defiance of Justinian, and of the Frankish kings, and of the Bulgars, had each been justified, considered by itself. But he shouldn't have committed himself to taking them on all at once.

The thunderheads were piling up fast.

CHAPTER XIV

Padway dashed back to Rome and showed Justinian's letter to Belisarius. He thought he had seldom seen a more unhappy man than the stalwart Thracian.

"I don't know," was all Belisarius would say in answer to his questions. "I shall have to think."

Padway got an interview with Belisarius' wife, Antonina. He got along fine with this slim, vigorous redhead.

She said: "I told him repeatedly that he'd get nothing but ingratitude from Justinian. But you know how he is—reasonable about everything except what concerns his honor. The only thing that would make me hesitate is my friendship with the Empress Theodora. That's not a connection to be thrown over lightly. But after this letter—I'll do what I can, excellent Martinus."

Belisarius, to Padway's unconcealed delight, finally capitulated.

The immediate danger point seemed to be Provence. Padway's runner-collecting service had gathered a story of another bribe paid by Justinian to the Franks to attack the Goths. So Padway did some shuffling. Asinar, who had sat at Senia for months without the gumption to move against the Imperialists in Spalato, was ordered home. Sisigis, who if no genius was not obviously incompetent, was transferred to command of Asinar's Dalmatian army. And Belisarius was given command of Sisigis' forces in Gaul. Belisarius, before leaving for the North, asked Padway for all the information available about the Franks.

Padway explained: "Brave, treacherous, and stupid. They have nothing but unarmored infantry, who fight in a single deep column. They come whooping along, hurl a volley of throwing-axes and javelins, and close with the sword. If you can stop them by a line of reliable pikemen, or by cavalry charges, they're suckers for mounted archers. They're very numerous, but such a huge mass of infantry can't forage enough territory to keep themselves fed. So they have to keep moving or starve.

"Moreover, they're so primitive that their soldiers are not paid at all. They're expected to make their living by looting. If you can hold them in one spot long enough, they melt away by desertion. But don't underestimate their numbers and ferocity.

"Try to send agents into Burgundy to rouse the Burgunds against the Franks, who conquered them only a few years ago." He explained that the Burgunds were of East-German origin, like the Goths and Lombards, spoke a language much like theirs, and like them were primarily stock-raisers. Hence they did not get on with the West-German Franks, who were agriculturists when they were not devastating their neighbors' territory.

✧

If there was going to be more war, Padway knew one invention that would settle it definitely in the Italo-Goths' favor. Gunpowder was made of sulphur, charcoal, and saltpeter. Padway had learned that in the sixth grade. The first two were available without question.

He supposed that potassium nitrate could be obtained somewhere as a mineral. But he did not know where, or what it would look like. He could not synthesize it with the equipment at hand, even had he known enough chemistry. But he remembered reading that it occurred at the bottom of manure-piles. And he remembered an enormous pile in Nevitta's yard.

He called on Nevitta and asked for permission to dig. He whooped with joy when, sure enough, there were the crystals, looking like maple sugar. Nevitta asked him if he was crazy.

"Sure," grinned Padway. Didn't you know? I've been that way for years."

His old house on Long Street was as full of activity as ever, despite the move to Florence. It was used as Rome headquarters by the Telegraph Company. Padway was having another press set up. And now the remaining space downstairs became a chemical laboratory. Padway did not know what proportions of the three ingredients made good gunpowder, and the only way to find out was by experiment.

He gave orders, in the government's name, for casting and boring a cannon. The brass foundry that took the job was not co-operative. They had never seen such a contraption and were not sure they could make it. What did he want this tube for, a flower pot?

It took them an interminable time to get the pattern and core made, despite the simplicity of the thing. The first one they delivered looked all right, until Padway examined the breach end closely. The metal here was spongy and pitted. The gun would have blown up the first time it was fired.

The trouble was that it had been cast muzzle down. The solution was to add a foot to the length of the barrel, cast it muzzle up, and saw off the last foot of flawed brass.

His efforts to produce gunpowder got nowhere. Lots of proportions of the ingredients would burn beautifully when ignited. But they did not explode. He tried all proportions; he varied his method of mixing. Still all he got was a lively sizzle, a big yellow flame, and a stench. He tried packing the stuff into improvised firecrackers. They went *fuff*. They would not go *bang*.

Perhaps he had to touch off a large quantity at once, more tightly compressed yet. He pestered the foundry daily until the second cannon appeared.

Early next morning he and Fritharik and a couple of helpers mounted the cannon on a crude carriage of planks in a vacant space near the Viminal Gate. The helpers had previously piled up a sandhill for a target, thirty feet from the gun.

Padway rammed several pounds of powder down the barrel, and a cast-iron ball after it. He filled the touch-hole.

He said in a low voice: "Fritharik, give me that candle. Now get back everybody. Way over there, and lie down. You too, Fritharik."

"Never!" said Fritharik indignantly. "Desert my lord in the hour of danger? I should say not!"

"All right, if you want to chance being blown to bits. Here goes."

Padway touched the candle flame to the touch-hole.

The powder sizzled and sparkled.

The gun went *pfoomp!* The cannon-ball hopped from the muzzle, thumped to earth a yard away, rolled another yard, and stopped.

Back went the beautiful shiny new gun to Padway's house, to be put in the cellar with the clock.

✿

In the early spring, Urias appeared in Rome. He explained that he'd left the military academy in the hands of subordinates, and was coming down to see about raising a militia force of Romans, which had been another of Padway's ideas. But he had an unhappy, hangdog air that made Padway suspect that that wasn't the real reason.

To Padway's leading questions he finally burst out: "Excellent Martinus, you'll simply have to give me a command somewhere away from Ravenna. I can't stand it any longer."

Padway put his arm around Urias' shoulders. "Come on, old man, tell me what is bothering you. Maybe I can help."

Urias looked at the ground. "Uh … well … that is—Look here, just what *is* the arrangement between you and Mathaswentha?"

"I thought that was it. You've been seeing her, haven't you?"

"Yes, I have. And if you send me back there, I shall see her some more in spite of myself. Are you and she betrothed, or what?"

"I did have some such idea once." Padway put on the air of one about to make a great sacrifice. "But, my friend, I wouldn't stand in the way of anybody's happiness. I'm sure you're much better suited to her than I. My work keeps me too busy to make a good husband. So if you want to sue for her hand, go to it, with my blessing."

"You *mean* that?" Urias jumped up and began pacing the floor, fairly beaming. "I…I don't know how to thank you … it's the greatest thing you could do for me … I'm your friend for life—"

"Don't mention it; I'm glad to help you out. But now that you're down here, you might as well finish the job you came to do."

"Oh," said Urias soberly. "I suppose I ought to, at that. But how shall I press my suit, then?"

"Write her."

"But how can I? I don't know the pretty phrases. In fact, I've never written a love letter in my life."

"I'll help you out with that, too. Here, we can start right now." Padway got out writing materials, and they were presently concocting a letter to the princess. "Let's see," said Padway reflectively, "we ought to tell her what her eyes are like."

"They're just like eyes, aren't they?"

"Of course, but in this business you compare them to the stars and things."

Urias thought. "They're about the color of a glacier I once saw in the Alps."

"No, that wouldn't do. It would imply that they were as cold as ice."

"They also remind you of a polished sword blade."

"Similar objection. How about the northern seas?"

"*Hm-m-m.* Yes, I think that would do, Martinus. Gray as the northern seas."

"It has a fine poetic ring to it."

"So it has. Northern seas it shall be, then." Urias wrote slowly and awkwardly.

Padway said: "Hey, don't bear down so hard with that pen. You'll poke a hole in that paper."

As Urias was finishing the letter, Padway clapped on his hat and made for the door.

"*Hai*," said Urias, "what's your hurry?"

Padway grinned. "I'm just going to see some friends; a family named Anicius. Nice people. I'll introduce you to them some day when you're safely sewed up."

Padway's original idea had been to introduce a mild form of selective conscription, beginning with the city of Rome and requiring the draftees to report for weekly drill. The Senate, which at this time was a mere municipal council, balked. Some of them disliked or distrusted Padway. Some wanted to be bribed.

Padway did not want to give in to them until he had tried everything else. He had Urias announce drills on a voluntary basis, at current wages. Results were disappointing.

Padway's thoughts were abruptly snatched from the remilitarization of the Italians when Junianus came in with a telegraph message. It read simply:

☼

WITTIGIS ESCAPED FROM DETENTION LAST NIGHT. NO TRACE OF HIM HAS BEEN FOUND.

(SIGNED)

ATURPAD THE PERSIAN,
COMMANDING.

☼

For a minute Padway simply stared at the message. Then he jumped up and yelled: "Fritharik! Get our horses!"

They clattered over to Urias' headquarters. Urias looked grave. "This puts me in an awkward position, Martinus. My uncle will undoubtedly try to regain his crown. He's a stubborn man, you know."

"I know. But you know how important it is to keep things going the way they are."

"*Ja.* I won't go back on you. But you couldn't expect me to try to harm my uncle. I like him, even if he is a thickheaded old grouch."

"You stick with me and I promise you I'll do my best to see that he isn't harmed. But just now I'm concerned with keeping him from harming *us.*"

"How do you suppose he got out? Bribery?"

"I know as much as you do. I doubt the bribery; at least Aturpad is considered an honorable man. What do you think Wittigis will do?"

"If it were me, I'd hide out for a while and gather my partisans. That would be logical. But my uncle never was very logical. And he hates Thiudahad worse than anything on earth. Especially after Thiudahad's attempt to have him murdered. My guess is that he'll head straight for Ravenna and try to do Thiudahad in personally."

"All right, then, we'll collect some fast cavalry and head that way ourselves."

Padway thought he was pretty well hardened to long-distance riding. But it was all he could do to stand the pace that Urias set. When they reached Ravenna in the early morning he was reeling, red-eyed, in the saddle.

They asked no questions, but galloped straight for the palace. The town seemed normal enough. Most of the citizens were at breakfast. But at the palace the normal guard was not to be seen.

"That looks bad," said Urias. They and their men dismounted, drew their swords, and marched in six abreast. A guard appeared at the head of the stairs. He grabbed at his sword, then recognized Urias and Padway.

"Oh, it's you," he said noncommittally.

"Yes, it's us," replied Padway. "What's up?"

"Well … uh … you'd better go see for yourselves, noble sirs. Excuse me." And the Goth whisked out of sight.

They tramped on through the empty halls. Doors shut before they came to them, and there was whispering behind them. Padway wondered if they were walking into a trap. He sent back a squad to hold the front door.

At the entrance to the royal apartments they found a clump of guards. A couple of these brought their spears up, but the rest simply stood uncertainly. Padway said calmly, "Stand back, boys," and went in.

"Oh, merciful Christ!" said Urias softly.

There were several people standing around a body on the floor. Padway asked them to stand aside, which they did meekly. The body was that of Wittigis. His tunic was ripped by a dozen sword and spear wounds. The rug under him was sopping.

The chief usher looked amazedly at Padway. "This just happened, my lord. Yet you have come all the way from Rome because of it. How did you know?"

"I have ways," said Padway. "How did it happen?"

"Wittigis was let into the palace by a guard friendly to him. He would have killed our noble king, but he was seen, and other guards hurried to the rescue. The guards killed him," he added unnecessarily. Anybody could see that.

A sound from the corner made Padway look up. There crouched Thiudahad, half dressed. Nobody seemed to be paying much attention. Thiudahad's ashy face peered at Padway.

"Dear me, it's my new prefect, isn't it? Your name is Cassiodorus. But how much younger you look, my dear sir. Ah, me, we all grow old sometime. Heh-heh. Let's publish a book, my dear Cassiodorus. Heigh-ho, yes, indeed, a lovely new book with purple covers. Heh-heh. We'll serve it for dinner, with pepper and gravy. That's the way to eat a fowl. Yes, three hundred pages at least. By the way, have you seen that rascally general of mine, Wittigis? I heard he was coming to call. Dreadful bore; no scholar at all. Heigh-ho, dear me, I feel like dancing. Do you dance, my dear Wittigis? La-la-la, la-la-la, dum de-um de-um."

Padway told the king's house physician: "Take care of him, and don't let him out. The rest of you, go back to work as if nothing has happened. Somebody take charge of the body. Replace this rug, and make the preparations for a dignified but modest funeral. Urias, maybe you'd better tend to that." Urias was weeping. "Come on, old man, you can do your grieving later. I sympathize, but we've got things to do." He whispered something to him, whereat Urias cheered up.

(to be continued in Issue 11)